SNOW
AT
MIDNIGHT

JESSICA McCLELLAND

RED SKY inc.

This is a work of fiction. Names, characters, places and incidents are of the author's imagination and are used fictitiously and not based on actual events, or persons, living or dead. Any resemblance to actual locals, organizations or events is coincidental.

Red Sky Inc.
Grand Junction, Colorado.

First printing: 2012
Second printing: 2018

PRAISE FOR THE KILLDEER SERIES

You'll be compelled to race through North of the Crazies by Jessica McClelland's easy and addictive prose, but that means you'll lose the detail and the accuracy that make her a truly fine writer. Her knowledge of the contemporary West and her abilities as a storyteller makes her a welcomed addition to the new class of crime fiction authors.

-Craig Johnson, author of the Walt Longmire Mysteries, the basis of A&E's hit series Longmire

Jessica McClelland's Snow at Midnight bursts out of the chute with a fresh new voice an authentic Montana sense of place, and a flawed but endearing protagonist readers will cheer for. Welcome aboard, Marley Dearcorn.

—C.J. Box, New York Times bestselling author of Force of Nature.

Snow at Midnight highlights not just a murder, but the nuances of Western culture: the conflict between old ranchers and new money, the independent self-sufficiency that comes from living an hour down a dirt road from the nearest hospital, the power struggles, the endless sky arching from the jagged horizon.

-The Daily Sentinel

BOOKS BY
JESSICA McCLELLAND

SNOW AT MIDNIGHT
DRAWN TO THE MEAN
THE JADE ARROWHEAD
THE BUFFALO FENCE
NORTH OF THE CRAZIES
JIM CREEK HILL
WATER RIGHTS

SNOW AT MIDNIGHT

CHAPTER 1

In Montana, Mother Nature will occasionally kick you in the teeth, just so you don't ever forget who's really in charge.

I sat in bed shivering under the covers, listening to the sounds of hail pounding the deck outside my house. The wind screeched. I could hear broken branches hitting the roof and scraping across the shingles. I flipped off the covers and groped my way to the small window, trying to figure out what fresh hell was currently barreling down on me. Night blacker than pitch hid the sight, but from the sound I could imagine what was happening. The trees surrounding my place were taking the beating of a lifetime. It was like the wind had teeth and it was chewing up everything it could find. Why is it disasters always seem to happen at four in the morning?

Since Montana was not famous for tornados, particularly in October, I squinted through the window and tried to get a hint of what was happening outside.

When I heard my sixty-foot cottonwood tree in the front yard start to groan and creak like it was in pain, I figured now might be a good time to run for the basement.

Then I recalled there was no basement. I wasn't in my cute little bungalow just outside of Helena anymore. I was back home. In Killdeer. Just in time for the apocalypse.

The wind intensified, if that was possible, and the big cottonwood let out a death knell. I could hear what sounded like gunshots and without even thinking I hit the floor. I wrapped my arms over my head and it occurred to me that it wasn't gunshots I was hearing. The cottonwood's roots were snapping apart.

"Of course it's Monday," I said to myself.

An eerie low rumble made the house tremble and I rolled away from the bedroom window, squirmed frantically underneath the big four-post bed, and pulled my feet under the sideboards just as the tree toppled outside. I know it was my panicked imagination working but it felt like the ground shook. I heard the picture window in my kitchen explode. The sounds of shattered glass tumbling to the floor made me cringe and grit my teeth.

At least the sturdy pine legs of the bed would give me some protection if the ceiling collapsed. That or the whole thing would crush me like a grasshopper under a Buick.

I squeezed my eyes shut and listened to the sounds of breaking glass and tearing fabric coming from the kitchen. So much for my new, variegated accordion window blinds.

The noise was so unbearable even both hands over my ears didn't help. It sounded like a two-mile-long, fully loaded coal train was climbing a hill through my living room. I waited for the sounds of more falling trees but luckily the wind seemed to have run out of things to destroy.

Then, it stopped. The wind didn't bother to gradually diminish. It shut down with a long, heavy sigh, leaving the valley with a shrug instead of a roar, with no explanation or apology.

I stayed put, keeping my feet tucked underneath the bed in case the sudden stillness was only temporary. But the peace held.

The rampage had ended as suddenly as it had started. I took a deep breath and rested my face in my hands. My long hair was plastered to my forehead from panicked sweat, and for a horrifying moment I felt a sudden flash of regret that I was divorced. A husband would be a handy asset right about now.

Sure. Until he saw where I had ended up during the storm.

I could imagine the conversation that would have gone on with my ex-husband, Allen.

"Marley, get ahold of yourself, girl, and come on out from under there before the neighbors see you."

I tried to get my heartbeat to slow down to a normal pace, and rested my cheek on the carpet. How long had it been since I'd vacuumed under here?

The phone rang. I flinched so hard I hit my head on the bottom board of the bed.

"Sure, I make it through the storm alright then give my self a head injury," I said, rubbing the back of my skull.

I scrambled and pawed my way free of the big four-post and snatched the receiver beside the bed on the fourth ring.

"Hi, Dad," I said.

"Kiddo, are you in one piece over there?"

3

"All in one piece," I told him. My T-shirt was soaked with sweat, too. But I didn't need to share that with anyone. "How bad was it up at your end?"

My father's voice changed from concern to excitement in the space of a breath.

"Holy cow, Marley. It was terrific! You should have seen the hail. Size of silver dollars, and my picnic bench ended up on top of the hay swather. That downburst was one for the record books. I'm going to call the paper to come and get some photos soon as it's light. I bet it makes the front page."

I smiled, more from relief than anything else. Hearing the sound of another human being, even over the telephone, was a sudden and welcome comfort.

I could see the headline. Nathan Dearcorn suffers loss of picnic bench. The Killdeer newspaper had its own ideas about what constituted a newsworthy story.

"Downburst?" I asked.

"I haven't seen one this bad, oh, since before you were born," he told me.

"So, sort of like a wind shear?"

"Only straight down instead of sideways," my father said. "Probably had wind get up to seventy-five, at least. Glad I don't have any alfalfa to put up just now."

"Well, I'm all in one piece, but I can't say the same for the kitchen window," I said.

"What? Did we get some damage there?" he asked, his tone creeping back to concern.

"Some, Dad. The living room window is on the floor now. I heard it give way when the cottonwood went."

He paused for a moment and I could hear him pulling open a closet. Probably reaching for his coat.

"Should I bring over my tools? I think I've got a piece of plywood—"

He hung up without saying goodbye, something my father never did. I frowned at the receiver.

"Dad?"

I reached for the lamp on the little nightstand and turned the knob.

Nothing.

I tapped the phone cradle to see if I could get a dial tone back. It was dead, too. Apparently a big pine tree somewhere in the valley had decided at that particular moment to take out a section of the ancient power line that snaked its way towards our ranch. It wasn't that much of a surprise. We were so far off the beaten path out our end of the valley, losing power and not having a working phone were irritatingly common occurrences.

I pulled a flashlight from the little nightstand drawer and switched it on. Light flared but it wasn't very enthusiastic. The batteries in the flashlight were probably older than me. I shook the flashlight, hoping the circle of light would brighten up, but if anything it only made things worse. I eased my way into the living room, stepping gingerly in case I felt any glass underfoot, and panned the area above the kitchen sink. The dim glow lit the depressing scene.

Glass was everywhere. I found a pair of hiking boots in the bottom of my coat closet and did the sensible thing. I rolled up my sweatpants, pulled on the boots and tucked in the laces before venturing farther into the living room. Glass crunched under my boots as I made my way to the sink.

5

An angry breeze battered the remnants of my window blinds and rain sloshed to the floor. A handful of hailstones had managed to pile up on what was left of the windowsill and a couple of stray leaves rested on top of the melting heap of ice.

No power meant no heat. The house was cooling fast. I pulled a Killdeer High sweatshirt from the closet and pulled it over my head to stave off the cold.

I surveyed the rest of the kitchen with the weak glow from my dying flashlight. My grandmother's antique white china teapot sat proudly on the counter, undisturbed. It was slick with rain but otherwise in perfect condition. It seemed that the damage hadn't been that bad after all.

Then I turned around and saw the screwdriver.

"Whoa."

The red plastic grip was the only part of the screwdriver that I could see. The rest of it was buried point first in the wall. It must have been what had shattered the window.

I eased my way across the floor and poked the flashlight through the hole that had once held a sturdy pane of glass. I could just see the damage outside. My huge cottonwood tree had missed the house, missed my old Honda and had scored a direct hit on the old toolshed. It was flattened. The impact had crushed one side of the shed, mangled the other, and must have propelled the screwdriver through the air and into my kitchen window.

"At least it wasn't the chainsaw," I said.

No point in going back to sleep. I did what most women would do in my situation.

I pulled my strawberry blonde hair back into a ponytail, pulled out a pair of rubber gloves and a broom and started cleaning.

I'd almost gotten the glass swept into a plastic bucket when I saw headlights bounce down the driveway. By the time my father bounded up the stairs I had rounded up the last of the glass and was starting on the water. My mop was soaked after one swipe.

"Marley?" My father was halfway across the living room before he called my name. When he was in a hurry, which was all the time, he would let himself in without knocking. Usually it bothered me, but today, not so much.

He came into the kitchen and looked me over thoroughly. His jeans were half-tucked into cowboy boots and his flannel shirt was buttoned randomly. His honeybee-yellow rain slicker puddled water on the linoleum.

Water dripped liberally outside from practically every surface. Leftovers from the storm.

"Some night," he said.

Satisfied that I was not damaged, he turned his attention to the window and let out a low whistle. I realized that his thinning gray hair looked darker when it was soaked, but in spite of the water dripping off his jacket onto the floor, I was terribly happy to see him.

I didn't care that the rush of relief at seeing my father made me feel a bit cowardly, too. I was almost thirty-four years old, and a grown woman, and fully capable of taking care of myself. But, sometimes a girl just needed her dad.

CHAPTER 2

"The shed's a total loss, but your car is fine," my father said as he stepped across the kitchen threshold and scanned the window frame.

"It's alright, Dad. Jack has a couple old toolsheds lying around that I'm sure he'd sell me for a good price."

My father circled the window and took in the damage with a practiced eye. He was adding up how much it would cost in his head, and subtracting the labor, which he would do himself, and any second now . . .

"We're looking at about sixty-five bucks here. Not too bad."

"Not bad," I agreed. I was hoping I could get the screwdriver out of the wall before he saw it.

A stray flash of lightning took a snapshot of the night. I winced and covered my ears. The thunder cracked, then dwindled into a low rumble.

My father searched his pockets. "I didn't bring a light with me. Left it in the glove box."

I gave him my flashlight so he could continue his examination. If I hadn't handed over my flashlight, he would have kept right on working without one. My father treated every situation like it was critical and urgent.

He even grilled a steak with so much focused intensity that when I was a child I thought he was watching the T-bone in case it tried to get up and run away.

"How are the neighbors?" I asked as I set the mop aside. I'd just make a bigger mess cleaning in the dark. "Did you talk to Paul before we lost power?"

"I was going to call the Gables, but the lines are down over at the ranch house, too. I know they are back from D.C. 'cause I saw Leif day before yesterday at the post office going on and on about that stepson of his getting a job at long last," he said. "I don't know about Paul Nesbit. I'm sure he's home, though."

Neither one of us owned a cell phone. Killdeer Valley had a notorious reputation for being a perpetual dead zone. It didn't matter how high you climbed or what ridge you stood on, cell phones didn't work with any reliability. Sometimes a signal could get through, but for the most part I always considered owning a cell phone to be nothing but a waste of money. Calling Paul, or the Gables, was out of the question now that the land lines were down.

I could see his outline, but not his face. He was propped against the counter holding the flashlight tucked in his armpit while he rummaged in his coat pockets for a pair of gloves.

A long row of tall, tired trees surrounded the phone and power lines that led to our valley, and I was sure the phone company maintenance crews and the power company workers hated us with a special kind of intensity reserved for those customers who are unintentionally a huge bother. Sometimes the utility crews didn't get the juice flowing again for days.

"I should drive by and check on Leif and Virginia," my father said, torn between the job at hand and the welfare of our neighbors.

"Tell you what, Dad. I'll go by and check on Paul and you go look in on the Gables. We can't do anything until it gets light and if we try to clean this up now somebody will just get cut. Why don't we meet back here in a half hour?"

"Good idea," he said cheerfully. He dug truck keys from his pocket. This was a welcome adventure for him and sometimes I wished that he had never sold the steers and given up ranching.

He toed his way to the front door and pushed it open, stealing off with my flashlight without a single backwards glance.

He was down the stairs and firing up his truck before I could even find my jeans. I pulled them on, after using the Braille system to navigate my bedroom, when the lightning flashed again and gave me enough light to see my canvas coat draped over the back of a chair.

In spite of the near total darkness I managed to find my car keys and make it down the stairs to my little Honda without falling. Branches and leaves had been ripped from the trees and covered the stairs, making the steps a tangled mess. I worked my way down the steps clinging to the railing, until my feet found the ground at last.

Lightning flashed. I jumped when thunder boomed through the valley, echoing off the high hills that crowded around my little house. The rain had left the forest heavy with damp and the fall air smelled rich with decaying leaves and sharp with the scent of broken pine boughs.

My car was plastered with soaked leaves but otherwise it looked like it had survived the storm.

I cleaned the windshield as best I could in the darkness and started the engine. I felt foolish sitting there for a minute or two just listening to the comforting sound of working man-made machinery. Living out in the woods had its advantages, but when things went wrong the isolation could be intimidating. A great many things had gone wrong in my life recently. Having a rogue downburst destroy my toolshed was only the most recent travesty. Lately, troubles had crowded out the triumphs.

Helena, in west-central Montana, was only a five-hour drive from Killdeer. But it felt like coming back home to the valley had brought me on a thousand-mile journey. Landing that job with the Montana Fish and Wildlife office nine years ago had been my greatest accomplishment and it had become my worst disappointment. I had been home for six months after being fired from my job up in Helena, but I still didn't want to talk about it.

My father and I somehow managed to get through everything else together without talking about it too much. We'd lost my mother when I was seven. She had been killed by a drunk driver, and my father raised me on his own with no help from anyone. Our family was just the two of us. No grandparents or aunts around to help out. My father and I were a team when it came to enduring hardship. We'd had a lot of practice.

I pulled out of my gravel driveway and turned towards the main road, my headlights swallowed up by the damp forest as I sloshed through the potholes and mud, dodging downed branches, and I headed towards Paul's house. If I didn't have any power, it was a sure bet he wouldn't either.

He was my closest neighbor and lived up on the plateau high above the Gable place. Paul's house was only six miles from mine but the drive took me longer than expected.

I used the time to try and come up with a nice way to ask Jack for the day off. I'd be able to call him in a couple hours. It was already close to four-thirty and he'd be up by six at the latest. I figured the excuse of having a downburst hit your house was a good enough reason, and I bumped down the washboard road certain in the knowledge that Jack would understand and allow me to have the day off to get some glass between me and the woods.

Jack Parks owned a landscaping firm in Killdeer, and he had hired me a few weeks after I'd come home. Landscaping certainly wasn't the job I'd expected to have considering all the experience I had as an office manager, but I was grateful for the work. Considering how bad I had left it up in Helena, I was happy that anyone in Killdeer would offer to hire me at all.

A day spent without pay was not ideal, but back at my little house I had a lot of work to do and I didn't really have a choice.

I could make sandwiches with all the lunch meat that was sure to spoil if the power stayed out all day, which was likely. The ice cream would be fine for a while, but as soon as I opened up the freezer it would start to melt and we would have to eat that too. I knew my father would not mind helping with that little chore.

The Honda groaned as I nosed it up the steep road towards Paul's. I rounded a sharp bend and the high beams found the wide porch of his home.

I killed the engine and left my keys in the ignition. Since I didn't have a flashlight, I left my headlights blazing so I wouldn't kill myself making it up the stairs, and I sat staring at the big house for a moment.

The stairs on Paul's house could be described as imposing. The entire house could be described that way. I guess when you had too much money you had to find ways to spend it all. There were worse things a man could do with multiple millions, and based on the town gossip, he had indulged in a buffet of sins where he had grown up back east, then turned his charm into a lucrative job. His spending habits hadn't changed since he had arrived in Killdeer four years ago. Paul certainly had blown millions since I'd known him. Probably at least couple million just on his home. But he had left his wild days behind him in Pennsylvania, and he had found other ways to spend his money since coming to the valley. Other than booze and floozies, the only thing left to chew up that much cash in Killdeer was running for political office. Or buying a doomed ranch. But Paul certainly wasn't a rancher.

Paul Nesbit had retired at the age of forty-seven from a career as the vice president of a large insurance firm in Pennsylvania. He'd managed to stay single, had no kids, and so all his money had gone into self-indulgence and shameless vice. That, and lately he had pumped large sums of cash into the race for mayor of Killdeer. It was terribly important to him that folks knew he had money, and he loved to throw it around. But, really, how big a house did one man need? Not for the first time I felt like my home territory was being invaded by those blessed with more money than I would ever see in a lifetime.

I climbed out of my car, closed the door and stood for a moment watching the windows. Funny, but I didn't see a flashlight waving through the rooms, and if there had been a flashlight I certainly would have. Paul had odd ideas about privacy. Well, he didn't really believe in it. So his house was not much more than a sixteen-room log mansion with windows the size of garage doors. It was Killdeer's most expensive fishbowl. I had never been to one of his parties, but getting invited to dinner at the Nesbit house was considered a social coup. I had heard that on one occasion the Oak Ridge Boys had provided the evening's entertainment.

I didn't move for a couple minutes, simply watched the front of the house. My Honda was old enough that when the engine was shut off the lights would stay on, and I took a moment to search the porch with the headlights illuminating the wide stone steps. Surprisingly the trees around his house had held up well and there wasn't much debris. I expected to see a lot more damage.

Things seemed much quieter here than they had when I'd left my place. The rough terrain behind Paul's house was thick with old ponderosa pines and the occasional cluster of quaking aspens. The leftover winds swirled through the pine needles, making them whisper.

I breathed in and smelled the faint sweet and sour tang of mountain juniper.

The breeze was shifting north to south in random, crazy swells, pushing the scent of junipers up from the steep cliff several hundred yards behind the big house. I couldn't see the cliff from the driveway, but I knew it was there.

The Gables lived below it, and no doubt my father was down there now, checking on them.

Other than the light, random breeze, the house was stone still.

I turned my head to the side and listened for movement of any kind. Everything was deathly quiet. I expected to see Paul floundering around inside his house with a bobbing flashlight. But there was nothing to indicate he was even home. I walked up on the porch and knocked on the screen door.

"Paul? You in there?"

He probably couldn't hear me. I pulled open the screen and knocked again, louder. Maybe he had slept through the entire storm?

I waited, but the big pine door stayed shut and not a single creaking board from within told me that Paul was on the move. I surveyed the porch. It was wide and long with enough room to host at least twenty people with martinis, and a little left over for cigar smokers at the end. Since the porch was sheltered from above by a second deck, it was mostly clean aside from the odd pile of aspen leaves scattered here and there.

I let the screen go and the heavy spring snapped it closed with a bang. I flinched from the sound. Well, if Paul hadn't been awake before, he certainly was now. I stepped back into the glow of my headlights and stopped to glance back at the house. Not one window was broken. Several branches littered the upper deck and one massive limb lay like a fallen soldier in Paul's neatly manicured rose garden to the right of the house. Other than the random piles of branches, not too much damage had been done. He'd been lucky. He had acres of glass and yet it had all survived intact. But everything was soaked through.

The wind had been kind here, but the rain had not. Puddles were everywhere. I sloshed through them with almost every step.

I headed to the left side of the house, my car headlights showing me the way, and pushed open the gate leading to the back yard. I'd worked a huge landscaping job on this house four and a half months ago in the cold spring of early June, and so I knew my way around. Paul kept a big utility shed tucked just inside the tree line behind his Olympic-size back yard, and I figured if he wasn't in the house maybe he was there, also searching for a working flashlight.

The clouds opened up tiny windows to the sky here and there, and moonlight splashed down intermittently on the wet landscape. It was enough light to see where I was going, but only just. The glow from my car was lost here. Still, I managed to fumble my way across the yard with help from the pale half-moon.

The little red tractor Paul used for mowing and brush control was parked where it belonged beside the back gate, and aside from the sticks and spattering of leaves, everything looked normal to me.

I was crossing the golf-course-quality grass when lightning flashed, making me jump. It was so close the crack of thunder immediately followed. I had a sudden urge to be as far away from these tall trees as I could get.

I stopped with one foot poised to take another step and lifted my head. My heart picked up the pace. Something made my skin prickle. I felt static tingle on my arms and the hair on the back of my neck stood up.

I felt a bit exposed standing in the middle of the yard with no one around for miles but the deer, and those who ate the deer.

I turned and bolted for the back porch. As I jumped on the single low step and backed up towards the door, the lightning flashed again. There was an explosion of light and I squeezed my eyes shut. Thunder cracked instantly.

It hadn't struck the house, but it was close. I was sure that last bolt had cooked the top of at least one tree close by. If these trees hadn't been soaked with rainwater they might have been burning by now from all the lightning strikes. I was ready to be done with this adventure.

"Paul?" I called, wincing as my voice bounced off the trees with more volume than I'd expected.

Nothing. Apparently he wasn't in the utility shed. Standing in the dark, alone on the porch, was making my skin prickle.

I wanted to turn straight around, go inside the house and call the neighbors more than anything. Then I remembered. *I* was the neighbor.

I swallowed hard and I shook my head, ashamed of myself, and turned to the door. The upper half of the back door was divided with two small windows. I cupped my hands over my eyes so I could peer inside. It was too dark for me to see anything clearly, but I had to make sure Paul was fine before I headed back home. He was probably sound asleep, oblivious to the outside world, and all that my yelling and banging had achieved was to give me a creepy feeling. Creepy feeling aside, it would be wrong to drive off without talking to him.

I twisted the doorknob, but it was locked. I frowned at that. I never locked my door, why should he? It irritated me that all of my efforts to check on my neighbor were going ignored.

I hammered on the door with my fist. Damn city people never could get the hang of country rituals.

"Paul? It's Marley Dearcorn. You awake?"

I cupped my hands again and pressed my nose to the tiny window. A flash of lightning sparked overhead, and I saw him.

An instant was all I had, but I saw it clearly. Paul was lying on the kitchen floor flat on his back with both arms limp. He wasn't moving at all.

CHAPTER 3

"Paul! Open the door!"

I watched the place where I'd seen him after the lightning flash, hoping for movement. I called again and pounded on the door frame. Nothing.

Maybe he'd slipped and fallen, hit his head or was unconscious. Whatever had happened I knew that he was in trouble.

He didn't, or he couldn't, get up. At that moment I wished frantically I had been born a big strong farm boy so I could break the door down with my shoulder. But my 120-pound frame wouldn't be nearly enough to do the job. I needed to get inside, and I had to do it fast.

I scanned the back yard, hoping for inspiration. A sledgehammer would do, but I couldn't see one anywhere. In a state of panic my eyes fell on the little tractor with its handy front-end bucket and I ran towards it without even thinking. The keys were stuck in the ignition so I finally had some good luck. I started the engine and with practiced hands raised the hydraulic bucket. The little tractor bucked forward when I stepped off the clutch, I turned towards the back porch raising the bucket as I gained speed, and I aimed.

The front tires of the tractor bounced up the low step and I hit the back door with the corner of the bucket. Wood shattered and glass flew. The door snapped off its hinges and fell inside the kitchen with a crash. I hit the kill switch and sprinted inside the house, scrambling over the fallen door to reach Paul.

He was sprawled on his back, his arms and legs rigid. He seemed to be choking, trying to breathe, but he wasn't moving.

I put my hands on his head to tilt his throat open and jerked back. His skin was shockingly hot to the touch.

Ignoring the heat I put my hands back on his head, tilted his neck back and checked his airway. My finger found no obstructions in his throat, so he wasn't choking on anything. He simply couldn't breathe. His body had locked up. He was an engine that had seized.

"Can you hear me?" I asked, leaning down.

He was struggling to breathe but he couldn't. I knew he had asthma, and I felt around the floor for an inhaler. Everyone who lived in Killdeer had seen Paul take a puff on his asthma medicine from time to time. He was allergic to everything.

I couldn't locate an inhaler anywhere beside him and thought he might have left it in his bedroom.

I scrambled to my feet and felt along the wall. I was frantic, and as I inched down the hall, hoping was heading in the right direction, I jumped with surprise when I heard the front door slam.

"Dad? Is that you?"

Of course it wasn't. My father was checking on the Gables and a good twenty minutes away.

I kept heading down the hall, hoping I was going towards the bedroom. It seemed to me that Paul would keep an inhaler in his bedroom.

I felt along the wall and a sudden burst of light shocked my eyes when I stepped around the corner. My headlights shone through the living room window and lit the house. I could see now, and I sprinted to the stairs, ran up them two at a time and headed for the far bedroom. I knew the master bedroom was at the end of the house on the top floor, because Paul had been such a stickler about cutting down a mature aspen that blocked his view from that window. If he had an inhaler, it would be beside his bed, I was sure.

I was relieved when I pushed through the bedroom door and saw that my car lights shone through the windows, illuminating the entire room. A bedside table with two drawers stood beside the massive bed. I searched the top. No inhaler. A bottle of wine sat opened on the table. The cork was still stuck on the end of a metal corkscrew. I dropped to my knees and jerked open the top drawer, pulling so hard the wine bottle rocked wildly and tumbled to the floor, shattering on the hardwood. Suddenly the room was filled with the pungent odor of red wine and fruit. And now the floor was covered with broken bottle glass. I tried not to kneel on the glass as I searched frantically through the drawers. They were full of magazines, tissues, and ink pens. But I didn't see anything else.

"Dammit, Paul, where did you put it?"

I scanned the floor. Maybe he had tried to use his inhaler and he had dropped it? I slid back from the table and pulled up the bed skirt. I felt along the floor and then my hand found something cool and smooth.

I snatched it and lifted it into the light. A white L-shaped cylinder with a prescription label taped to the side rested in my hand.

"Finally," I said. I shoved the inhaler inside my canvas coat pocket and ran back down the stairs. If he needed it I would have it ready. I was pretty sure Paul was having the worst asthma attack of his life.

I groped my way back to the kitchen and felt along the floor until I found him. He didn't have a shirt, and when I knelt beside him I could feel the heat radiating off his skin.

"I've got your inhaler," I said.

I lowered my ear next to his mouth to see if he could respond at all, even if it was with a whisper. At that moment, his breathing stopped. I felt my throat tighten with panic. His entire body seemed completely paralyzed. I had to do something. He was dying.

I felt for a pulse. My hands were shaking. Placing my fingers lightly on his neck, I felt nothing, and began CPR at once.

I used both hands and didn't bother with anything but compression, like we'd been taught at the Fish and Wildlife training seminars. Mouth-to-mouth resuscitation wouldn't save him, but compression might, and that's what I did. I could feel the intense heat from his body radiating into my hands. It was like he was burning up from the inside out. I pumped his chest as hard as I could, using all of my body weight to get enough pressure to compress his rib cage. He was a big man and it took all the strength I had to force his heart to beat.

Almost at once my body began to tire. I could feel Paul slipping away, but I kept at it, hoping he would come around.

I wanted to yell at him to keep trying but I didn't have the energy to do it. I kept hoping for some sign I was helping him, but he didn't respond at all.

After what seemed like a very long time, I saw headlights splash across the back yard just as my tired shoulders started shaking from the effort. I tried to keep going, but I could tell Paul was gone. I stopped CPR, not because I wasn't willing, but because my arms just gave out. I'd only managed to do compression for at most twenty minutes or so. I doubted that it had made a bit of difference. Paul's body had simply given out.

My father's strong hands came down on my shoulders and pulled me off the kitchen floor. I hadn't even heard him come through the door. He sat me down on a chair at the kitchen table and told me to stay put.

My father carried a heavy-duty flashlight he always kept in his truck, and I watched as he leaned over Paul's body and checked for a pulse, shining the bright light over the big man as he tried to tell what had happened.

"I thought he had an asthma attack," I said.

"He seems pretty red to me," my father said.

I hated to look, but I did. Paul's skin did look red. Almost like he had suffered heatstroke.

"Maybe it was a heart attack?" I said.

My father stood up and rubbed his forehead with the back of his hand. "I'll go call Loy," he said.

He had a CB radio in his pickup truck and it seemed like only a few minutes passed when a paramedic stepped through the destroyed kitchen door.

I know it had to have taken the paramedics three-quarters of an hour to get to us from Parkman, breaking every speed limit on I-90, but the rules of time were bent and things were moving past my awareness with warped intensity.

I spoke to the paramedics, slowly and carefully explaining what I'd found, and when I heard them say that Paul was dead my father led me through the house to the front steps and sat me down so I wouldn't have to look at a corpse any longer.

I sat on the cold stone steps and the trees surrounding the house pulsed with light from the ambulance's rotating beacon.

By the time Sheriff Loy Shucraft pulled into the driveway I was still shaking. My arms didn't seem to want to work anymore and neither did my mouth. Explaining what had happened was growing more and more difficult.

Loy had been sheriff of Killdeer for three years, but he and I had known each other almost our whole lives. The fact that I was talking to a friend was a small comfort, but I was willing to take any comfort I could possibly get.

Loy told my father to keep me on the front steps and he disappeared inside the house. After a few minutes I wasn't shivering from shock, I was shaking from the cold. Sitting on the stone steps was draining what little warmth I had left in me.

Finally I heard Loy's heavy steps coming through the house and he came back to tell us what he knew. The look on his face when he leaned over me was grim.

"Well, Nathan, it looks like your daughter found Paul not too long after he'd suffered some sort of episode. Maybe a heart attack, or a stroke. He had asthma pretty bad. It could have been related."

My father stood up and tried to walk away, and by proxy lead the sheriff out into the driveway and away from me, but Loy didn't budge. The sheriff and I had graduated high school together and Loy had always been of the mind that I was one of his best friends because I was level-headed. He seemed to be sure I could handle what he was about to say.

I blinked and fixed my gaze on his sturdy frame. His lake blue eyes scanned me, one hand resting on his gun belt and the other propped on his knee. He was trying to make it easy on me, but he had a job to do after all.

"Marley, from your statement, you did CPR for nearly fifteen or twenty minutes. That sound right?"

I nodded, not sure at all but trusting that he'd worked out the time frame based on what my father had said.

"It was too late for you to save him," Loy said. "You could have done CPR for two days and it wouldn't have made a bit of difference. Marley, you did all you could do. It wasn't your fault he died."

"He was hot," I said, my throat sounding hoarse.

"What do you mean, hot?" Loy asked, his eyebrows scrunching.

"His skin was hot. Burning. But that doesn't make any sense. Why would he be so hot?"

"Marley, Hun, do you think you could be mistaken?" Loy asked, his wide face looking perplexed.

I let my eyes fall to the steps beside me and I shrugged. "Maybe."

I wasn't.

I gave my father a look and his eyes clouded up with sympathy. He cupped my elbow and lifted me from the steps. "We're done here, Loy. I'm taking Marley home. You have any other questions you come by the ranch house and ask me. She's had a rough morning and I think this can wait till later."

"Nathan, I'd like to hear what else she has to say," the sheriff said, backing up a bit like a cutting horse dealing with a flighty calf.

My father looked irritated. "And you can wait till after she's had some breakfast and some rest."

Loy squared his shoulders and my father squared his jaw and I stood between them shivering in the chill air. They said nothing for a moment, then Loy let his eyes fall on my face and his shoulders slumped down. I must have looked pretty wretched, because the burly sheriff stepped aside and indicated with a nod we could go.

"I should be here for another hour or so, then I'll come by Marley's place," Loy said, pointedly. "If she has anything else to say I'll get the rest of her statement there."

My father relented. "Fine."

We started towards my father's truck.

"One more thing, Nathan," Loy said. "Did you come in the back door or the front door?"

My father stopped and I could see him going over it all in his head. He glanced back at the sheriff. "The back. I went in the back."

"Did you try going in the front door?" Loy asked.

My father frowned. "Nope. Didn't bother. I figured if I couldn't see anybody on the porch they were around back. Why?"

Loy shrugged. "It was unlocked, that's all."

I stopped walking towards the truck and turned to look at Loy. "But, the back door was locked up tight. Why would he leave the front door open?"

"It's probably nothing," the sheriff told me. "Go on home and get some rest, Marley. I'll be by later."

I stood looking at the house for a moment, feeling foolish that I'd broken down the kitchen door for no reason. It didn't make any sense to me that the back would be locked when the front wasn't. But, not a lot about this morning was making any sense to me anymore.

I let myself be tugged into motion and my father led me to his truck. It wasn't spoken, but understood between us, that I wasn't in any shape to drive. I could leave my car at Paul's for a few hours. We pulled out of the driveway as another sheriff's truck rounded the bend, lights flashing, but no siren. I guessed it was Loy's new deputy arriving at the scene, driving slowly, because he knew there wasn't any need to hurry at this point.

CHAPTER 4

We drove back to my little house in silence, my father not uttering a word, until we pulled into the gravel drive of my place and he saw something he didn't like. He swore, soft enough that most people would miss it, but not me.

"What's wrong?" I asked.

I followed his gaze and saw a familiar white truck parked in my driveway, the green swirl logo of Reliant Landscaping painted on the door. Jack Parks stood at the foot of my stairs, his lanky frame hesitating. He looked like he was about to head up the steps. My father practically growled when he stepped out of the truck and slammed his door.

"Jack, good to see you. What can I do for you?" My father's lips were white from pressing them together.

I opened my door and reluctantly followed. When Jack saw me his eyes popped. "Marley, you look like hell. Everything alright over here?"

"She's had a tough morning, Jack," my father said.

"My scanner picked up all the talk between Loy and his dispatcher," Jack said. "I called out here but your lines are down."

"Just a bit of wind," my father said, hustling me past Jack towards the stairs.

Jack looked at the huge cottonwood tree sprawled in my front yard and the flattened toolshed. "Uh-huh."

I pulled my canvas coat tighter around my shoulders and stopped to talk, being polite, though my father seemed determined not to be. "I appreciate you coming over, Jack."

My boss looked at me closely. "You sure you're alright, Marley?"

My father stepped in front of me. "She's fine. Shook up. There was a bit of trouble up at the Nesbit house and we were seeing to it."

I looked at the back of my father's head with raised eyebrows. A bit of trouble?

Jack's face changed. "Oh, sorry to hear it. Everyone in one piece at Paul's place?"

My father shook his head, staring at Jack with an expression bordering on irritated. "No. Paul had a spot of bad luck and he's passed away this morning."

Jack's serene expression flinched to shock for a moment, but went back to placid quickly and his brown eyes rested on me. "Paul's dead? What the hell?"

I nodded. "I found him this morning just before sunup. Loy said it looked like a heart attack. I don't suppose I could take the day off, Jack?"

"Sure, sure. Course you can," he said, moving to stand beside me.

My father put an arm over my shoulders and headed me towards the steps. "She's had a rough time. I'm sure you understand that she needs some rest."

Jack's even voice didn't falter, but his feet moved slowly as he stepped out of our path. "You need any help with the damage on the house?" he asked. He was looking at me and I shook myself internally to respond.

"No, Jack. Thanks. Dad's going to see to that. But I sure could use a new shed at some point."

"I can find something over at the shop we can bring out, if you like. And maybe I'll have the boys come by later and cut up that cottonwood. I can give you a good rate on the removal."

My father chuckled. It was a condescending sound. "I'm sure you could."

Jack shuffled his long legs and ran a hand through his thick brown hair. "Well, I'll let you get some rest, Marley. See you tomorrow, then?"

"I'll be at work tomorrow," I said, with more conviction than I felt.

Jack gave my father a sincere smile. "Okay, then. Well, take it easy, Nathan."

My father didn't bother to respond. In fact he made a point not to.

Jack was pulling out of the driveway by the time I'd kicked off my shoes and curled up on the couch. I braced myself for the verbal barrage from my father that usually occurred directly after he saw Jack Parks, but oddly, my father silently set to work on the kitchen window and kept his thoughts to himself. It was the first time since I'd started working for Jack that my father had come face-to-face with the man and not said anything derogatory afterward. It was a mystery to me, but to say that my father didn't care for Jack was like saying the Sioux at the Battle of the Little Big Horn hadn't cared for Custer.

I watched my father work for the better part of an hour, staying out of his way at his insistence. I felt my eyes get heavy and I must have drifted off into a hard sleep for a good portion of the morning, because when I woke my father was gone.

I pulled myself up and tried the light switch. Nothing. It was a safe bet we'd have no power for the rest of the day. Getting a power line crew to come all the way out to our end of Killdeer always seemed to take a lot longer than it should. I imagined they probably didn't like working in our little valley very much. There were too many trees, too many potholes in the gravel road, and only a handful of people to service. No, the valley wasn't a priority and we were used to going without electricity after destructive storms. Not for the first time I found myself wishing that the mayor lived on our end of the valley. I was willing to bet if he did, we would have the lights back on a lot sooner.

I didn't feel like having peanut butter and jelly even though I was starving, and I was afraid to open the refrigerator. Once I did, everything would start to spoil.

I wandered into the kitchen and saw that my father had made quite a bit of progress on the window. The frame was clean and ready for a new pane of glass, the wood was sanded and prepped, and I felt a strange jolt of amusement that I could look through a hole in my kitchen straight into the back yard. I felt the breeze blow through the woods and into my house. A mossy aroma drifted in. Luckily, it was shaping up to be a mild fall day. The sun was warming things up and it had to be almost sixty degrees. Good thing too, as my entire living room was at the mercy of the elements.

A chickadee fluttered down from the big ponderosa pine outside and landed on the window frame. It seemed just as entertained as I was by the sudden lack of glass. It cheeped at me once, then puffed up and flew back to the tree, a tiny streak of black and white.

I realized my father was most likely in town getting a replacement pane of glass. I should have gone to help, but I'd needed the nap.

My stomach growled and I resigned myself to a cold shower. No electricity meant no hot water, but if I was going into town to feed myself I needed to clean up.

I hadn't taken a shower that fast since college, and I was shivering and drying off when my ears told me someone was coming up the steps to my front door. I snatched a robe and managed to tie it as someone knocked.

I padded to the door and when I peeked out the window I saw Sheriff Shucraft standing on my steps, eyes bloodshot and expression irate.

I pulled open the door a crack and stuck my nose in the opening. "Just let me get on some clothes, Loy. I'll be right with you."

I made the mistake of leaving the door open a bit, and when I came out of my bedroom Loy was standing in the living room with his fists crossed over his chest. He was glaring at my wall.

More accurately, he was glaring at the screwdriver stuck in my wall.

"This could have killed you."

He said it like an accusation.

I stepped beside him and pulled the screwdriver from the Sheetrock. It took both hands.

He turned his peeved expression on me.

"Your yard is a mess. There are tools all over the place, and I see you lost your window. There's a dead squirrel plastered to your deck, and you are damn lucky that cottonwood tree didn't crush your house."

His tone rankled me a bit. Like I had any control over flying hand tools. "There isn't a dead squirrel on my deck. You made that up."

"Marley," he said, turning to give me the hairy horse-eye glare. "It seems to me you should be living closer to town."

"And it seems to me that you should respect a lady's privacy while she changes."

His eyes sparkled and he let a corner of his mouth curl up. "Nothing I haven't seen before."

It was my turn to glare. We all did stupid things in high school. "Don't you have some important police work to do?"

Loy smirked.

I sat down on the couch to tug on my socks. "So what killed Paul?"

My choice of words seemed to surprise him. He turned serious and tried to squeeze his bulk into the wooden rocking chair across from me. His gun wedged against the armrest and he shifted around for a few seconds, trying to get it loose, before giving up and standing once again.

"It looks pretty straightforward," he said. "Paul had severe asthma and the paramedics seem to think he had some sort of cardiac failure. He showed all the signs of a heart attack victim. It may have been induced by the bad shock he got when the downburst hit his house."

The downburst hadn't really hit his house. It had reserved my place for that honor.

It didn't seem to me that there had been enough damage at Paul's house to say the storm had been a shock.

"Heart attack?" I asked. "But he's so young."

Loy looked at the ceiling. "The paramedics seemed to think Paul may have had some sort of allergic reaction, but who knows?"

"Sure. Who knows?"

Loy rested his hand on his gun. He did that whenever he was about to ask a question he didn't like.

"Marley, did you notice anything odd when you first got inside the house?"

I glanced at him for a moment, and then looked at my socks. "Yes. I thought it was strange that I didn't see a flashlight anyplace beside him."

"I see," he said, shifting his feet. "Anything else?"

"Anything else?"

Loy tensed and I was suddenly paying very close attention to him. "The new guy we hired? You met him at Lil's once I think. Nick. Well, he's big on crime scene situations and forensics, and he was practically dusting the goddamn acreage for fingerprints. I sent a toxicology kit up to Missoula, but he seemed to think we should do a full autopsy. He said he just wanted to cover all the bases. Speaking of that, we found a busted bottle of wine in the bedroom. Did you happen to notice that?"

He pushed his baseball cap back with one big hand. He was the only sheriff of Killdeer in living memory who wore a brown baseball cap on duty rather than the standard cowboy hat. Some of the more traditional folks frowned on this fashion choice, but I liked it.

"I was the one who broke it," I said, feeling foolish I hadn't told him about it back at the house.

Loy's expression was carefully neutral. "What were you doing in Paul's bedroom, Hun?"

"I thought he needed his inhaler. I was looking for it."

He looked slightly relieved and his shoulders relaxed.

I gave him an exasperated look. "Loy, I was not in his bedroom for any other reason, so just get that thought out of your head right this instant."

"I wasn't having a thought," he said, protesting. "I was trying to determine the sequence of events."

"Oh. Well, have I helped you out at all?" I asked, perturbed that he would even consider the possibility that I would have been seeing Paul in a more than friendly capacity.

He checked his watch and fiddled with the volume switch on his radio, clearly embarrassed that he had let his concerns be so transparent.

"You helped me out. I would say that the storm woke him up, and he couldn't sleep so he got himself a glass of wine to calm down. Then he must have started to feel poorly and that had to be when the lights went out."

"Why did he go down to the kitchen?" I asked.

"There was a rotary phone in the kitchen. Even with the power out, a rotary phone will still let you call. I think he was trying to phone for help," Loy told me.

"Then he collapsed in the kitchen. I must have shown up not too long after that," I said, feeling a cold shiver from the image.

"That's what we came up with," Loy said. "But not exactly in that order."

I gave him a look that said I wasn't entirely convinced. The whole situation seemed so unreal.

I sighed and rubbed my temples. "He wasn't that old."

"Listen," Loy said with care. "If you need to talk to anyone about this, just call the station and I will have Valerie page me. I can come right over. You may find it won't be all that easy to get past the shock of seeing someone you knew die like that. But I've seen a lot more of it than you have, and if you need—"

I cut him off with a wave and a small smile. "I'll call. Don't worry. Dad won't give me a moment's peace. Thanks, Loy."

He had asked all of his questions, so why was he still hovering over me?

I sat forward a bit and softened my smile. "So why did you really drive all the way over here just to talk to me?"

He let out an exasperated breath. "Marley, listen. I know how you are. But this isn't a case. There is nothing here that needs to be investigated. I don't want you worried about what happened."

My soft smile faded. "What do you mean, you know how I am?"

Loy put his hand back on his holster. "The game wardens gossip worse than cops. Whenever we have our monthly law enforcement meetings with the county staff, we do business and then we . . . well, we swap stories, shoot the bull. Trade information. You know."

I was getting a bad feeling about where this conversation was headed.

"And what did the game wardens from Parkman tell you about me while you were shooting the bull?" I asked.

His face turned one shade redder. "They told me you always took more interest in the criminal cases they were investigating up in the Helena office than you should have."

I kept my temper, though I had to struggle to do it. "And you believed that?" I asked.

Loy shrugged off my question. "All I'm saying is this isn't a case. We don't need to investigate anything. I know you practically ran that office in Helena, and you were in tight with the investigator. Also, I know you always had a lot more curiosity about things than was healthy and maybe that had something to do with why you got fired. You always were poking into stuff, Hun. Even in high school you were like that."

"And what does that have to do with Paul?" I asked.

"Nothing. Not a thing. So, I don't want you to fret over this. Understand?"

I let that simmer for a moment before I opened my mouth. I had learned a measure of humility coming back to Killdeer six months ago. I wasn't so quick to protest accusations these days. I had learned that protesting didn't do a bit of good anyway.

I pasted a smile on my face. "Sure. I understand. You don't want me to fret."

It was his turn to rub his eyes. "Get some rest, Marley. I can come by and check on you later if you like."

"I think I'll be fine." I'd had enough rest.

"Good. That's good. You'll call if you . . . ?"

37

"I'll call," I said. "Thanks. But, really, I won't let this get to me."

He seemed satisfied, gave my shoulder a quick squeeze and tipped his hat.

He obviously wanted to say more, but he didn't. He forced a smile, gave me a quick bear hug and finally clomped down the stairs to his truck.

I heard the engine fire and he was a quarter mile away before I recalled I didn't have my car. I was stuck, with no one to give me a ride back out to Paul's house. Unless I wanted to wait for my father to get back with the window, I was stranded. I could sit around, or I could start walking. It looked like I would be getting some unexpected exercise today. If I had only been thinking I could have asked Loy to give me a lift.

"Damn and damn," I said. "It's hard being dumb."

CHAPTER 5

The walk back to Paul's house was pleasant, considering the morning's events. I hadn't bothered with a watch. It was strange not having any particular schedule to keep on a workday, so I channeled my energy into getting back to my car as quickly as I could, and I made great time. Back when I had been working at a desk every day I had been ten pounds heavier and a walk to the grocery store seemed like a long way. Not anymore. I was suddenly grateful for all the time I'd spent landscaping with Jack. I was in the best shape of my life.

I saw a sheriff's truck parked beside my Honda when I crested the steep hill, but I didn't recognize the truck as belonging to Loy. The new deputy was probably inside the house.

When I walked up the driveway I could see the house in daylight, and I knew right away that my property had taken a great deal more damage in the form of downed tree branches and hail-shredded leaves. Luckily the trees next to my driveway had sheltered my Honda from the hail. But the area was still a mess. If Jack set our crew to work at my little house, I guessed we could have it back to normal with a full day's labor.

I stood looking at Paul's property from the long driveway for a good few minutes, and I decided our full crew could have it cleaned up in half a day. It was in far better shape here than at my place.

I felt an odd surge of obligation at that thought. Paul had hired Jack to take care of his property and here it was, looking terrible.

I walked to my Honda and opened up the passenger-side door, being careful not to ding the deputy's truck. I always kept some of Jack's business cards in my glove compartment, and I pulled one out and walked over to the stout mailbox mounted by the front steps. The cards in my glove box had my name written on the back so that Jack would know I'd been the one to refer the customer to him. I opened the mailbox and set the business card inside it, knowing whoever would come to take ownership of the big house might need to hire someone to clean up the property. I didn't know if Paul had any family. Any relatives who came to deal with his death might find a bit of comfort knowing they wouldn't have to clean up the mess at the house on top of everything else they would be dealing with. And Jack would get some much-needed business.

My feet crunched the driveway gravel as I headed for my car. I heard a scrape from the front door and glanced behind me as a youngish sheriff's deputy bobbed down the front steps. His black hair was cut short but still managed to stick up at odd angles. Probably from too many dramatic gestures with restless hands. His pale skin seemed flushed. He walked straight at me, fixated on me like I was a target.

"I guess you'd be Nick," I said.

He came to a stop inches from me. "I am. You are Marley Dearcorn."

I couldn't argue the fact. I gave him a nod. I didn't like him. He seemed too eager, or maybe it was that he smelled like he'd been sweating ginseng and echinacea all morning. A very serious health nut.

He looked me up and down, weighing and measuring me. "I was hoping you would get back here to pick up your car."

I pulled my car keys from my pocket to indicate how right he was. "I'll just move it now. I'm sure it must be in your way."

He pulled a fat notebook from a sagging back pocket and flipped through several pages of neat script. His pants hung off his narrow frame, giving him a Barney Fife appearance, as though he worked out. A lot. But all it was getting him was leaner and not necessarily meaner.

"You need to answer a couple questions for me."

I watched him fiddle with the notebook. He looked up at me, expecting a response.

"Okay," I said.

He nearly grew an inch in height, and I realized he was so excited he was standing on the balls of his feet with anticipation. Technically, Loy had taken my statement early this morning, and his follow-up questions at my house should have been enough. Either this deputy was eager to prove himself or else he didn't trust the statement I had already given.

"Sure. I can answer a few questions," I said, keeping my voice as even as I could.

Unfazed by my bleak tone he pulled out a mechanical pencil worthy of MIT and poised the tip over his bulging notebook.

I'd worked for Montana Fish and Wildlife branch office in Helena long enough to recognize waterproof paper when I saw it. The stuff was not exactly cheap. Nick had an entire notebook made of the special paper.

He was starting to get on my nerves.

"What did you see when you first got here?" he asked, his eyes wide.

I suddenly felt the urge not to cooperate. "Well, it was dark."

His lips twitched and he worked his eyebrows. Clearly, I wasn't in the spirit of the thing.

"Elaborate."

It was not a request.

I took a breath to steady my nerves and noticed I was clenching my fists too tight. I eased my shoulders a bit and shut my eyes for a moment, letting my mind take me back to the predawn nightmare I'd lived only a few hours ago.

"It was not as bad as I expected it to be," I began.

"Not as bad?" he asked, his eyebrows traveling up his forehead with confusion.

"My place was wrecked by the downburst," I explained. "The gusts were still pretty erratic when I left my house. But when I got here I didn't see as much damage as I'd expected."

He considered writing that down, then appeared to change his mind and gave me one more chance.

"Right. What about after you got inside the house?"

That was not so easy to remember because I had spent the morning trying to forget.

"I thought it was odd I couldn't see a flashlight through the windows."

42

"Why?" he asked.

I pressed on. "I figured Paul had to be awake, and since he didn't have power either I thought he would have a flashlight or a couple of candles burning."

The deputy scribbled something and nodded that I should continue.

"I thought it was strange that the back door was locked," I said.

"Why is that strange?"

"Everybody leaves their doors unlocked here in the valley."

"Which is a stupid thing to do," he said.

His tone was so condescending I wanted to stand on his instep. How could I explain that was the way we did things out here? Deputy Nick was obviously not from a small town.

"When I looked through the kitchen window I could see Paul lying on the floor."

"How did you see him if the power was out?"

"The lightning flash was enough to light up the kitchen."

He scribbled. "Then what?"

I shifted my feet. "The door was locked but I knew I needed to get inside, so I used the tractor."

"Why didn't you just break a window?" he asked.

I was getting tired of feeling stupid. "I was in a hurry."

He ignored that. "You told the paramedics you did CPR for twenty minutes."

"I did do CPR for twenty minutes."

He looked me up and down.

The examination made me bristle.

"You weigh, what, 120? And you're female. I figure you'd be able to do effective CPR for about ten minutes before you dropped."

"I'm a landscaper," I said, my face getting red. "It's not like I paint other people's toenails for a living. How long do you think you could do CPR?"

He scribbled. "And then you told Sheriff Shucraft that Paul's body was hot. What did you mean by that?"

"He wasn't a body when I got there. He was still alive."

That made the deputy look up. "Right. Sorry."

I probably should have told him I'd run upstairs looking for Paul's inhaler, but I didn't want to drag this discussion out any longer than necessary. I was already on the verge of saying something snide. The last thing I wanted to do was antagonize a man with a badge.

I forced myself to ease back on the accelerator. "Paul stopped breathing when I was leaning down, listening to him to see if he could speak. He couldn't and when I checked for a pulse I didn't feel one, so I started CPR right away."

"And you did compression for twenty minutes," he said again.

I stared at him. I could feel my chest tightening up. I hadn't been friends with Paul, but I'd known the man, and seeing him die had not been easy.

The deputy was oblivious to what I was feeling.

"Do you think the shock could have made you lose track of time or something?" he asked.

"No," I looked straight in his eyes. "It didn't."

Nick—I still didn't know his last name— closed his notebook. "I think we're done here. You can go."

He walked back up the steps and I was officially a nonperson once again. He ducked under the yellow crime scene tape, and it occurred to me that Deputy Nick had probably strung the stuff all the way around the house. Crime scene tape for a heart attack?

The deputy let the screen door slam behind him as he went back inside the house. I felt like I'd just been interrogated. Maybe he had heard about my sudden departure from Helena and had formed his own opinions about me in advance.

Nobody in Killdeer came out directly and said that they didn't trust me any longer, but everywhere I went I couldn't shake the feeling I was now an outcast in my own hometown. It had taken me weeks to find a new job. But, I had avoided looking for a new job until I had almost completely run out of cash. I'd been too ashamed to apply for work. I couldn't stand the thought that the folks who populated Killdeer suspected that I was a criminal.

Did they suspect I was a criminal? I simply couldn't say one way or the other. Sometimes I felt like everyone was looking at me, pointing and talking behind my back. Then again, maybe it was all in my head.

CHAPTER 6

I needed a shoulder to lean on and a hot meal more than anything in the world. So by definition, I needed to see Irene Baker. She could never be described as sweet, or softhearted, but she was solid and pragmatic and exactly the person I needed to talk to.

I started my little Honda, gunned it hard enough to kick up gravel, and headed towards town. I needed to see a friendly face, and though Irene was typically as friendly as a persistent horsefly, she was also steadfast. I drove straight to Lil's café.

The parking lot was full, as usual. I went inside and sat at the counter in my usual spot. Center stool, straight across from the coffeepot.

Without a word, the owner of the café plunked a coffee cup in front of me and filled it with a steaming hot brew so dark you could paint a house with it. I loved the coffee at Lil's.

Irene had bought Lil's café a year or so before I had moved to Helena. She was adamant about keeping the name. The café had changed hands a dozen times during its existence, but every new owner insisted on keeping the old name. Nobody knew, or remembered, who Lil had been.

Nobody cared.

It was the best food in town and if you ever needed a place to rent, a guy to help you cut up a deer during hunting season, or needed advice on how to get skunks out of your garage, you went to Lil's. All you had to do was ask around. Somebody there would know what you needed, or know who did. Lil's was the unofficial town bulletin board.

"Bad day," Irene asked, replacing the coffeepot on the warmer.

I nodded. "The new deputy just spent ten minutes talking to me like I am an idiot."

"Screw him," she said.

"Irene Baker. You don't mean that," I told her.

Irene slammed a roll of quarters down next to the cash register. She popped open the drawer, did some quick counting and then peeled the coins into the till with the skill and speed of a concert pianist.

"When have I ever not meant what I said?"

I searched her face. Irene had ice-blue eyes, no-nonsense short blonde hair and a fortyish face as serious as a hatchet. Her look could peel the bark off a tree stump. Someday I would learn not to question her.

Lil's was busy, even though it was in between the lunch rush and the early dinner crowd. Irene had owned Lil's for ten years but in all that time it hadn't changed a bit. It was your average café, complete with swivel bar stools and mismatched dining room tables.

A hot omelet, flanked by two sausages, appeared on the counter in front of me. I hadn't remembered ordering yet.

"Nick talks to everyone like they're an idiot," she said.

Her nimble fingers made short work of a disorganized stack of customer receipts. "Who cares what he thinks?"

"I care." Harvey Wilson was slumped at the end of the counter in his best overalls, greasy John Deere baseball cap worn sideways and potbelly protruding proudly. He eyed Irene.

"Nobody asked you, Harvey." Irene slammed the cash register drawer shut.

He chuckled and fingered his worn toothpick, turning his attention back to the daily dose of depression we liked to call the local paper. The headline read *Bull Moose Attacks Logging Truck.* Apparently the news about Paul hadn't been discovered until after the morning printing.

I poured cream in my coffee.

"I thought the paper would be all over the story about Paul by now," I said.

Irene watched me stir my coffee. My face must have shown that I was not too keen to talk about what had happened.

"You can bet they will run with it tomorrow," she said.

I sipped my coffee and gave her a sour look over the rim of my cup. "Something tactful, I'm sure. Like a headline that says David Jordan runs for mayor unopposed. What will folks talk about now that they won't have the race between Paul and David to worry about?"

"Well, Marley, really," she said, shaking her head. "It was like watching two five-year-olds fight over space in a sandbox. It was a joke and everybody knows it."

She shook her head. "Paul and David just hated each other. They only ran for office out of spite."

"You don't think they wanted to give something back to the town?" I asked.

"I'm not sure either one of them could handle the job of cleaning the toothpaste out of a bathroom sink, much less the position of mayor for a city."

"Killdeer qualifies as a city?" I asked.

Irene shot me a look.

I set my cup down, feeling tired.

"So, Dearcorn, did Paul have any last words?" Harvey asked, leaning towards me over his newspaper.

"Yeah, he said tell Harvey Wilson to pay his tab down at the Broken Spoke," Irene told him, her eyes sharp. She wasn't about to let Harvey needle me about what I had seen.

The grungy farmer worked his toothpick, looking like he was trying to decide if he was up to taking on Irene this afternoon. Wisely, he went back to his half-finished bacon instead of saying anything else.

Irene snapped her fingers at a waitress gliding past with a plate of eggs and rye toast, pointed to a man in the corner and indicated with a nod his iced tea was in need of attention. Nothing got past Irene.

"So, did he have any last words?" Irene asked.

"What? No, of course he didn't. He couldn't say anything at all because he was too busy dying," I replied, a bit harsher than I had intended.

"I can't say I had anything against him personally, but will he be missed?" she said, pulling out a new box of coffee filters and peeling off the lid with a nimble gesture. "I think Killdeer was just too small a town for the likes of Paul Nesbit."

"He seemed to be trying to fit in," I said.

She smirked. "He pretended to fit in. He made a show of it, playing at being a reformed man while going back to the same old love 'em and leave 'em behavior that got him into trouble in Pennsylvania in the first place. And he was allergic to everything. God forbid a strawberry touch something he was going to eat here in the café. I stopped carrying strawberry pie because of him."

"I miss your strawberry pie," Harvey said. "You gonna start carrying it again?"

"He wasn't exactly a choirboy or anything, but have a little respect, maybe?" I said to Harvey.

"Not a choirboy? Do you know how many secretaries in this town will be crying their eyes out over the fact that he's dead?" Irene asked.

I slid my empty plate to the side. "Paul wasn't that bad. You don't think a man can change?"

"A man? Change?" Irene asked. "Not without having suffered severe head trauma. And even then, probably not. Paul was a dog. I doubt seriously that moving to Killdeer changed him one bit."

Irene had never suffered a nasty divorce. An unscrupulous lover had never left her at the altar. As far as anyone knew, she had never even been the victim of sexual assault. No, Irene just didn't like people much. Which was odd considering she owned the busiest diner in Killdeer.

"You think Paul could have won the race for mayor?" I asked, wanting to change the subject but not quite sure how to do it.

It felt like all the customers in Lil's were scrutinizing every word I said. Maybe I was simply being self-conscious, but then again, maybe not.

Now I had been involved with a man's death. I was fairly sure this wouldn't help my reputation much.

Irene rubbed her forehead with long fingers and seemed to mellow slightly. "You know, I think he could have won. Shows you how stupid people are. Paul was going to beat David in the race, based on what all my customers have been yammering about for the last month."

"Really?" I asked.

"David was running out of money," she said, propping her bony elbows on the counter and scanning the café for signs of trouble. She ran a tight ship, to say the least. Her waitresses were mostly terrified of her.

She set my empty plate in the gray dish tub under the counter. "Paul was outspending him a hundred dollars to one in this race. You saw that huge billboard ad Paul bought?"

I nodded. It had once been an advertisement to discourage meth use, but Paul's face had replaced the ad a few weeks ago. His black hair and black beard made him look more like a pirate than a candidate, but his gleaming smile came off more roguish than malevolent.

Irene sipped a fragrant herbal tea. Her doctor had said it would help her nerves. "It cost him four thousand dollars to buy that billboard spot. You think for one minute David would have the kind of cash it takes to compete with that level of spending?"

If anyone knew the power of the dollar, it was Irene.

"Not a chance," she answered her own question.

"David may have inherited that lovely house from his parents, but that was all he ever inherited. Paul was going to win, I'd say. He was always kissing babies and showing up at the Rotary meetings, renting himself out to any club in town that would have him."

"He even went to that snooty knitting circle at Wee Wooly's Yarn Shop and tried to knit a scarf," Harvey Wilson said, not able to resist butting back in. "Paper had a write-up about it."

"What a disaster," Irene said. "But Paul charmed the cashmere pants off of Wendy, and you and I both know that if Wendy liked Paul, Joe would like Paul and the bank would back him. I would bet he managed a big campaign donation out of that one. Oh, Paul was hitting the hot spots all right. I would be surprised if David had any hope of winning. Shame really. You know how much that job means to him."

"I thought David was washed up as mayor when Loy busted him for that DWI back in '08," Harvey said.

"I think it actually helped his career," Irene said, her tone disgusted.

"How can that help a political career?" I asked.

"Just think about how many members of the city council are members of the detox club. You know what the kids say about Killdeer. There's nothing to do here but drink and scr—"

"Mayor Jordan went through detox?" I asked with surprise.

"Six weeks' worth in June of last year," Harvey said.

"No wonder Paul was favored to win," I said.

Irene sipped her tea. "I personally think David Jordan is the lesser of the two evils. He may be a lush, but he always tries to do what's best for the town and I can't say that Paul would have done that."

She glanced up and her eyes narrowed suspiciously as two wannabe hoodlum teenage boys came through the front door.

"Richie Williams, if you are coming into my café you will pull your pants up to a decent hitch around your waist. You understand me, young man?"

The two gangsta youth stopped dead in the door, their expressions radiating disdain. They looked around and realized every eye in the place was suddenly fixed in their direction. They shuffled oversized sneakers for a moment, adjusted ball caps worn artistically sideways, then the apparent leader relented and hiked his pants up to his waist. "Yes, Ms. Baker."

Irene finished her tea with one swallow, her civic duty done for the day, and patted my hand.

"Your house okay? I heard about your shed and the picture window, but other than that was there very much damage?"

For a battle-ax, Irene could be surprisingly kind.

I put money on the counter and stood up. "Dad will probably have the window replaced, the kitchen redecorated and the front yard landscaped by the time I get home. You know how he is."

For a moment I saw it. At the mention of my father, Irene's face always softened a bit and took on a wistful expression. She smiled and started punching numbers on her cash register. "That's eight bucks fifty, Harvey."

"How come little Miss Dearcorn didn't have to pay for breakfast?" he asked, pointing at me with his toothpick.

"'Cause she ate the cook's mistake omelet," Irene answered. She nodded at the five-dollar bill I had put down. "And she tips better than you."

"Maybe I'll run for mayor and clean up the corruption in this town," Harvey said, digging his greasy wallet out of his overalls.

"You need any help at all, call me and I'll come out to give you a hand," Irene said.

"Thanks, but I think this morning I'll head down to the Big R and pick up another pair of drop-down blinds and call it good for the day," I said, reaching for my brown canvas coat. "If I don't have power this evening, you'll see me again for supper."

Irene set about washing her cup in the little side sink behind the counter and gave me a smile. "Tell your father I asked after him."

I left, thinking how strange it felt to have a day off when I shouldn't, and decided it might not be a bad idea to search for a new pair of shoes along with the blinds. I needed something to cheer me up.

CHAPTER 7

I parked in the mostly empty parking lot outside the Big R store and went inside, lost in thought. It was the beginning of the month and it seemed like all the bills ganged up on me at once. If the drop-down blinds were too expensive I'd have to settle for drapes. I opened my checkbook, saw the balance and realized shoe shopping would be out of the question.

As I headed towards the interior decorating aisle I had my head down and was busy checking the balance in my savings account, wondering if there were some hidden deposits I'd forgotten to log. I noticed the jeans I'd put on this morning had a stain. And a hole in the left knee.

My steel shopping cart bucked back like a spooked horse and hit me in the stomach. I gasped and saw stars sprinkle across my vision, took a moment to breathe, and saw Virginia Gable staring at me like I'd just run over her dog.

"Virginia," I said with a nod.

"Marley, you really should pay more attention to where you are going."

Virginia was in her middle forties, and not nearly old enough to be my mother, but it didn't stop her from talking to me like she was.

"Sorry, Mrs. Gable."

She squinted. Virginia hated to be called Mrs. Gable.

"Why aren't you working?" she asked, her hands wrapped tight around the handle of her cart. I noticed it was full of things I would have liked to be able to afford. Her Welsh corgi sat next to her feet, obediently watching her every move. His leash was purple.

"I'm taking the day off." I gave the dog a look. Normally, people left their dogs in the car when they went shopping.

"He's a service animal. I have low blood sugar and when I feel faint he barks to remind me to lie down." She patted the corgi's head. "Don't you Saint Christopher? That's my good boy!"

She needed a dog to tell her when she should lie down?

The dog panted and wiggled with delight from her heavy praise. It always made me cringe when people talked to their animals in baby talk.

I gave the corgi a sympathetic look. He couldn't help it that his owner was a Twinkie.

Virginia sighed, stood up and primped a perfect lock of severely dyed blonde hair back into place behind her ear. It showed off her diamond earrings nicely. "I'm sure Mr. Parks wouldn't want to know that you are spending your free time shopping."

I paused a beat before letting her have it. "A downburst hit my house last night and exploded my living room window."

She had the decency to blink. "Oh. Of course." She adjusted her Falcon Realty badge until it was precisely even. It gleamed.

She sniffed, her face suddenly waxy. "Your father mentioned when he stopped by at such an ungodly hour this morning that you'd had quite a bit of damage at your home. I'm not certain why he felt the need to come barging in on us."

I felt my dislike for Virginia creeping to the surface. "He wanted to be sure you and Leif were alright. The phones were down."

She pretended to examine a hand and I noticed her long, manicured nails looked perfect. My nails were short and usually had dirt under them. I wrapped them under the cart handle.

"Leif answered the door. I came out of the bedroom when I heard voices and there was your father, standing in the foyer, dripping."

I allowed myself a smile. "So you and Mr. Gable didn't have any damage?"

She scanned the shelf, pretending to read the cans of deck stain. "No. I imagine the cliff gave us some protection. All we had was rain."

The Gables lived behind Paul's house at the base of a sharp limestone cliff. Glaciers receding from the area thousands of years ago had left behind a perfectly smooth wall of stone, sheltering the land below the cliff and providing the perfect location for a secluded home. It was an extraordinary location. Leif Gable had built a house tailored for the landscape, a beautiful three-story log design with a wraparound deck that looked out towards the forest and seemed to blend seamlessly with the place. He'd given it to Virginia as a present almost five years ago. They had moved to Killdeer from Washington, D.C., and had started a new life together. Leif was a generous, truly nice man. We all wondered what he saw in Virginia.

She let her eyes drift towards me in a carefully controlled manner and her face was expressionless. "I understand that you were the one who found Paul."

I grimaced. It was no surprise she knew what had happened. Falcon Realty staffers were plugged in to a tight network of gossips.

I suppressed a sigh. "Yes. I was."

Her phone rang inside her cavernous purple handbag. She ignored it. "So. He must have had a heart attack? Stroke?"

I shrugged. "I couldn't really say."

I pressed my lips together and stared at her. She wasn't getting another word out of me about Paul and that was all there was to it.

Virginia was clearly irritated, but I let my expression show her I wasn't going to elaborate.

She clamped her mouth shut and looked straight ahead. "Come, Saint Christopher."

She pushed her cart forward and didn't say another word as she walked away, the corgi flanking her loyally. Her pumps made clicking sounds on the tile that sounded like springing mousetraps.

Virginia didn't care for anyone who didn't understand how the pecking order worked in Killdeer. Apparently my duty was to give her the inside scoop, and fill her in on all the morbid details, but I'd failed miserably. Or maybe she was hoping to dig up some gossip about Paul. It was no secret she had disdained him. If there was a line of respectability, Paul would find it and springboard over it with glee. Having inside information about his death would have given her something to talk about for weeks at the Chamber of Commerce meetings.

I was glad I had been evasive. I decided that I would stick to that if anyone else wanted to pump me for details.

I bought a pair of new window blinds and headed for home, thinking it would be better to help my father repair last night's damage than dare to open my refrigerator.

The radio announcer was giving the afternoon traffic report with a thick cowboy drawl. "Temperance Koltiska and two coal bed methane workers collided at the intersection of Main and South Fork twenty minutes ago. Tempe's truck busted an axle, so if you need to go to the stockyard, you'll have to go down Steamboat Drive to get there."

As I slowed my car to avoid busting my own axle on a deep pothole, I glanced to the side of the road and saw a flash of movement. I tapped the brake and peered through my passenger-side window. Something had taken shelter in the ditch, and as soon as I saw what it was, my heart sank.

The deer had managed to creep off the road and hide in the tall fall grass of the barrow ditch. It was almost invisible. I saw its gleaming eye, wide and wild, staring at me from the camouflage of Canada thistle. It had dragged itself from the road and lay watching me. I stopped my car and sighed. It was hurt. Pretty bad from what I could see. I pulled to the side of the road, parked and stepped out to take a closer look, and when it didn't bolt for the trees I knew it was mortally wounded.

I could smell the stench of fear. As I got closer to the deer, a doe maybe three years old, I could see that she had been there since before the previous night. A hollow of grass was crushed down all around her.

Both back legs lay behind her body, useless. For one terrible moment I was reminded of Paul, lying in the center of his Italian tile kitchen floor, paralyzed. I swallowed back bile and fought against the memory, willing it to recede.

I rubbed the back of my neck and knelt down. "Poor thing. Hit by a car, weren't you?"

Her eyes rolled and both nostrils widened. She smelled me and the fear was telling her to run, but her broken body couldn't oblige and she lay helpless in the grass.

I shut my eyes and listened.

I didn't carry a gun in the car. Of course, it was against the law to dispatch a wounded game animal in any case, so even if I'd had a gun I wouldn't have used it. But I lived in Montana and there was no shortage of people willing and able to do what I could not. All I had to do was wait.

I stood by the roadside for perhaps ten or fifteen minutes before I heard the sound I was waiting for.

Truck tires.

A black Jeep rolled into view. It came from the south, traveling down the rutted road easily on all-terrain tires. It slowed to a crawl when the driver caught sight of me.

I stepped away from the ditch and gave the driver a half-smile, and I could see a man behind the wheel watching me impassively.

The driver flipped a U-turn, parked the Jeep behind my little Honda and stepped out.

He was exactly what I was looking for.

"Hi," I said. I waited for him to come to me.

He stood beside his vehicle for a moment, and I could see he was sizing me up.

"Got trouble, Miss?"

His accent was odd. Almost sounded British. Maybe this man wasn't what I was looking for.

"You live around here?" I asked, uncertain. I sure as hell wasn't going to ask some British tourist on vacation to shoot a wounded deer for me.

"I do." He still didn't move, just stood where he was, watching me.

He seemed like the hunter type. After nine years working for the Fish and Wildlife office in Helena, I could usually spot them.

His Jeep had an elaborate gun rack across the backseat, and I could see at least three rifles, or maybe one was a shotgun. He stood with upright calm, his black pants and black jacket making him look more like a Secret Service agent than a local yokel. His eyes were hidden behind a pair of Top Gun sunglasses.

"I don't suppose you own a gun," I asked.

He smiled a little at that. "I own a few."

I shuffled my feet and cast a long slow glance into the ditch. His eyes followed mine and I saw his face register what I was asking without words.

"Ah. Right," he said, studying the deer.

He opened the back door of his Jeep and pulled out a black shotgun. Did this man know there were other colors besides black?

I headed for my car, reaching for the handle without giving him another glance.

He stopped and looked at me. "This was what you wanted me to do, yes?"

I hesitated.

Usually, when someone was about to break the law, the person who had just asked him to do it didn't hang around. But he was not an American, clearly.

Maybe he didn't know about proper hillbilly etiquette. "You know how to euthanize an animal?"

He nodded. "You could say that."

He moved with such ease I guessed he had to be very strong. But his steps were so light he made half the noise that most people usually make. No dragging feet and shuffling around with this guy. He smelled like gun oil. Not exactly unheard of in Killdeer, but with him it seemed like the smell of weapons wasn't something he carried a couple days a week. I got the impression it was how he smelled all the time.

"Thanks," I said. I stopped and fidgeted, turning towards him. I felt the odd desire to explain myself. "You know it's not exactly legal, but it would take a game warden a half a day to make it out here if I called."

"No need. I don't suppose you got a name?" he asked, looking at me with no expression.

I blinked. "I'm Marley. Marley Dearcorn." Why was I so rattled?

"It's my pleasure to make your acquaintance, Miss," he said.

Was he kidding? Who talked like that?

He held the shotgun barrel down with one hand. He handled it like I handled a knife and fork. Like second nature.

"Marley," he repeated. "That's an odd name for a wee gal such as yourself." He was a head taller than me. Most people are. But he seemed taller because of the way he carried himself. He practically crackled like a downed power line.

"It was my grandfather's name. He died the same day I was born, and my father loved him very much." Why was I telling this to a total stranger?

"How did he die?"

"What?" I asked.

"Your granddad. How did he die?"

"He, ah, he was killed actually. I don't really talk about it much."

He didn't smile. "Course. Not a problem. What brings you out this way?"

"I live here," I said. "Just past Dearcorn ranch my father has a caretaker's house. I'm staying there."

He appraised me methodically. "I ask on account of I haven't seen you before. I tend to remember faces. I would certainly remember seeing you."

I felt my cheeks warm. "I've only been back in town for six months. I don't seem to remember seeing you around here, either."

He let the corner of his mouth turn up. "I keep a low profile."

I was suddenly feeling a bit exposed. I had just told him where I lived and my name in the space of a three-minute conversation. What the hell was wrong with me?

"Well, just keep a low profile while taking care of that deer. If law enforcement sees you do it you could get a very substantial fine for your trouble."

"Not likely," he said, easing past me and deliberately opening my car door for me.

I didn't take my eyes off him as I slid into my seat. I got the impression he enjoyed it that I was staring at him.

He barely looked at me as he closed my door.

He walked to the nose of my car and towards the ditch with casual indifference.

I started the engine, fiddled with the stick shift for a moment and finally relented and leaned across to roll down the passenger window. He watched me as I struggled to crank the old window down, and judging by his expression he was amused. He took a few steps back and tilted his head down so that he could see me.

I wished that he would take off his sunglasses. "I didn't catch your name."

He pumped the shotgun once. "You can call me Finn."

"Well, thanks, Mr. Finn. I hope the next time I see you it is under better circumstances."

He shook his head. "Not Mister. Just Finn."

I started my car and threw it in gear. He walked off the road, into the ditch, and I hit the gas. I had no great desire to see him shoot the deer and I heard not a few rocks fly when my tires spun on the gravel.

I glanced in my mirror only to see him watching me. He waited until I was well around the next bend before I heard the shotgun discharge.

CHAPTER 8

"What's the matter with you, girl?" I asked myself as I made for home.

Finn. What kind of a name was that? And what was I thinking just volunteering all that personal information? Especially to that guy. He was about as personable as a brick and probably ate steroids for breakfast.

I parked in my little driveway, beside my father's pickup truck, and lugged the window blinds up the stairs.

Just as I came through the door my father called out to me. His lively voice made my heart to a normal, healthy rate.

"Power's back on, Kiddo. Whatcha got there?"

"New blinds," I said, laying them on the sofa. "How's the window?"

"Just about done. Look, see here? The darn glass took me a half hour to pull out of the window frame. Whoever put that last window in used so much glazing compound it's a wonder I could pull it out at all."

"That was you, Dad," I said.

He thought for a moment. "Right. It was, wasn't it? What was I thinking, huh?"

Indeed. I knew exactly how he felt.

I noticed that he'd patched and painted the hole where the screwdriver had been. He hadn't given me one word of grief over the incident, unlike the sheriff.

"Dad, do you know a man named Finn? Not Mister. Just Finn. Drives a big black Jeep with a hard top and a gun rack?"

"Sure, sure," my father said while he packed up his tools. "Nice fella. Works up at Area Forty-nine. Why?"

"Area what?"

"Some weather facility the government built on the hill up towards Fable. Guess they figured a little town like Fable wouldn't mind having a big weather station close by, because who's going to complain, right? A couple pot growers and a crazy retired actress, is all."

Nice fella?

"Area Forty-nine?" I asked, pulling the blinds out of their box.

My father grinned. "It doesn't quite rate on the same scale as Area Fifty-one, being here in Killdeer, does it?"

"Dad, about this Finn character . . ."

"Nice enough. Keeps to himself. He sure saved my neck a couple weeks before you came home."

"Oh?" I asked, suddenly irritated all over again. Who was this man who seemed to have materialized out of thin air?

"I was bringing the hay swather back from town. Had to get new bearings. You know how long it takes to drive that thing to the ranch from Warren's repair shop?"

"A bloody long time," I said.

"A bloody long time," my father echoed. "I got a flat tire and that Finn fella came along and helped me change it. Drove me to the ranch and back so I wouldn't have to walk all that way to get my truck so I could carry the tire. Funny, he seemed to be coming along just at the time I really needed a hand."

"Imagine that."

My father started rounding up his tools. "Why you asking about him?"

I fiddled with the directions for the blinds and tried to locate something called an anchor screw inside the box.

"You didn't have any trouble today, did you?" he asked.

I glanced up. My father was watching me carefully now.

"Just a deer that needed put down. Mr. Finn, ah, Finn offered to lend a hand."

"Lucky he happened along, then."

I found the anchor screw and gave my father a reassuring smile. "Lucky indeed. He sure seemed to know his way around a shotgun."

"I think he's some sort of law enforcement character."

I dug around in the box for the second screw. "What kind of law enforcement?"

"Something to do with security for that weather station. If it really is a weather station. Anyway, he doesn't talk much. Probably why they hired him in the first place. Because he doesn't talk much."

"He's good at that," I observed.

"Looks like you've got it under control here, Marley," he said.

"I'm off to get some early supper and then it's game four in the World Series. Want to come over and watch?"

I usually liked watching baseball with my father, but I wanted to get my house put back together.

"I think I'll get to work on the fridge and go to bed early. Thanks for helping me with the window, Dad, but I had best get this place organized now. It was nice of Jack to let me have a day off, but he's going to make me pay for it tomorrow."

As usual, my father's expression clouded over at the mention of Jack Parks. Someday I was going to get to the bottom of why an amiable man like my father could harbor such open dislike for a person. Maybe, as was often the case, my father knew something that I didn't.

CHAPTER 9

Morning brought clear skies and a sunrise worthy of a Charles Russell painting. It also brought the promise of steady, backbreaking labor for the next couple of weeks. Killdeer had been randomly ravaged by the winds that had generated my downburst. Some of the houses in town were victims of the same sort of damaging winds that had toppled my cottonwood tree, and others were simply cluttered with debris and would require attention from those possessing strong backs and weak minds, as my boss liked to say.

I had once made my living sitting at a desk, wearing slacks and blazers. But now I tied my hair back into a rough ponytail and pulled on a pair of heavy leather gloves, and that was all the dressing up necessary for the day.

I rode with Jack to his shop where he kept the tools of his landscaping trade, such as the backhoe and concrete forms, and we set about hitching up the hydraulic trailer to the work truck. It was going to be a busy day.

I was wrestling with the lock pins when I heard the phone in the shop start ringing. Jack sprinted inside, leaving the door open, and I could hear his side of the conversation.

"Reliant Landscaping."

"David, I think we can be there in about an hour. That work for you?"

I heaved a sigh and crammed the lock pin into place. David was almost certainly Mayor David Jordan. I allowed myself a moment of dread and self-pity before hopping into the cab and slamming the door.

Jack slid into the driver's seat and had the decency to offer me an apologetic look.

"David has a big pine down in his front yard. He wants it gone by this afternoon."

"I don't suppose you would let me go work in Mrs. Gunderson's yard today? She needs to have her pond drained before winter."

Jack patted my shoulder sympathetically. "I'm pulling the whole crew in for this job and I need you to run interference."

I nodded, knowing exactly what that entailed. Being the mayor seemed to give David the impression that he needed to be right in the middle of any job directing the process. For whatever reason, he couldn't keep his nose out of the work, and so the task of keeping him out of the crew's way always fell to me.

"We have to get there pronto, Marley," Jack said. "David is mayor, and now that Paul's dead he's going to stay mayor and I really need that big tree trimming job the city is bidding out next month."

I grumbled, but set my mind to the task at hand and kept my mouth shut.

We drove in silence for a bit, and then Jack turned to me and blurted out the question I'd been afraid he would ask.

"Marley, are you doing alright?"

I shifted in my seat. "You mean since I found Paul?" I said.

Jack stuck a stick of gum in his mouth and chewed it ferociously. "I mean since your house was beat up and you were almost killed by a screwdriver."

"How did you know about that?" I asked.

"Loy," he said with a shrug. "He mentioned it at Lil's. He was pretty upset about Paul, I guess, and he needed something to talk about to keep his mind off it and told me about you and your, how'd he put it? 'Her unfortunate encounter with the contents of her toolshed.' He almost looked pissed off."

I could see Loy saying it. I shook my head and laughed a bit. "Loy always did have a way with words. You know he could have been a professor at the University. He's got the brains. Why he went into law enforcement I will never know."

"Loy? A professor?" Jack said. "Not a chance. He's way too smart to be a cop, but he's just too dumb to quit."

I had to agree with that. Loy had succeeded at being a good sheriff because it never did occur to him to fail. "Since when are you and Loy such good friends?" I asked.

"Since he told old man Martin Shelly to pay me the eight grand he owed me for that concrete job we did at his hotel," Jack replied.

I guess the sheriff coming to your door and asking you to pay your bills was more intimidating than a civil suit. Particularly if you had a habit of letting your cows "accidentally" break into your neighbor's alfalfa field right before harvest time. I shook my head. It occurred to me that I knew far too many personal details about the folks who lived in my little world.

We drove in silence while I tried to find a way to ask my next question as diplomatically as possible. We passed a long row of lodgepole pine trees, and it broke my heart to see how much damage the pine beetle infestation was doing to the forest around Killdeer. At least a third of the trees were the telltale red color the needles turned when the tree was dying, or mostly dead. I thought that it was about time the Forest Service brought in some workers and cleared out the dead trees. If they didn't get to work on the job soon, our pine trees would get even worse.

"So the books look good for now?" I asked, hoping I sounded casual.

Jack smiled. "I'll be able to pay my crew, if that's what you're asking."

"I never doubted it," I said, and we both laughed.

There were weeks I worried about getting paid. But somehow Jack always made sure I had a check in my hand even when I knew he couldn't afford to pay his phone bill, which was considerable. Jack lived on the very edge of solvency, and I knew from my hours of putting invoices into the computer for him that Reliant Landscaping made money, but it never seemed like it was enough. Still, I was always holding a paycheck at the end of the week, and so were Donny and Shepherd, Jack's two crewmen.

Being a landscaper was messy, difficult work, but I was grateful I had a job.

After I'd come home, the Billings Gazette had run a front-page article about the Fish and Wildlife branch office in Helena botching a huge investigation. Someone in the office had tipped off a poacher who had been selling elk horn and velvet to a black market contact.

The investigator in our office was close to making an arrest and the entire operation was hush-hush. But something had gone wrong. The poacher had pulled up roots, destroyed or dumped all the evidence hidden in his garage, and had done it not seventy-two hours before the game wardens planned to make their move.

Word got around after my return that I'd been fired, and although nobody ever came out and said it directly, I couldn't shake the feeling that everyone in Killdeer had jumped to the conclusion I'd been the one who had tipped off the poacher.

The truth behind my sudden dismissal from my job was something I had promised the investigator I would never discuss. The investigator, Bruce Duvekot, was my friend. He also had a wife and two kids to support, and I was single with no one else depending on me. Bruce had botched the investigation, but I had been right in the middle of it and the situation was grim. It had been an easy choice to make when it came down to which one of us would be fired. Since I had promised Bruce I would never talk about what had happened, he had kept his job, but I'd been forced to do something I thought I would never do. I'd lied about an investigation to protect a friend. That shadow of deceit had followed me home and I still felt as if I was never going to be able to shake that burden off. Maybe I felt so comfortable working for Jack because he never asked me about it, and I knew he never would.

Jack parked the work truck in front of Mayor Jordan's house and I felt my eyes grow wide when I saw the front yard. A sixty-foot western white pine had been torn up by the roots and lay across the sidewalk leading to David's front door.

It looked like a living building had been pushed over in the yard. Branches had broken off randomly and were still scattered on the sidewalk and covering the street.

David came sprinting down his front steps towards us with an eager face and gloved hands. He was wearing a pair of safety goggles.

I blocked him and lifted a clipboard, fixing a look of dire seriousness on my face and laying it on thick.

"David, we should go around to the back of your property now so you can give me a detailed accounting of the damage."

Mayor Jordan looked crestfallen. "But doesn't Jack need me to help cut the branches off the tree first?"

I shook my head, feigning urgency. "He said it is very important I get this documented before we do anything else. We have to do an assessment of the damage before they can start working at all."

David came very close to whining. "But the back yard has hardly any damage at all."

"Jack told me specifically that you need to walk me through your property, so we can draw up a proper and accurate bill."

I started walking. David followed reluctantly, casting backwards glances at Jack and looking terribly disappointed. He obviously thought that getting to play with the other boys and running a chainsaw sounded like a lot more fun than being stuck with me.

I couldn't have agreed with him more.

CHAPTER 10

For the next three hours I was assaulted with inane chatter from a man with the energy and enthusiasm of a heavily caffeinated UPS driver and the social tact of a roller-derby girl. For a politician, David had a knack for always saying the wrong thing at the worst time, and on top of it was clueless to the fact that Jack certainly did not want his help. I did the best I could to keep my mouth shut while I tried to keep him away from the crew so they could actually work. I finished the assessment of the damage in about a half hour, and spent the rest of the time just making up terms that sounded technical, derailing David each time he tried to escape, and generally preventing the mayor from touching any tools so he wouldn't hurt himself.

I filled everything out in triplicate. This would be the most detailed invoice Reliant Landscaping would ever produce.

I managed to check the progress of the crew from time to time, trying to judge how much longer I would be stranded with the mayor.

"Jack had the boys clip the upper branches with the little chainsaw, and he is starting on the root system of the big tree," I said, making a show of moving as far away from the downed tree as I could.

David shoved his hands in his coat pocket. "I could help with the smaller branches."

I shook my head. "Most people assume that once a tree falls over it is perfectly safe to hack away on the limbs until it is chopped up and hauled away. But Jack is a certified arborist and he knows better. It's rare, but sometimes losing the weight of the big branches at the top of a downed tree can cause it to right itself unexpectedly. Anyone standing in the root hole would be crushed. Jack never lets anyone on his crew work in the root hole. He is deadly serious about it, so I'm sorry but I can't have any clients next to the job site."

The mayor moped around the yard, occasionally offering suggestions, but otherwise keeping himself away from the work. It was safe to say my wrangling was successful.

Jack, Donny and Shepherd stayed on the job until sunset that day, finally hauling the last of the small branches to the dump. I was sweeping up the pine needles when David ambled over and stopped beside me.

"Where's Jack?"

I pointed to the truck not ten feet behind David where my boss was cramming branches into the refuse trailer. "He's taking the fourth load to the city compost pile."

"Sure," David said, ignoring that.

Apparently, it was much easier to talk to me than to Jack. Or maybe David felt more comfortable arguing with me over his bill than confronting my boss.

Oh, goody.

"I just wanted to thank him for dropping everything to handle this mess for me. I know he's sort of a busy man."

That was like saying a Black Angus bull was a bit twitchy. I smiled in a customer service sort of way. "We are glad to do it, David."

I let myself have a moment of pleasure from the fact that I lived in a place small enough I was on a first name basis with the mayor.

David stared at the root hole where his white pine had once stood, proud and invulnerable. The boys were busy shoveling dirt in so it didn't look like such a scar.

"I guess when the wind goes out for a walk it can do whatever the hell it wants to do," David said, a note of admiration in his voice.

I had to agree. My front yard was a testament to what the wind was capable of doing.

"Funny that it chose my house," he said, hiding his sudden unease with an artificial laugh. "What random, dumb luck."

I was starting to wonder if the mayor was about to hit on me.

He reached up to straighten a tie that he wasn't wearing, looking nervous.

I kept my smile, wishing he would go away.

He dropped his hands and rubbed them on his legs, remembering that he was in his work clothes. "You know the election is in a few weeks, and it wouldn't do to have my house looking like a slob lived here. It looks great now."

"We like to hear that," I said.

David kept looking up and down the street. He was talking to me, but not looking at me. "Don't worry about that open window on the top floor. It's not part of the tree damage. It got wet years ago and now it won't close all the way. Someday I'll get it fixed."

"Well, it is always important to take care of a piece of property," I said, thinking that running unopposed was a better way to win than having a nice front yard and a perfect house. It was convenient as hell for David that Paul had picked this week to die. I found myself watching the man closely.

The mayor surveyed his domain. "True. I know it sounds odd that I worry about the election, now that Paul's . . . well, you know. But I guess I've had my mind so set on this campaign I can't seem to do anything else even though he's dead."

"You really thought Paul had a chance of winning?" I asked, regretting my words instantly. He had no reason to confide in me.

David looked at me, then away, letting his eyes fall on the empty spot where the tree had stood proud and strong not two days before. "If there is one thing I have learned, Marley, it's that nothing in life is certain."

"Amen," I said, feeling my internal alarm go off. Any second now David would be asking me for a campaign contribution.

"Paul would have been a terrible choice for mayor of Killdeer. I can only see his death, such as it was, as God's retribution for his sinful past behavior."

I was stunned. "Really? So you think God killed Paul?"

"In a manner of speaking, I guess I do," David said, his small eyes coming to rest on me. "You could stand a bit of religion yourself. I never see you in church."

I lifted my broom and finished sweeping up the rest of the pine needles.

He smirked righteously.

I gave him a hard look. "I guess I stopped having any use for God the day a drunk driver killed my mom."

David murmured something about the Lord's will, then crossed his arms and rocked back on his heels. "Tell Jack I will keep him in mind down the road as other jobs come open. The city sometimes needs contractors, so let him know he's really proven himself today, and I appreciate it."

I had managed to cram the entire Reliant Landscaping invoice into one envelope and I pulled it out of my jacket pocket. I handed it to David with a smile. "Jack appreciates your business. Would you like to write us a check now?"

The mayor took the envelope and tucked it under his arm. "We arranged payment earlier on the phone. It's taken care of."

I certainly didn't remember Jack taking down any credit card information when the mayor had called us that morning, but decided not to bring it up. The last thing I wanted to do was spend more time with David Jordan.

"Tell Jack the check is in the mail," he said, replicating his earlier laugh.

I forced myself to smile. "I'll do that."

I started sweeping again.

"Marley?" he said, his tone suddenly bleak.

I glanced up. His cheerful expression had vanished and he watched me with sudden intensity.

"Do you think Paul really had a heart attack?"

I let my face poker up and fiddled with the broom handle casually. "What do you mean, David? You think he didn't?"

The air swirled around us playfully, lifting a handful of aspen leaves and spinning them like a natural top across the big yard. How the wind could change from harmless to deadly in the space of a few hours was beyond my understanding.

I watched him closely. He was breathing shallow, like he was afraid he'd spook me if he moved too suddenly. His eyes darted around the yard, searching for a safe place to stare.

I tilted my head to the side like a cocker spaniel, trying to look dumb and harmless, and gave him an encouraging smile. Got something you'd like to share, David?

He drew breath like he was about to speak, but his face twitched and he let out a long sigh.

I felt the stirring of something in my chest and glanced down at the sidewalk.

In spite of the weight of the huge tree, the sidewalk had miraculously survived. I was sure the concrete would have been broken to bits directly underneath the big pine. But Jack said that the equal distribution of weight applied across the large surface area of so many branches had kept the sidewalk from breaking.

People were like that, too. When they had a heavy weight to carry, it seemed lighter if they shared the load with others.

"You think Paul was helped along into the next world?" I asked.

"He sure didn't have many friends," David said, uneasy. "But he was trying pretty hard to get some. Maybe he was trying a bit too hard."

Well, everyone knew that.

But what was David getting at?

His lip quivered almost imperceptibly.

He ran a hand through his thinning blond hair and laughed a bit too loudly. "Sure it was a heart attack. I mean, what else could it have been?"

I didn't say anything, just watched him. David seemed to regain his composure and turned for his front door. "I've got a city council meeting to prepare for, Marley. I'll let you get back to it. Tell Jack thanks again."

I wasn't sure if his open competition with Paul was causing him to feel self-conscious or if he was feeling genuine sadness. The two men had been at each other's throats for months, but to suddenly find himself without an opponent must have been a rude shock. Maybe David felt the rest of the town would think it odd that the popular candidate was suddenly dead only two weeks before the election. I decided that people worried too much about what others might think. Myself included.

As I knelt to scoop up the rest of the pine needles I realized that uncomfortable tightness in my chest hadn't diminished. Now that I thought it over, it did seem a bit odd that Paul had died so suddenly. Bruce, my friend who was the investigator up in Helena, always said he didn't believe in coincidences.

I shook my head and told myself that it was time to put the incident behind me. I knew how uncertain life could be from day to day. And I also knew what snooping around asking questions could get you.

The gossip Loy had picked up from the game wardens about me was mostly true, as much as I hated to admit it to myself.

I did have a tight relationship with the investigator up in Helena. But not for the reasons everyone imagined.

We spent time together because whenever he was stumped by a difficult case he would sit down with me and talk it out until we had the problem cracked. The experience had left me with a desire to solve puzzles. But sitting behind a desk acting as a sounding board was very different than being in the field. For one thing, I was not a trained investigator. I was a glorified ex-secretary who had been demoted to shoveling dirt. So the last thing I should be doing now was pushing my bad luck by asking any questions about Paul, and the best thing I could do was to keep my head down and my nose out of it.

Right.

Keep my nose out of it.

That would be like asking a Labrador retriever to stay out of the water.

CHAPTER 11

Work ended, gloriously enough, and I dragged myself home. I ate dinner straight from a box of something I'd popped in the microwave, leaning against the kitchen sink, and I mused about the days I'd been married and had actually eaten supper sitting down at a table. Those days were long gone. I certainly wasn't looking to replace Allen. Marriage was never easy, and catching him in bed with a waitress from Kalispell hadn't helped matters one bit.

I stopped chewing the last water chestnut from my Kung Pao chicken at the sound of tires crunching gravel on the driveway. The doorbell rang and I tossed the paper container in the trash.

Loy Shucraft stood in the doorway, grinning, a big bouquet of flowers clutched in his wide hand.

I sighed.

"Are those calla lilies, Loy?"

He looked at the flowers speculatively. "You know, I believe they are."

I glanced down at myself. Muddy hiking boots, smudged blue jeans and a sleeveless white T-shirt that looked closer to gray. "I'm not exactly dressed for company."

He gave me that grin, the one that always told me he was up to something, and walked straight past me into the kitchen without invitation.

"Get your jacket," he said, his hands busy putting the flowers in my good Crock-Pot.

"I've got a vase, somewhere," I protested.

He waved me away and plumped the arrangement with his big hands. It actually looked very nice.

I gathered up my stained canvas jacket and shot him a suspicious glare.

"Ready?" he asked.

I shook my head. "I know I'm going to regret this, but yes."

We left, me not bothering to lock my front door, and climbed into Loy's sheriff truck and headed down the road at a slow pace.

I checked my watch with what I hoped was obvious irritation. "This is not a date."

He laughed. "Marley, what am I going to do with you?"

I remembered to put on my seat belt.

Loy drove at a slow pace. He was savoring the remains of the kind weather, his arm dangling out the window. We rounded the bend in the narrow road that climbed the hills east of my father's ranch. At the crest of the hill was a turnoff that snowmobile riders used in the winter to off-load their machines. We pulled in. I noticed the sun was threatening to set, and when Loy stopped the truck I gave him another look. This one said that I was not amused. He laughed again and shut off the engine.

I crossed my arms. "Really? Do you know how bad it would look if someone saw the sheriff making out with a girl in his official vehicle?"

"Look over there, you see?"

I leaned forward in the seat. "Is that the weather station I've been hearing about?" I unbuckled my belt and scooted forward earnestly now. We were on a high ridge that flanked my dad's ranch. Our elevated position gave an excellent view of the ridge across the valley.

"Yes. And it's not a weather station." Loy took out a pair of very expensive binoculars.

"It's bigger than I thought it would be," I said. The station was sprawled across the opposite ridge and I counted at least five buildings, plus a double row of satellite dishes lined up like the world's most expensive snow fence.

He handed me the binoculars. "Keep watching that south side. Don't take your eyes off of it for a second."

"How long should I watch?" I asked, setting the binoculars on the seat. I didn't need them, having been blessed with better than average eyesight. I wasn't irritated any longer and truly wanted to know what to expect.

Loy rubbed his palms together like a kid. "It varies. Sometimes it happens right after sunset, sometimes it happens right before. But it always happens. Every single night."

I couldn't take my eyes off of the station now. I did as I was told and paid strict attention to the south side of the complex. I counted the dishes. Twenty altogether, of various shapes and sizes. They weren't the usual white that one would expect. They were a dusky gray color and almost looked blotchy. It wasn't until the last of the sun's rays glinted off them that I realized they were painted with subtle camouflage. It wasn't the typical green and muddy brown used for Jeeps and artillery that we always saw on the news, either, but multiple shades of gray.

I was about to ask Loy why they would be painted with such dull colors when I took a hard look at the landscape around us. The hills were packed with trees. But on the top of the ridges the dolomite and limestone rock formations peeked out from the growth, and it occurred to me that the weather station looked exactly like another pile of rocks. Or it would look that way from above.

I kept my eyes fixed on the dishes, waiting. Simultaneously every single dish in view rotated towards the east, stopped briefly, then tilted up so that each one was pointed towards the same location high in the dusky sky. They stayed that way for a few seconds, looking like they were huddled together, intently listening to someone telling them a secret. I rolled down the window to get a better view, and just as suddenly they rotated back into their original position and became still, trying to act casual, giving every impression that nothing special had just happened.

"How about that, huh?" Loy asked.

I turned to look at him, feeling a mix of awe and confusion. "Wow."

"I noticed it a few months ago, and I've been coming up here since then to try and figure it out."

I shook my head. "I don't even know what to say."

"I thought you'd think it was pretty cool. What do you think it means?"

I tried to guess, shrugged and decided we didn't have enough information. "It happens every night?"

Loy took the binoculars back and stowed them under the seat. "Every night. I thought you would be able to see something that I couldn't."

We looked at each other and I smiled a bit. It was almost like sneaking into the high school swimming pool all over again.

"What does it look like to you?" I asked him.

He rubbed his chin. There was a bit more stubble than usual. Loy had not been taking very good care of himself lately. "It looks like they are all pointed to exactly the same place, like they are targeting a certain location in the sky."

I thought about it. "Maybe those dishes are transmitting important weather data to a satellite."

"Right," Loy said with a snort. "Weather data."

I shrugged. "It didn't look any different to me. I didn't see anything that you didn't."

Loy looked a bit disappointed, but eventually he nodded and gave a chuckle. It was harmless fun for him, a mystery he probably didn't really want to solve because then it wouldn't be fun anymore.

He started the truck and we drove back to my house. Loy walked me to my door and took off his hat. He hadn't showered in a while either. His hair was matted and I was surprised at how tired he looked.

"Marley, listen," he began. His voice was higher than usual and I could tell he was about to say something he didn't want to say at all. His palm rested on the butt of his pistol. "About this deal with Paul."

I crossed my arms and leaned against my door frame, giving him time to get to it.

"It was just his time to go. Right?" he said, his jaw set. "I am more sorry than you can possibly know that you are the one who found his body. I wish it could have been anyone else other than you."

I tried, and failed, to offer him a smile.

"But it wasn't. So listen, you need to understand that as far as the sheriff's office is concerned this case is straightforward and he died of natural causes beyond anyone's control. There is nothing you could have done differently that would have saved his life. I don't want you preoccupied over this and beating yourself up, telling yourself you could have done more."

I nodded, feeling a bit like I was getting a psych evaluation. "Okee dokie, Sheriff. Don't worry, Mayberry will get back to normal in no time."

"Goddammit Marley, you hear a word I just said?"

Something was wrong. Loy never, ever spoke harshly to me.

I watched him carefully, his pulse was racing, and he looked like he was sweating.

"Sure, Loy. I hear you. But you wouldn't have gone to all the trouble of coming out here just to tell me that Paul's death wasn't my fault unless there was something else bothering you."

He heaved a sigh, frustrated and angry.

It told me more than his words. Loy wasn't simply irritated, he was worried. But why?

"Alright," I said, lifting a reassuring hand. "I don't want you to think I take your concern for granted. You didn't have to take the trouble to make sure I was alright, but you did, and I thank you for that."

He eyed me cautiously, waiting for me to say it.

"But," I began.

He growled and shook his head. "And this is the part where you tell me you are a big girl and can take care of yourself. Well, I know that."

"I can take care of myself," I told him.

"Seeing your neighbor die isn't something that happens to the average person every day. But it does happen to *me* every day."

He reached out and gripped my hand for a second, giving it a squeeze before letting go. His palms were sweaty. "I know how difficult it can be to deal with it when you see someone come to such a hard end. But more than that, Marley. When it comes to something like this, the best thing you can do is to let it go."

Loy hadn't driven me all the way up the ridge to show me some synchronized satellites. He was trying to tell me something. He knew that during my time in the Fish and Wildlife office I'd seen my share of criminal investigations. I'd seen what the pressure could do to a game warden when he was in a tight spot. Loy had that same look. The look a warden would get when he realized he'd just stumbled across an illegal kill site, and the poacher was still there, and armed better.

I decided not to aggravate him. "Consider it dropped."

He squinted at me, standing his ground on my porch. "And if you need to talk to someone—"

"I'll call."

For a moment he looked like he almost believed me.

We said our goodbyes and he clomped down the stairs to his sheriff truck.

Loy drove down the road slower than usual, and he must have looked back three times before he was out of sight. I went into my kitchen, made some hot chocolate and settled into my rocking chair to think it over.

I must have sat there for close to an hour, because when I finally looked up and came back to reality it was almost time for me to be in bed.

Getting to sleep wasn't easy. I tossed back and forth for a good forty-five minutes before lying on my back and taking a few deep breaths to try and quiet my busy mind.

I had to admit that what I'd just experienced had been traumatic, but was Loy using the recent unhappy events as an excuse to try and insert himself into my life again? Or was he simply a concerned friend?

I couldn't be sure one way or the other. Our brief relationship was fifteen years in the past. I'd dated Loy a total of three months back when we were in high school, but neither one of us had ever tried to rekindle that romance. Had he really carried a torch for me all these years?

Scolding myself, I finally resolved to get some sleep and I put the whole ordeal out of my mind. After all, if there was some good reason why I should be worried about what had happened over at Paul's place, surely Loy would have told me what it was. Wouldn't he?

CHAPTER 12

The next morning came as a surprise. I was sure it was still sometime in the middle of the night and I had the distinct feeling that I was owed about two more hours of sleep. But the alarm went off and I rolled out of bed dutifully. Jack called while I was brushing my teeth.

"Eat your Wheaties. We are working on a big project today. Donny and Shepherd are delegated to post-storm cleanup duty so you and I can go play nicey-nice to a well-paying customer."

"Nicey-nice?" I asked around a mouth full of toothpaste.

"You know, pretend we can work miracles for folks with way more cash than sense, and deal with unrealistic expectations on top of it."

"Where are we going, Jack? Not the bank again," I said.

"Nope. We're going to the Caucasian Reservation. Comb your hair and wear a tight shirt."

He hung up, leaving me holding a dripping toothbrush over the kitchen sink.

"Wonderful."

I rushed through breakfast and sped to the shop. There was good money to be made today and we obviously needed to get a move on.

When I slid into the truck beside Jack he grumbled something about hoping we had enough gas to make it there and back.

Jack referred to our destination as the Caucasian Reservation, but it was actually called the Wild Mustang Golfing Community. Everyone called it the Mustang Ranch, much to the chagrin of the owners. It was the most exclusive, and hence expensive, subdivision in the county. Acres and acres of manicured green grass were sprinkled here and there with mansions so obscenely opulent I would have been embarrassed to live in any of them. Jack said it was a reservation for rich people, because we had to put the bastards someplace, after all. It was safe to say that Jack loved, and hated, people with money.

We drove the fifteen-minute trip mostly in silence. I was able to guess where we were headed. Jack drove us to a new house just finished by a local rancher lucky enough to have discovered that his old broken-down ranch was sitting on top of enough coal bed methane gas to make him a millionaire. Lewis Pritchett was a good man in his late fifties, who had never done a single selfish or cruel thing in his life, and had suddenly found himself to be one of the richest men in the county. I thought it couldn't have happened to a nicer guy, save for my own father. Sadly, there was no methane gas on our land.

When we got to Lewis's place, Jack pulled right into the driveway and parked the truck with a bit more abruptness than usual. He was not happy about being here. There were jobs in town needing a good tree trimmer, and his boys were not certified to do any climbing, so Jack had to put off the work until he had things under control here, and it was irritating him greatly.

I opened the glove box of the truck to dig out a new invoice sheet and frowned when I saw what sat inside.

"What the heck is that doing here?" I asked.

Jack leaned over to see what I was looking at.

A snub-nosed pistol rested on top of the stack of invoices. It was a revolver, a small five cylinder with no hammer and no safety. It was the type of pistol that would fit neatly inside a woman's handbag. Since it didn't have a hammer, there was nothing to snag the pistol when drawing it out of a pouch or a purse. It was ideal for carrying concealed.

"That was how Mrs. Gunderson paid me for her shrub removal job," he said.

"She's eighty-two years old," I said, surprised and a little disconcerted.

Jack shrugged. "It's worth three hundred bucks. She said her eyesight's too bad these days for a pistol. She likes her little Browning shotgun better."

I stared at the pistol, trying to get a mental picture of tiny Mrs. Gunderson drawing down on a purse snatcher. "Maybe you should keep it back at the shop."

"Maybe we should quit jawing in the front yard and get to work," he said.

I got out of the truck and closed the door just as Lewis Pritchett appeared. He was wearing a pair of beige Carhartt pants and a flannel shirt. Being a millionaire had done nothing for his fashion sense.

"Lewis, good to see you," Jack said, extending a hand. "What are we looking at doing here today?"

I noticed Jack had left a half-empty bottle of aspirin on the floor of his truck and I decided I'd give the man a lot of room today. He was a walking headache, and every few minutes he pinched the bridge of his nose like he was trying to let off steam.

"Jack, I've got an emergency," Lewis said, pumping Jack's hand with enough force to dislocate the average shoulder. Good thing Jack's shoulder was above average.

"Lewis. You spell it out and we will get on to work."

The rancher took a huge breath and I felt the corners of my mouth turn up. He was positively beside himself with worry.

"I've got a meeting of the Killdeer Historical Preservation Society tonight and the yard is a mess. All the members are coming and I can't have the place looking like this when they show up."

Jack took a deep breath of his own. "Alright, Lewis. What would you like us to do?"

I could tell by his tone that my boss didn't really consider this an emergency worthy of taking him away from a half dozen lucrative job sites. I could also tell that as we spoke, the bill for this emergency job was doubling.

"I don't care what you do, I trust you," Lewis said. "Just make it gorgeous. Cecilia Winthrop and her niece Rebecca will be coming tonight, and the last thing I want to do is make a bad show of it. The society means a lot to me."

The society wasn't what meant a lot to him. It was Cecelia's niece, young Miss Rebecca. Lewis had been trying to win Rebecca's affection for close to a decade now, and every time he made an impression with her it always seemed to be a bad one.

It was painful to see a grown man panic.

Plus, all of his effort was futile, too. Rebecca was in love already, with her work. She was a pediatrician and commuted to Parkman every day. She was determined to be a success and didn't have time for a personal life. Her aunt had paid for medical school, so Rebecca trudged along dutifully to the meetings because it pleased Cecilia to be involved with something. Pleasing Cecilia was high on Rebecca's list.

Jack told Lewis what we would be doing today to make the yard worthy of a visit from the Historical Preservation Society, describing menial maintenance with flowery terms, and Lewis seemed pleased. He disappeared inside the house and I could hear him talking in excited tones. I watched the windows for a few moments and saw an army of cleaning women attacking the home's interior with all the determination of Rommel's desert tank brigade. I shook my head and hoped that I would never fall in love with someone who would turn me inside out like that.

I worked steadily into the morning without interruption, weeding, pruning and generally performing basic yard maintenance. I was not surprised to see the battered gray work truck pull into the driveway with Donny and Shepherd inside. They got out of the truck and set to work. Jack shot Shepherd a look and indicated with a nod that he was now in charge.

"Just try to look busy, because he won't know the difference," Jack told me, as he gathered up his water bottle and gloves.

"Lewis is inside driving the housekeepers like they are the Fifth Cavalry," I said.

Jack snorted. "I'll bet. Listen, I'm heading into town so if anything comes up, Shepherd will see to it. Alright?"

I didn't grumble about it, but I hated it when the older of the two boys was in charge. Why Jack kept him on the crew was beyond me. Shepherd was surly and sometimes flat refused to take orders at all.

"I've got to go see Mom this weekend over at the nursing home in Parkman, and so I won't be able to work Saturday doing any trimming. So, my weekend is shot to hell. If Lewis comes out and asks where I am today, tell him I had a trimming job come up that couldn't wait."

"It'll be fine," I said.

My boss hopped in his truck and vanished, heading into town, frantic to cash in on the easy money waiting for him. I knew he would work until the sun set that night.

I gave a nod to Donny. Shepherd ignored me, which was preferable, and the three of us bent to the task at hand wordlessly. Donny's thick blond hair almost hid his entire face as he edged the grass along the cobbled sidewalk using the little gas-powered weed eater. Shepherd was wearing his hair in a buzz cut these days, and he was still recovering from a wicked sunburn, which seemed unlikely so late in the fall. Even in October Killdeer still had its brutally hot days once in a while. Both boys were lean and tough, the side effects of making a living with your body. I realized with some satisfaction that I was not such a bad specimen myself these days. Eight hours a day of heavy lifting had given me something I hadn't had since I'd helped my father on the ranch. I'd heard it was called muscle.

I was in the back yard working on a particularly nasty patch of overgrown hedge when someone walked up behind me. Lewis was ambling over for a chat. He seemed to be a bit calmer now that work was proceeding and it looked like his house would be in order by the time the important company arrived.

"Marley, I wanted you to know how sorry I was to hear about you finding Paul and all. Shame, really. He didn't seem like he was sick."

"No. He seemed fine to me, too." Right up until the moment he wasn't. "I guess we never really know how much time we have left."

This hardly gave Lewis pause. "That's a fact. Sad though. Isn't the first time that place has seen tragedy."

I tested the shears I was using on the hedge. They were losing their edge.

"Oh? How's that?" I asked, not really listening. Just doing what I could to hold up my end of the conversation.

Lewis scrunched up his face the way some folks do when they are thinking back to an old memory. "There was a real bad fire tore through that valley, some time ago now. Firefighters lost their lives. Got burned up in the forest under the cliffs where Leif Gable built that big house."

I tried to imagine what that must have been like, and shuddered a bit. "That's a story I haven't heard before."

"Funny thing was, one fella made it out alive. Ended up on top of the cliff just behind where Paul's house sits today. Nobody ever did figure out how the hell he managed to get all the way up there. That cliff's supposed to be impossible to climb."

He turned his head slightly. "I expect if you was properly motivated, though, you'd find a way up it."

I called the area to mind. "You can't even tell there was a fire there. The trees are all tall and healthy around Leif's house. It's the one place in Killdeer that hasn't seen any pine-beetle-killed trees. How long ago did it happen?"

"I was a kid then," Lewis said. "Sad for them boys that got killed. And now Paul. What a shame. Seemed like he was fine whenever I saw him." He spit once on the ground and surveyed the hedge I was trimming. "Looking good there, Marley. Let you get back to work now."

I watched him walk away and thought about the valley behind Paul's house. I recalled the cliff face and realized what an accomplishment it must have been to scale those rocks all the way to the top. They were as smooth as a parking lot.

"You going to stand around all day or actually do some work?"

I spun around. Startled. Shepherd was glaring at me from beside the house and I hadn't noticed him there.

Sheepishly I lifted the hedge shears. "These could use some sharpening."

Shepherd snatched the shears and tested the edge. "I'll do it then. Get to work on something else."

Obviously, I wasn't qualified to sharpen a pair of hedge shears. I let it slide that a kid who wasn't even old enough to drink was ordering me around. I should have stuck up for myself, but it would only cause more friction between me and Shepherd and we already had plenty of that.

I decided to finish power raking the back yard and was reaching for the rake when Shepherd's voice startled me once again.

"And Paul wasn't the healthiest guy around, for your information," he said with a sour expression. He'd apparently been eavesdropping on my conversation with Lewis.

I didn't look directly at him, but focused on the rake. "Really? How's that?"

"Let's just say he was at that prissy yarn store one day not too long ago when my mom was there. She said he was his normal self and trying to learn how to knit in a class with a bunch of women. Fag. Anyway, she said he all of a sudden got real pale and freaked out and had to get out of there because he looked like he was going to puke or something. Didn't sound like a guy who was all that healthy to me. I'm just saying."

I pondered that.

Prissy yarn store could only mean Wee Wooly's. He'd gone in there to get Wendy's support for his campaign. I already knew that from listening to Harvey Wilson gossip down at Lil's. But Harvey hadn't said a word about Paul taking ill while he was there. Maybe Paul was sick after all.

It was a bit late to be worrying about that now.

Still, my curiosity was piqued. If he'd suffered some sort of physical episode at the yarn shop, maybe Wendy had seen it and could tell me something about it. It was silly, but I wanted to know what had gone wrong with Paul that his body would simply self-destruct when he always seemed so healthy.

I wouldn't have cared if I hadn't been the one to find him.

But I had found him, and by virtue of that I did care. Maybe a little too much.

CHAPTER 13

Thursday morning arrived and I drove past Wee Wooly's on my way to Jack's shop. The hand-lettered sign on the door told me they were closed for the week for inventory. I stood outside and pressed my nose to the glass, but no one was inside diligently counting skeins of yarn, and I suddenly felt frustrated that my curiosity wouldn't be fulfilled. I drove to work feeling irritated. I shouldn't have been so disappointed by a simple little thing like Wendy's shop being closed, but I was. I felt a burst of determination to track her down and find out what she knew.

The day was merciful. I was spared working with Shepherd, and Jack and I did something I loved to do more than just about anything else on the job. We went to pick up boulders.

It took almost an hour to drive out to the Blue Sky rock quarry, bouncing down a road that got graded by plows once a year, if that.

The quarry was nestled at the base of the mountains and I loved every minute of the drive. Jack and I talked politics and religion, and speculated on the sex lives of various movie stars. When we got to the quarry it was deserted and we set about parking the trailer and pulling on gloves.

Jack had open access to the quarry, was able to load the rocks he wanted for his landscaping jobs, and weigh the loads himself. The owners of the quarry knew Jack would pay his tickets. Even when money was tight, he always paid his quarry tickets.

"Some good ones today," Jack said, circling the two-acre mound of boulders. The quarry owners had started the business a scant three years ago to supplement a cattle rancher's income, and then they had sat back and let the money roll in. They made as much money on the sale of rocks as they did on cows some years. Since they worked under the honor system, the only real labor involved in keeping the quarry active was when they hired a man once a month to come out and replenish the supply of rocks and stones as customers thinned the piles.

The quarry rocks had been sorted into three sections by size. Small, medium, and oh-my-God. We were after the medium boulders today. The rose granite was particularly popular with Jack's clients at the moment, and we located and marked two or three about the size of the average family coffee table that we would take.

I pulled out the six-foot carbon steel pry bar so it would be within reach, and Jack started the big yellow tractor with a front-end loader we used to lift the rocks. I climbed on the pile. Smoke spewed out the stacks of the tractor as Jack turned it to face the pile of boulders. The rocks were stacked deep today, maybe six to eight feet high. I positioned myself on top of the first boulder we were determined to take and he revved the tractor. His technique was simple. He lowered the bucket, hit the gas and crashed into the pile with as much speed as possible.

In theory the rocks we didn't want would shift to the side and we'd be able to reach the ones we did want. I had to stand on top of the prize boulder so Jack would know where to aim.

Of course it was not exactly safe, me standing on top of the pile and hoping that something didn't go wrong. But Jack said I had a knack for knowing when to jump, and he demonstrated a confidence in my ability that gratified me.

At least I had the brains to set the twenty-five-pound pry bar aside until I would need it.

I stood directly on top of the first boulder we wanted and waved to Jack that I was ready. He goosed the tractor and aimed the bucket straight for me. I heard the big engine rev and watched carefully as the bucket skimmed the surface of the hard ground, building speed.

The bucket hit and I felt the mound of rocks shift beneath me. Two white boulders started to buck to the left unexpectedly and I hopped off the stack and to the ground just as the pile gave way and crashed.

Jack slammed the tractor in reverse and lowered the bucket.

"You okay?" he called from the cab.

I nodded and gave him a thumbs up.

He waved back and positioned the tractor for another attack.

I climbed back onto the stack and stood on top of the boulder we wanted. It was dislodged, and one more solid hit would knock the less desirable rocks aside so we could reach it.

Jack hit the gas and lowered the bucket and the tractor slammed into the stack.

The white boulders groaned and shifted, their rough edges ground against each other and sparks flew in all directions. Some of the boulders cracked and the smaller rocks actually split apart from the force of the impact. But he was a pro, and the rocks we didn't want rolled aside to expose the big pink boulder. I felt the pile move and I wondered what my father would think if he could see me doing this.

Probably a good thing that he never would.

Jack parked the front-end loader and got out, coming towards me with the hooked chain. It was time to snag our prize.

"This one's going to the bank," he told me.

"It's a beauty. I wonder what the underside looks like?"

"If it's as nice as the top, we can't lose no matter which way we place it," he said happily. Jack was really in his element when choosing his landscaping rocks.

I helped him wrap the chain around the nose of the boulder. It was too big to lift out with the bucket, but we could drag it into the open dirt and then use the tractor bucket to push it in the trailer.

I pulled the heavy chain around the tip and was trying to secure the hook, without much success, when Jack knelt beside me to give me a hand.

"This going to Joe's bank?" I asked.

"Yep. I like working for Joe Martinez," Jack said as he tugged the chain into place. "He always pays me on time."

I tested the chain, tugging on it hard. "You know his wife, Wendy?"

He stood up to ease the crick out of his back and stretched carefully. "Sure. I know Wendy."

"What do you think of her?"

"Pretty woman. Not much substance to her, though. I wouldn't want to be Joe."

That surprised me. "Why not?"

"Well, Wendy is such a hothouse lily. She has that little yarn shop, but other than that, what else does she have going for her?"

I snorted. "Well first of all, she's thin and beautiful. And she's sweet. Living in that big house Joe built hasn't changed her one bit. She's still got a kind heart." Their house was a mansion. They lived close to Mr. Pritchett at the Mustang Ranch.

"Sure," Jack said speculatively. "Money is nice to have. But Wendy is the type of person who would fall apart if it weren't for Joe. Who wants to be married to someone like that?"

I mulled it over. Jack could be right. But I certainly hoped Wendy had enough awareness to tell if there was something wrong with Paul. For my own selfish reasons I was hoping that she would be willing to talk about what had happened at her yarn shop the day Paul seemed to take ill.

"Joe seems to like being married to her, though," I said.

"Joe would kill anybody who came near Wendy," Jack replied with all seriousness. "She may be a willow wisp, but Joe is a tank. If anyone ever touched Wendy he would take them apart piece by piece and bury the bits where even the coyotes wouldn't find them."

I started to ask him another question, but he was already heading back to the tractor to drag the boulder from the pile.

"Move aside, Marley," he called over the roar of the tractor. "I'm just gonna yank it out and that chain might come loose."

I nodded and walked a good twenty yards away from the pile as Jack muscled the big boulder free.

We loaded several tons of rocks, some for the bank and some for a little side project Jack was doing for a woman he was trying shamelessly to impress. That was one thing I liked about him more than anything else. Jack wasn't afraid of anything. Not even romance. If he liked something, he went for it and told everybody that was his goal. I wished sometimes I could be more like him in that respect. It wasn't easy to admit to myself that deep down I still cared what other people thought about me.

We worked well into the afternoon gathering the stones for the bank. After the trailer was loaded we drove back into town, Eddie Money playing on the CD player in the cab.

"How was your mom over in Parkman?" I asked, making conversation to pass the time.

Jack grimaced. "She's worse. That nursing home is such a train wreck. Doctor only comes once a week. Nobody gets the residents their medication on time. Sometimes the trash cans in the rooms don't get emptied for days. You can tell a lot about a place by how often they empty their trash cans."

I had to agree with that.

"Still, after having a stroke, I guess it's better for her to be in there than living at home with a nurse. At least she is around other people full-time," he said.

"That's got to be expensive."

He whistled. "And how. It's four thousand a month. Good thing her social security kicked in."

"It's good of you to go by and see her regular," I told him. I didn't say it, but I knew Jack didn't go to Parkman just to visit his sick mother.

Usually he made a long detour and went over to the casino up on the reservation before he came home. If there was one weakness in my boss, it was his habit of hoping to cash in on the big jackpot. Sometimes I wondered how it was he managed to pay his bills and keep up his regular visits to the casino. Maybe he was lucky?

"Aw, it's my mom. Course I go see her. Besides, they got cute nurses," he said with a grin.

We both laughed about that as we pulled into the bank. We set to work unloading rocks, and left them piled haphazardly to be finished the following day. It was past four and almost time to quit.

The day came to an end and I drove towards home, past Wee Wooly's, and wasn't surprised to see the windows dark and no one moving inside. I did what I could to suppress my renewed irritation. Where was Wendy? It seemed odd to me that she would simply lock up her shop and disappear.

I toyed with the idea of calling her at home, but if I started asking her questions about Paul she would know I hadn't called simply to catch up. Wendy and I had been close friends in high school, but after we graduated she had married Joe, I had married Allen and we drifted apart. Funny how suddenly having a man in your life took you away from your friends.

Tracking her down at home was out of the question. If I wanted to talk to her I would have to wait until she came back to work.

It had been a long day. Driving home to eat dinner out of a box leaning over the kitchen sink didn't sound all that appealing. I decided to stop at Lil's.

Irene knew practically everything that went on in Killdeer. Maybe she could clue me in as to why Wendy had suddenly dropped out of sight.

CHAPTER 14

I took a seat at the counter, oblivious to the bustle going on in the packed café.

Irene slapped a menu in front of me and leaned down to whisper in my ear. "That man from Area Forty-nine is here."

I pivoted in my seat and saw a flash of thick blond hair and black shirt in the far corner. His back was to me, luckily. So he didn't see me rudely giving him the once-over. I shrugged and turned back to Irene.

"So?"

She smirked. "So? He's only the most intriguing person to walk in this place in fifteen years. Wouldn't you like to know what they do up there all day? He carries a gun, you know."

I had to admit, there was a part of me that did want to know what went on at the station. Anyone interesting enough to induce Irene to say the word intriguing did deserve some speculation.

"I'll bet it's pretty boring up there," I said.

Irene wasn't buying it. She poured me a raspberry iced tea and took my menu away without my having opened it.

"You're having the mushroom and Swiss burger," she said.

"Okay."

She scribbled on an order slip and crammed it up on the ticket holder. "I'm trying a new lean ground beef. Tell me if you think it's too dry."

The cook, a plump man with straight black hair, pulled the order slip and read it while shoving full plates into the heated pickup window at the same time. How anyone could manage so many different tasks all at the same time was a mystery to me.

"Why don't you go talk to him?" Irene said. Her sharp eyes darted toward Finn and her mouth curled in a smirk.

I sipped my tea. "Sure. I'll just sit down beside him and say, 'The Blue Whale Sings at Midnight.'"

Irene rolled her eyes. "He's not a Russian spy. He's just a man, Marley. I don't care what he does for a living, men still have needs."

I rolled my eyes back at her. "Dirty old woman."

"Not those needs," she said with irritation. "He's been in this town almost nine months and he hasn't really made any friends to speak of. I just think someone should go talk to him and try to be . . . friendly."

I shot her a look. "And that someone would end up telling you all about the conversation and then you'd be up on all the gossip from Area Forty-nine."

She grinned. "Something like that."

I shook my head. "Count me out. He's surly at best and I don't think he really wants any friends."

"How do you know he's surly?" she demanded at once.

"My father talked to him," I said. Then I held up a hand. "Don't get excited, they talked about hay swather bearings and flat tires."

Irene didn't need to know I'd spoken to him once as well. As far as I was concerned the man was about as personable as a guard dog.

My mushroom and Swiss burger appeared in front of me and Irene settled in to warm the counter beside me with her elbows. She gulped a strong cup of coffee, black, no sugar.

I frowned at her coffee cup. "I thought you had switched to tea?"

"With everything that's going on around here? This is all that gets me through the day without punching someone."

"By everything you mean what happened to Paul?" I said.

She put a hand on my arm and squeezed. "Honey, I know it must be hard for you to hear about it all the time. Folks can't seem to talk about anything else. I am starting to get sick of hearing about him."

"The burger is great," I told her, sensing that she was poised to tell me something.

Irene was waiting for an opening to spill what she wanted to say. I gave her an encouraging nod, which was all it took.

"Did you know that David's real estate firm is already handling the sale of Paul's house? That seems a bit shady if you ask me. But Paul left everything to charity, and that includes his house and all the land. So Falcon Realty is selling it on behalf of the estate, and you know their agent will get a big fat commission."

I paused before taking another bite. "But isn't that a conflict of interest?"

"I thought so too," Irene went on, hardly drawing breath. "But Falcon Realty gave the account to one of its junior agents and David swears up and down he is giving her the full commission and taking nothing for the agency, in order to show that he isn't trying to capitalize on the death of a former political rival."

I tossed that information around in my head awhile.

"Who's the agent?" I asked.

"Your dad's next-door neighbor. Virginia Gable," Irene said. She nearly spat the name.

"I didn't know she was considered a junior agent." I pictured Virginia's perfect blonde hair and Gucci wardrobe and thought she'd always looked more like she owned Falcon Realty than David Jordan did. It was no secret that she basically ran the business while David concentrated on being mayor.

"Virginia bullied David into letting her have the account. I talked to Billy Collins about it just yesterday when he came in for barbeque ribs, and he told me that office is in a state of denial. They have themselves convinced it's proper for the agency to be involved with the sale of Paul's property."

"Isn't Billy the office assistant for Falcon?" I asked, trying to place the name.

"Nice kid. Too nice to be working for Falcon, if you ask me," Irene said.

"Well, how does he know what goes on between Virginia and David?"

Irene leaned in a bit and lowered her voice. I was about to be the recipient of privileged information.

"Billy heard them shouting about it. They were both talking about what a shame it was that Paul didn't have any family his estate could go to, but that they both agreed letting it all go to charity was a Christian thing to do." Irene humphed when she said this.

"But then it got nasty. Virginia said she would take the contract but David was worried how it would look, him being Paul's opponent, and all. He said Virginia just hit the roof over that. She threatened to quit if David didn't give her the account. She's got enough influence in that office now that she can get away with a move like that. You know the commission from the sale of Paul's property will be substantial."

Several thousand dollars' worth of substantial, I thought.

"He's leaving," Irene said, surreptitiously casting an eye behind me.

We both fell silent and watched as the mysterious Finn-in-black left the café.

I glanced around and realized everyone else having dinner was just as captivated by his departure as we were. Once he was gone, the usual level of conversation resumed and I overheard not a few folks speculating about our quiet visitor.

I sighed. The people of this town really needed to start watching Dancing with the Stars or something.

I insisted on paying for the raspberry iced tea, thanked Irene for the meal and left, my head down and my thoughts spinning. I was so preoccupied by the revelation that David's real estate firm would be cashing in on Paul's death I didn't even see the deputy until I was pulling my car keys from my pocket.

"Oh, hello Nick," I said with a frown. He was leaning against the hood of my Honda, his arms crossed and his face hostile.

"Miss Dearcorn," he said with a nod. "And it's Deputy Wilcox."

I noticed he was holding something tucked in his left hand. I came to a stop and smiled. No need to be rude.

"What can I do for you, Deputy Wilcox?" I asked with as much sweetness as I could drip into the sentence.

He sensed my sarcasm and produced a small plastic vial with what looked like a Q-tip inside.

"You can give me a DNA sample."

I nearly laughed until I saw that he wasn't kidding.

"What for?" I asked, abandoning my sweet voice in favor of my righteously indignant tone

"We just need to verify that the facts you gave us match the evidence at the scene of Paul Nesbit's death."

I gaped at him. "Which facts, exactly?"

"All of them," he said.

I did laugh then. "Nick, I'm not giving you a DNA sample," I said.

"And that tells me you've got something to hide," he said.

"What? What information could I possibly have that I would keep from you?"

He shrugged. His shoulders moved like coat hangers under his baggy shirt. "You tell me."

"I think I've been hiding the fact that I think you are an incompetent boob pretty good," I said.

I shouldn't have said it, but it popped out before I could stop myself.

He pushed the swab out the tip of the vial and came towards me.

I took a step back reflexively but he trapped me against my car and gripped my arm.

He twisted my wrist back until it stung. I was so stunned I completely froze. He lifted the vial towards my mouth and reached for my jaw.

Just as his fingers touched my face a hand came down between us and I felt myself shoved to the side. I stumbled and tried to catch myself but I was headed for the ground fast. A strong arm circled my waist and propped me upright against the side of my car. I caught my balance, and turned just in time to see Finn relieving Deputy Wilcox of the plastic vial. And his footing.

Nick hit the ground and I winced as air woofed out of his lungs. He scrambled backwards and got to his feet, his face red and twisted with anger.

Finn watched him, hands at his sides. Casual.

"That's assaulting an officer!" Nick yelled. "It's illegal to lay hands on a law enforcement official."

"And it's illegal to take a DNA sample without a warrant," I said.

Nick ran his hand through his crew cut and bent to snatch the plastic vial from the ground. "Next time I see you," he said, glaring at me over Finn's shoulder, "I'll have one."

The deputy marched to his county truck, slammed the door shut and squealed both back tires pulling away.

I ran my fingers over my forearm where Nick had grabbed me and realized my hands were shaking.

I drew a deep breath and retrieved my car keys from the asphalt. When I stood up Finn was watching me impassively.

"Um, thanks," I said quietly. I was still so rattled I didn't trust myself to take my hand away from my car just yet. It was solid and sturdy and comforting, not unlike the man standing in front of me.

"Not a problem." His face was still expressionless, but his voice had raised a pitch or two and that was all that betrayed any emotion whatsoever.

I happened to look towards Lil's, and I saw a chorus line of faces watching us from the window. They saw me looking and instantly bent back to their clam chowder and salads as if nothing had happened. Great. Might as well be on the six o'clock news.

I gathered my composure, what was left of it, and tried to give Finn a smile.

"You always seem to come along just at the right moment." I tried to laugh. It came out more like a squeak.

Finn gave the parking lot a sweep with his eyes. Probably checking the perimeter for ninjas. "I've got a knack for it," he said with total seriousness.

"Lucky for me."

An awkward silence fell on us. Awkward for me. He seemed not to notice.

I cleared my throat. "I should get home. Ah, thank you."

He stared at me, unsmiling. "Glad I could help. Stay out of trouble, Miss Dearcorn."

If only that were possible.

I pulled open my car door but paused before climbing in.

"Finn," I called after him.

He stopped and glanced back. He wasn't wearing his sunglasses this time, and I was amazed at how blue his eyes looked.

"Where are you from? Are you British?" I asked.

He smiled almost imperceptibly.

"Johannesburg. I'm South African."

With that he walked away, leaving me staring after him stupidly.

I climbed in my car and pulled out of the parking lot, certain that the next time Irene saw me she would be livid that I had driven off without giving her details of what had just happened. But the fact of the matter was that I wasn't entirely certain myself.

CHAPTER 15

I drove home, flustered over Finn's unexpected appearance in the parking lot and flabbergasted over his actions towards Deputy Wilcox. It wasn't like me to be nervous around men, but there was something about Finn that seemed to amplify my ability to feel awkward. I tried to put it out of my mind and concentrate on the road. It was dark enough that I needed to switch on my headlights. The last rays of light were slowly diminishing behind the mountain and casting the valley in a long shadow.

By the time I reached my driveway I knew the day's drama wasn't quite finished. Virginia Gable was parked in my driveway.

I sighed and turned off my car, willing myself to open the door and be polite. Every time I saw Virginia I felt like a kid at school who'd been busted passing notes and was now sitting in the principal's office. Talking to her was draining. I stepped out of my car and tried to give her a warm smile. My face felt brittle.

"Marley," she said, clipboard in one hand and animosity painted on her face as usual. "I came to get your signature on this claim form."

"Claim form?" I asked. I stopped and folded my arms, showing plainly that I had no intention of signing anything until I bloody well knew what it was.

Her Welsh corgi took this opportunity to leap into the driver's seat of her SUV and leaned on the horn. It blared, startling her. "Saint Christopher! No! Bad doggie! Mommy is very disappointed in you."

The corgi lowered his ears and obediently slunk into the passenger seat. I did my best not to laugh.

Virginia cleared her throat. Her jaw muscle quivered. She recovered her composure and shoved the pen towards me. When I made no move to take it she sucked her teeth with disdain.

"It is a claim form for the damage you did to Paul's house when you broke the porch door with the tractor. The insurance company is billing you for the cost of the repairs, and I need your signature so the repairmen can get to work."

I stared at her for a moment. "You have got to be kidding me."

"If you would just sign here—"

"Virginia," I said, looking her straight in the eye. "If you think for one second that I am going to pay for the damage you are out of your mind."

"Marley, you damaged the property, and you are responsible for the cost of the repairs to that property. Do you deny that you broke the door?"

"In service to the greater good, sure I broke the door," I told her. "If your definition of liability is to hold people accountable for actions they perform while trying to save the life of a fellow human being, then you are one cold fish."

That brought her up short. She actually sputtered.

"And another thing," I said, just getting up to steam. "If people thought that by trying to help their neighbors who are in life-threatening situations they would be sued, there would be a lot fewer Good Samaritans out there and a lot more dead people."

"This isn't about morality," she said. Her lips were twitching with anger.

"You are wrong there." My face was starting to feel hot. "That is exactly what it's about. If you want to bill me for damage I did while trying to help Paul, go ahead and try. See how far it gets you."

Virginia tilted her head and tucked the clipboard to her side protectively. "Marley," she said, her voice coated in honey. "You are right, of course. This is a very unfortunate situation. Now, I might be in a position to help you. I suppose I could talk to the insurance company on your behalf."

I waited for the other shoe to drop. It was, no doubt, a double E steel-toed work boot.

"If you tell me exactly what happened, maybe I could use your side of the story to convince them that you really should be left out of this," she said. "Describe the events, in detail, and I will see what I can do."

What sort of a ghoul would want to know the details of a man's death?

"Virginia, there isn't that much to tell."

"Maybe you should let me be the judge of that." Her eyes glittered.

I looked away from her to hide my disgust. Saint Christopher was busy decorating her driver's-side window with slobber and nose prints. Good for him.

Obviously there was more going on here than simple curiosity. Virginia was up to something, and she was using the threat of an anonymous insurance company to rattle me so that I would cooperate.

"Okay." I took a deep breath and for once in my life I really thought about what I was about to say. I picked my words very, very carefully.

"I got to Paul's house and the power was out."

She pounced on that. "How did you know that he just didn't have the lights turned off?"

I felt my stomach tighten. She wanted to hear it all, beginning to end. "The electricity was off at my place. I guess I just assumed it would be there too."

"Go on." She jotted a note on her clipboard with an expensive pen. I thought she and Nick Wilcox could start a mechanical pencil club.

"I walked around the house and it looked like it hadn't been hit too hard. But when I knocked nobody answered."

She encouraged me with another head tilt.

"I went to the back door, and when I knocked I saw Paul lying on the floor of the kitchen and he wasn't moving."

She nodded that I should continue.

"I thought he must be in trouble if he was on the floor like that, and I guess I panicked and just found the first thing I could that would get me inside the house fast."

"The tractor."

"It worked," I told her.

She scribbled on the papers. "And when you got inside the kitchen what did you find?"

"I found Paul unconscious. He wasn't breathing."

Virginia looked at me over the top of her clipboard. "What did he look like?"

"I'm not sure I understand." Why was this important to her?

She tapped the clipboard with her pencil. "I know you are not a doctor, Marley. But did it seem to you that he had simply had a stroke? Heart attack? How did it look to you?"

I was beginning to feel like this conversation wasn't about an insurance claim. "He looked like he was dying."

She sniffed. "Marley, you have got to give me something better than that, or else a team of lawyers from the insurance agency will be sending you a certified letter within days."

I was beginning to doubt that there was an insurance company. Virginia was doing the classic carrot-and-stick routine with me. She was threatening me, then offering me a way out if I helped her. I just had to figure out why.

"Well, if I had to say what I really think, it looked to me like Paul had just fallen over dead from a heart attack."

She scrutinized me. "Why would you say that? Describe the condition of his body. Did you see any blood? Was there any sign he'd fallen? Tell me how it looked to you."

"There wasn't any blood anywhere. He didn't look like he hit his head on anything. What else could it have been? Sometimes it happens like that, even to young people like him."

"Can you think of anything, anything at all, that would lead you to believe he died of unnatural causes?"

"Unnatural causes?"

She sighed. "Marley, the resale value of a home goes down considerably if rumors start circulating that the former owner passed away because of foul play."

"Foul play means murdered, doesn't it?" I asked.

She turned a curt smile. "I don't know if you have heard, but I am handling the sale of Paul's house. Now, you won't be telling anyone that Paul died of any other cause than a heart attack, will you? Natural deaths don't take nearly the bite out of the final sale price of a home that a murder would."

My opinion of Virginia suddenly dropped another notch, if that was possible. She didn't care about the man. She only cared about the bottom line. All this haranguing was just her way of finding out if I was going to cost her money.

"No, Virginia. It was natural." I tried to hide my disgust, and didn't do a very good job of it.

She searched my face. "I think I can make the insurance company understand you shouldn't be held responsible for this. It was only dumb luck that you were there at all."

Something about the way she said it made me pause. I decided to change my tone. If I appealed to her vanity there was a chance she might let something slip.

"Virginia, I really appreciate this. I'm sorry I got so angry. You are sticking your neck out for me and I can't thank you enough for doing that."

"You shouldn't forget it," she said, freshening up her red lipstick. She dropped the tube back in her bag. "I didn't have to come to your defense like this."

I nodded vigorously. "Oh, I know that. It was very good of you to do it."

Restored to her magnanimous state, Virginia turned to climb into her gleaming black BMW.

I waited until she was about to shut the door. "What's the name of the insurance company?" I asked.

She stopped and stared at me, one well-manicured hand resting on the door. "Excuse me?"

"The insurance company. What's their name?"

She gave me a blank look. "Why do you want to know that?"

"Well, if I get a letter from them I wouldn't want to make a mistake and throw it in the garbage."

She opened her mouth and then swallowed. "You won't be hearing from them."

She slammed her door, started the engine and drove away without looking back.

I watched her roll down the washboard dirt road until her dust trail was out of sight. Virginia had given me quite a lot to think about.

She was right. If I hadn't shown up when I did, Paul would have died alone on his kitchen floor and no one would have discovered him for at least a couple days. The only reason I'd to his house in the first place was because of the downburst. But nobody could have seen that coming.

I stopped my rambling thoughts for a moment and tried to focus. The pine trees whispered around me, and I found myself wishing that they could share all of their secrets.

Something seemed out of place. But what could it be?

I closed my eyes and forced myself to remember every detail of when I'd first walked inside that dark kitchen.

The door had been locked from inside, and Paul was on the floor, stiff and not moving.

I frowned. Wouldn't a man suffering a heart attack be moaning or writhing? At the very least wouldn't he be convulsing? He hadn't moved a muscle when I'd gotten to his side. The only sounds I had heard were the awful strangling noises he'd made.

I concentrated, willing myself to see the scene again with as much detail as I could remember.

It wasn't that Paul was immobile; it was almost as if he was completely paralyzed. His body was so rigid it was as if he was dead already. And he hadn't uttered a sound. Not even a moan. The only thing that had let me know he was still alive at all had been that terrible, awful ragged breathing.

I remembered the moment my hands touched his face to open his throat for CPR and feeling the sudden sensation of tremendous heat. Why had he been so hot? Was it his body shutting down?

I shook my head. My instinct told me Paul's body wasn't shutting down, it was almost as if his body had been under attack.

All of the CPR and first aid training I had endured working for the Fish and Wildlife service had taught me that victims of trauma usually went into shock, became very cold, and the best thing to do was to cover them with a blanket. But Paul hadn't been cold. In fact he'd been the exact opposite.

It made sense to me that Paul knew he was sick when he tried to reach the kitchen. But, sick from what?

Whatever had killed him couldn't have been that much of a surprise. I had a suspicion that if he were sick, Paul would have known about it. It made going to see Wendy all the more important to me. If she could tell me what it was he succumbed to in her yarn shop that day, maybe it would help me understand what had really been the cause of his death. And in understanding it, maybe I would feel a bit better about the fact that all my efforts to help him had amounted to nothing.

Something else was bothering me. Why had I heard the front screen door slam when I was rushing upstairs to the bedroom to search for his inhaler? Could there have been someone else at the house? That didn't make any sense at all. Most likely, it had only been the wind. But then why had Loy asked me all of those questions about what I'd seen? He hadn't said anything directly, but all of the questions he'd asked made me think that the burly sheriff was not simply investigating a natural death.

I climbed the steps to my front door, feeling conflicted. Loy had told me to let it go. That is exactly what a smart person would do.

Maybe I was overreacting. More than likely Paul had suffered a fatal asthma attack and there was nothing more to it than that.

If that was the case, why had Deputy Nick Wilcox tried to take a DNA sample from me with no explanation?

I stood on my deck for a moment and listened to the sounds of evening.

Everything seemed peaceful, but who knew what went on in the forest under the cover of darkness?

It was probably a terrible mistake, but I had to know what had really happened to Paul. First, I would talk to Wendy. If she could add anything helpful that might allow me to understand what had really occurred, I would pass along the information to Loy, and then I would drop it.

At least, that is what I told myself. It seemed like a good idea at the time.

CHAPTER 16

Friday morning brought horizontal rain. It rained so hard and fast that when I finished pouring my first cup of strong coffee I wasn't surprised to see my father's truck pull into my driveway.

He bounded up the steps, never seeming like he had the patience to just walk anywhere like a normal person, and pounded on my door.

Instead of waiting for me to open it, he came inside so I wouldn't have to bother with a little thing like coming to the door. I reminded myself to speak to him about letting himself in all the time.

"Hey, Kiddo. Some storm! You see that rain this morning?" A yellow aspen leaf was stuck to the side of his head.

I smiled. "Want a cup of coffee, Dad?"

He shook his coat and drops of rainwater fell on the kitchen floor. "Nope. Just wanted to check on you before I go see about The Line. Can't remember if I parked it up against the trees or not. Can't have the damn thing blowing all over hell and gone. Just wanted to make sure everything was good here."

The Line was a quarter-mile-long unbroken length of rolling aluminum sprinkler pipe. It resided in my father's forty-acre pasture that he planted each year with alfalfa, and sometimes corn.

My father had given up the cows four years previously, but he amused himself with hobby farming small pieces of the ranch now and again. Each spring he went a bit mad with glee when the plowing time came.

"Hey, Dad," I said, trying to slow him down a bit and perhaps have a regular conversation. "Have you seen Wendy around lately?"

He paused to think. "Wendy Martinez? Can't say I have."

I felt irritated all over again. What would I have to do to get a chance to talk to that woman? "I noticed her shop was closed up all week."

He scratched his soaked forehead. "Haven't heard anything. You thinking of taking up knitting? That doesn't seem like you."

I laughed at the notion. "Not likely. I guess I just wondered why she's been gone."

"Well, she goes to that Friends of the Library auction they hold every year. I know they always spend a lot of money and Joe gets smashed."

I searched my memory. "Is that tomorrow night?"

"Next Saturday. Week from tomorrow. You really want to talk to her I'll bet you will find her there."

I wasn't crazy about waiting all week to ask her a simple question, but unless she reopened her yarn shop, it was the best chance I would get. "Thanks, Dad. But isn't it a formal event?"

"You must have at least one dress left over from your office days," he told me. The aspen leaf finally let go from the side of his head and drifted to the floor.

129

I shrugged. "Maybe one. If I can find the time, I may go."

"Might do you some good to get out of the house and wear girl clothes once in a while. Marley, I would sure like to see you get out of the landscaping business."

"It's the only job I could get," I said.

"It's the only job you tried to get," he said.

"I'm not sure that anyone else in Killdeer would have me."

"I think you might be surprised if you just gave it a shot," he said.

He kissed me on the forehead and left, banging the door closed before clomping to his truck through the October monsoon.

I picked up the phone and called Jack. As I suspected, he was halting work for the day. He told me not to bother coming in. Two days off in one week? As fall turned to winter and snow started to blanket the ground, our outdoor landscaping projects would gradually dry up until they disappeared altogether. I was not a fan of snow removal, but landscapers had to do something in the winter to make up for lost revenue when nobody needed to have grass mowed and shrubs trimmed. As I hung up the phone I thought that perhaps my father was right. Maybe it was time to look for another job.

With nothing better to do with myself for an entire day that should have been spent earning a paycheck, I slipped into a pair of grungy jeans and an old T-shirt and cleaned my house with severe determination.

I scrubbed the bathtub until it gleamed, waxed the kitchen floor, took all of the dishes out of the cupboards and washed the shelves and then scrubbed the kitchen sink. I washed the drapes from the living room and vacuumed until I was sure my electric bill would be double. I took a lunch break, then tackled the laundry and stripped the bed down to the mattress pad. After all the laundry was finished I rebuilt the bed and finished off the project by dusting everything. By late afternoon I was satisfied my house was as clean as it could be and I decided to go for a short walk. The rain had subsided and everything outside looked washed, too.

I pulled on a pair of hiking boots and headed for the little path that wound up the hill to the south behind my house. It was a twenty-minute struggle to the top, but worth the work to reach. The path was mostly stone, gravel and scree, so I managed to avoid getting too muddy. I found my familiar spot on a granite outcrop directly at the summit of the hill and sat down to catch my breath. I'd slipped and slid my way to the top, hampered by the slick grass and soaked autumn leaves that littered the trail. The outcrop was wet, but not soaked, and I didn't mind the damp. I looked out over the expanse of trees and smiled with a bit of selfish pride. Everything from the tall stand of aspen trees flanking the road towards Killdeer, down to the low pasturelands that touched my little house, belonged to my family.

My father owned well over a thousand acres, which was small for a ranch, but to me it was a king's estate. No matter what happened to me I had always been able to come back to this place and feel the comfort of the land. It was my home, but more than that. It was a sanctuary.

I watched the sun dipping low and stayed to enjoy it only a few minutes more.

It wasn't a good idea to try and navigate the trail back down the steep slope in the dark.

I made it back to my little house just after the sun had disappeared behind the mountain, and left my dirty boots outside on the deck.

I amused myself for the rest of the evening searching through my stash of formal dresses. I had a party to crash and I wanted to look nice. All my nice outfits were wrapped in sheets of plastic straight from the dry cleaners and I hadn't touched them since I'd come home.

Most of the dresses were passable, but not for a formal event. Instead of the office wear I had used in my professional life I turned my attention to the dresses I'd once used for dinner parties, back when I had been married and had done that sort of thing. I narrowed my choices down to three. A red, short-sleeve satin scooped-neck cropped just below my knees. A lavender silk drape that came with an embroidered scarf.

The last dress I considered was a cream off-the-shoulder tight mesh with a white silk shell that I'd splurged on years ago. The mesh weave was a sturdy fabric made of interlocking vines and I had managed to find a pair of shoes that matched the fabric perfectly. I hoped the shoes were somewhere in the bottom of my closet.

I looked back and forth between the three of them before deciding. Definitely the cream dress.

I took it out of the plastic and hung it in the bathroom. A week's worth of showers should steam out any wrinkles, and a quick toss in the dryer an hour before the auction should make it fresh as new.

The Friends of the Library auction was Killdeer's one ritzy event of the year.

Our town prided itself on the well-kept little library nestled in a quiet cul-de-sac on the southern edge of town.

It boasted a state-of-the-art circulation system with security devices at each door and a scanner that automatically checked out the books and printed receipts for the patrons. It had the largest collection of regional nonfiction in two counties, and it was practically a brand-new building. Oh yes. Killdeer loved its library. This event always managed to raise thousands of dollars for the library foundation. I had only been to it once and I had never gone back. It was a bit intimidating to see the wealthiest people in the county bidding five hundred dollars on a pitcher full of margarita mix. I was lucky if I had five hundred dollars to pay my car insurance.

This seemed like a lot of trouble to go to just to talk to an old friend at a party. I considered simply driving out to Wendy's house and knocking on her door, but somehow it didn't feel right. Wendy might not appreciate my barging in so I could pump her for information about some politician she barely knew. It seemed more appropriate to give the impression I had accidentally bumped into her, and then proceed to make small talk about the day Paul had been at Wee Wooly's. I knew I would feel self-conscious at the auction spending the evening surrounded by people who had plenty of money to spend, but if I couldn't track Wendy down any other way, I was willing to endure a little financial jealousy to get five minutes of her time.

CHAPTER 17

An uneventful weekend came and went, and I found myself pressing down the switch on my alarm Monday morning, feeling better than I had any right to feel. Just the idea that I was on a mission to find out what had really happened to Paul gave me a little nudge towards fine.

Jack was still playing catch-up with the climbing jobs, so all I had to do was basic winter prep. I went from house to house, visiting all of our regular clients, and did the menial maintenance jobs that people hate to do themselves. I rolled up hoses, blew leaves off of patios with the leaf blower, drained artificial ponds and gathered up the last remnants of dropped tree limbs that could be carried by hand and dumped into the trailer. I hardly saw a single human being the entire day.

When the day ended I couldn't face Kung Pao chicken from a box and stopped at Lil's to face the music.

As expected, as soon as I sat at the counter a pair of angry ice-blue eyes fixed on me, just inches from my face.

"What the bloody-blue-blazes was that scene in my parking lot last week?" Irene said.

I shrugged. "I told you Officer Wilcox had it in for me."

"And then you drive off without one word? Marley, you have no idea how that looked from where I was standing."

"Can I have the Reuben? Hold the fries?"

Irene snorted. "Not until you tell me everything that happened."

She folded her arms, a signal that she wasn't kidding. I knew if I ever wanted to eat again, I'd have to spill.

"Okay," I said, relenting.

Irene leaned in to catch every word.

I decided to start at the beginning. "Loy told me that this new deputy has a real CSI forensics fixation."

"Wilcox?" she asked.

I nodded. "He is always dusting for prints, looking for fibers, that sort of thing. Well, he wanted me to give him a DNA sample out there in the parking lot. And I didn't want to give him one."

"Why should you? It's not like Paul got hit over the head with a candlestick in the drawing room, for crying out loud. He had a heart attack."

"That's what I thought too," I told her. "But the funny thing was, when I got there, Paul seemed to be going through more than just cardiac failure. His skin was too hot."

"What does that have to do with anything?" she asked.

"No, Irene. He was burning up. It was like someone had just taken him out of the oven and put him on a cooling rack. It was literally burning me to touch him."

Irene came around the counter and sat beside me on one of the round Naugahyde stools.

"So? I still don't know what that has to do with anything."

"Wilcox most likely took Paul's body temperature when he examined the scene, and I think it was probably still really high, so I guess he suspected that I hadn't done CPR on Paul, that I was lying about it for some reason."

Irene, bless her heart, didn't erupt into storms of protest. She simply nodded. "And he wanted to make sure you had really tried to help him."

"That's the only thing I can think of," I said. Saying it out loud, it sounded like a weak theory, even to me. I tugged at the rubber band I'd wrapped around my strawberry blonde tangles. My hair spilled out of the tie over my shoulders.

"Well, that explains Wilcox," Irene said. "But what about Mr. Area Forty-nine? He was in the middle of you two so fast I didn't even see where he came from."

"He's from South Africa."

Irene shot me a look. "That's not what I meant. It's almost as if he was watching for trouble. How else could he have seen what was about to happen between you and the deputy?"

I shook my head. "I have no idea. But he's strange. Nice," I said quickly, when she cocked her head to the side with an expression of concern. "Nice enough, anyway. But he's odd. I think he's been in law enforcement for a long time."

"That can make a man strange," she said.

"I have been wondering about something," I said.

Irene did a quick sweep of her café with eyes that saw everything. Satisfied all was right with her realm, she settled back down and leaned into me a bit. "Honey, are you sure you are ready to start dating again?"

"What?" I said. "What does that have to do with Paul?"

"I'm not talking about Paul anymore," she said. She waggled her eyebrows at me three times with a suggestive look.

"The man-in-black? Irene, come on."

"He's cute," she said. "And you're cute, too, Marley. Any girl as pretty as you shouldn't be without a man. It's a waste. You with those big green eyes and trim little . . ."

"I was wondering about what could have made Paul sick," I told her.

Irene shook her head at me. "You have got to stop thinking about it."

"But what if he was sick? What if he knew that he was sick, or someone else in town knew he had a condition of some sort?"

"And if he did, would finding out what it was make you feel any better?" she asked.

"Yes, it would. I tried to help Paul. I tried so hard my arms gave out. If I knew that he had some medical condition that cost him his life I'd be able to sleep a lot better at night."

Irene thought about what I had said. Then she put a sympathetic hand over my arm and patted me. "Marley, even if Paul wasn't sick, there was nothing more you could have done. Nobody could have."

I didn't believe that. I had to know the truth.

"Irene, had anyone ever said anything to you, anything at all that would have led you to think Paul was ill?"

She shook her head at once. "Nobody. And believe me, if someone who came in here had any thoughts on that, I would have heard about it."

I certainly believed that.

"Shepherd seemed to think he might have been sick," I said.

"The scruffy, abusive jerk who loves picking on you?" she asked. "What does he know about it?"

"Shepherd's mother was at Wee Wooly's the afternoon Paul went in there to try and knit a scarf."

"Knitting isn't anything to be ashamed of," Irene said defensively.

"I didn't say it was. Shepherd said that his mother saw Paul have some sort of episode at Wee Wooly's. He got pale and sick without any warning. Maybe Wendy Martinez saw something that is important."

"And you think if you talk to Wendy about it, she will tell you what happened," Irene said.

"It's the only thing I have to go on so far."

"Good luck finding Wendy," Irene said. "I haven't seen Wee Wooly's open for days, and if she is going in and out of there to do inventory like the sign says, then I'm Sigourney Weaver."

"I'm going to talk to Wendy the first chance I get. I think I may have to wait until the auction on Saturday night."

A broad grin spread across Irene's face. "Oh, is that so? Marley Dearcorn is going to the Friends of the Library auction. Well who's your date?"

"Date? I don't have one. I'm going alone."

"Oh, no you're not," she said. "It's couples only this year."

"Couples only?"

"That's right. The Foundation had this wonderful idea to make the auction a couples event. Unless you have a date, you can't get in."

"Why?" I asked.

"I guess they had too many people come last year and they ran out of the shrimp scampi, so they decided to weed out the riffraff."

I felt a sudden surge of panic. "But who am I going to go with?"

She gave me a lascivious look.

"No," I said at once. "The guy from the weather station? I don't even know how I would get in touch with him. No way."

"Well, your dad won't go, I can tell you that," she said.

"I know, I know. He hates that sort of thing. I'll find someone. If I have to I'll take my dad's lawn boy."

Irene laughed. "If you get desperate enough, you'll think of something."

Unfortunately, she was right.

CHAPTER 18

Tuesday came and went. I spoke to Mrs. Gunderson, and though she was happy to chat with me about her lost crop of tulips (we'd try again next year), she didn't know anyone who would be willing to be my date for the auction.

Wednesday went by, and still the yarn shop was shut down, so it was looking less likely that I would be able to bump into Wendy at work.

I handled jobs that didn't include contact with clients. So my quest to gather gossip about Paul's health was fruitless.

By Thursday morning I had resolved to find a date for the auction, which was an alarming two days away. I worked a long day and then fell into bed with no idea who I would ask to be my escort for the evening. It had been a long, frustrating and not very productive few days.

I suffered a weak moment and toyed with the idea of asking Donny, the younger of the two landscapers on our crew, to be my date. Luckily I came to my senses and realized it would be impossible to live it down when he laughed in my face.

By Friday afternoon, as I was just finishing up the final touches on a brick patio in Mrs. Shedd's back yard.

I had to face the fact it was time to resort to drastic measures. I had told Irene I didn't know how to get in touch with Finn, but that wasn't entirely true. There was one way.

I drove home, happy that there was still enough light to see the road, and enough light to see a little Honda parked in an obvious place.

I stopped my car on the side of the road, not very far from where I had seen the wounded deer in the barrow ditch the previous week, and waited.

It was nearly twenty minutes before I heard the sound of tires on gravel coming from the south. When I saw the black Jeep, I'll admit, I felt a clammy sweat suddenly coat my skin.

"For heaven's sake, girl," I said to myself. "What's the worst that can happen?"

I felt ridiculous sitting in my car waiting. I stepped out and leaned against the driver's-side door, pretending to be nonchalant.

I watched as he flipped a U-turn and parked behind me, exactly as he had done before. I stayed propped against my car. I had more pride than to go lean into his Jeep window like a teenage girl.

He watched me for a moment, motionless. I gave him a small wave and he opened his door, walking towards me with more graceful swagger than a man had any right to have. I knew it was ridiculous, but I imagined that Finn had never once in his entire life tripped over anything.

"Finn."

He gave me a very slight smile. "Marley."

Well, he wasn't a politician, was he? Conversation wasn't as important when you were in his line of work. Whatever that was . . .

"Finn, I wanted to thank you for helping me out with Deputy Wilcox the other day."

"Not a problem. He tune you any more cack after that?"

I stared at him. "If that means has he bothered me, then no. I haven't seen him."

Finn chuckled. "Sorry. Sometimes I forget myself. I grew up outside of Johannesburg. Most of my friends were in the surfkin mob."

I nodded, thinking that this was the first time he'd volunteered something personal.

"I need a favor," I said. That wasn't exactly how I had imagined this would go, but he seemed to respond to that.

"Name it."

Finally, a man who didn't shy away from a dangerous mission.

"I am going to an auction on Saturday night. It's a fund-raiser. And, and I need a date. I was hoping that you would like to join me." I need a date? Golly, Marley. How could the guy resist?

He looked at me with a mixture of surprise and perhaps a little bit of disbelief.

"I'll understand if you can't make it," I added when he didn't respond. "But I would really appreciate it if you can."

He stood there, his face completely impassive. A hundred possible responses ran through my head. Sorry, but I'm pouring concrete for a surface-to-air missile pad. I'd love to go but I'm washing my grenade launcher Saturday night. I have a dentist appointment . . .

"Sure," he said. "What the hell. Why not?"

I pushed away from my car. "Really? That's great. Well, uh, how do I find you?"

"What time is the auction and where?" he asked.

"Six-thirty at the library. But—"

"What do I have to wear?"

"Well, it's semiformal so—"

"I'll find you. Be ready at six."

I tried not to laugh. This wasn't exactly a military operation. It was cocktails and finger food. But he was doing me a favor, so I just nodded and vowed not to burst out laughing if he asked me if there was a weapons check next to the coat closet.

"I'll be ready at six," I said.

He seemed satisfied that he could count on me to be prepared, nodded and headed back to his Jeep without another word. He drove off, not looking back.

I rubbed my palms on my jeans, realizing that I was covered in dust and mud. Hopefully Finn had enough imagination to picture me cleaned up. I didn't always have brick dust in my hair.

I drove home, slightly giddy, and spent the remainder of the day thinking about how to handle the next evening.

When morning came I still felt a small flutter of excitement.

I tried to tell myself it was because Saturday night I would finally start getting some answers. Then maybe I could take Irene's advice and let it all go.

Saturday afternoon I shaved my legs. I told myself that this meant absolutely nothing. Women did it all the time. The fact that I shaved my legs had nothing to do with the fact that I was going on a date. It wasn't even a date, really. It was a mission. I was on a mission. I needed information about Paul, and the auction was the only way I could do that. And the only way I could get to the auction was to go on a date. Simple. I had it all worked out.

And then, at precisely 5:59 and 15 seconds, Finn pulled into my driveway.

CHAPTER 19

I stood at the window and watched him park his Jeep.

It was positively gleaming.

He'd washed his vehicle.

I suddenly didn't feel so silly for shaving my legs.

I went outside and paused at the top of the stairs, dramatically. His expression didn't change at all, and I felt suddenly stupid for striking a pose. That sort of thing was probably lost on a man like Finn.

He stood next to the driver's-side door and stared at me, not making a move to come closer. Well, that was annoying, but I was willing to let it slide. He was here, wasn't he?

I slipped on a long camel-colored wool jacket and walked down.

He didn't say hello, didn't move, and simply watched me, waiting.

Then I saw his expression. His eyes were fixed on me.

"That dress is boss."

"You like it?" I asked. I hoped that the word "boss" meant good.

"I do." He nodded with military precision. "It will take us seventeen minutes to drive to the library."

I supposed that meant we should leave now. He opened my door and as I climbed in I couldn't help but notice that he was, once again, dressed head to toe in black. Black slacks, shiny black boots that looked more urban than cowboy, a black turtleneck and a wool blazer. The blazer was black, too.

He made it work.

He started the engine and I could see when I glanced over my shoulder that the vehicle had been stripped down inside. There was only one rifle in the gun rack, as opposed to the usual arsenal that I remembered seeing previously. I could see from the impressions in the leather on the backseat that multiple heavy items usually sat there, but they had been taken out.

We drove in near silence. I commented on the weather, facetiously, but he didn't take the hint and said one or two words the entire ride to the library. I thought he kept glancing at my legs, but I never once actually caught him doing it. I had never met a man as difficult to read as Finn. It was an agonizing seventeen minutes.

When we parked at the library I spotted Jack's truck down the street, and I made a mental note to remind myself to find him in the crowd and give him a rough time for coming to such a posh event. Jack usually hated these auctions, and I was surprised he would bother to show up at all.

The building was packed with people.

As we purchased our tickets and walked inside, I had a flash of self-consciousness.

Since coming home I had purposefully avoided socializing.

My father told me I worried too much, that the fears I harbored over any rumors circulating about me since I'd been fired were overblown, but I still felt a wave of panic as we crossed the room. I took Finn's arm. He seemed pleased by that, but I'd done it for my own comfort.

Nobody gave me a second glance. Finn, on the other hand, was openly stared at with not a hint of discreetness. I might be nothing special, but he certainly was.

We mingled. That became boring in a matter of seconds. All of the women seemed to be following Finn with their eyes. Had he made any eye contact with the packs of curious females he'd have been set upon. I don't think he knew it, but keeping his gaze on me was all that stood between him and being torn to bits.

We checked out the items being offered up for auction. For such a small library the items on the rows of tables were astonishing in their quality. It was a mix of art, fine leather apparel, handcrafted wooden furniture and useful hunting and fishing equipment. I kept searching the crowd, but there was no sign of Wendy. Not yet, anyway.

The tables that were not filled with auction items were piled with desserts, dainty pastries, and tiny sausages on sticks. Waitresses in snug skirts drifted by with trays of wine and champagne.

Finn was holding a small plate crammed with six different types of chocolate sweets. He grinned at me shamelessly.

I looked at my own plate, filled with diagonally cut celery sticks, a tiny parsley quiche and two small bread wedges. I looked down at Finn's plate again. He was scooping a caramel brownie on top of his chocolate truffles. I looked down at my own plate. Something about that picture didn't seem right to me.

I backed up to snatch a couple chocolate truffles and ran right into someone.

"Leif! I'm sorry," I said.

Virginia's husband, Leif Gable, was maneuvering for the same dish as I and we'd collided.

"No, no," Leif said, patting my shoulder. "My fault, Marley. You first."

He pointed to the dish and I smiled as I scooped two truffles onto my plate. When I was finished he took the last three.

"This is a great turnout," Leif said. He stepped back to allow others access to the table and I moved to stand beside him.

Leif was a little older than Virginia, but he hummed with life and energy where she seemed to siphon it.

She wore expensive, designer-label clothing and Leif dressed in comfortable outdoor wear. Virginia spent a fortune having her hair done every week, and Leif shaved his head smooth.

Not for the first time, I wondered what such a nice man saw in Virginia. She was a viper. He had a genuine smile.

"Leif, this is my . . . friend . . . Finn. He was kind enough to join me tonight."

Leif balanced his small plate and shook Finn's hand firmly. "So how's the weather station?"

Finn gave a small smile. "Stimulating."

Leif chuckled and popped a truffle into his mouth. "I'll bet," he said around the mouthful.

The two men shared a grin, and somehow I got the feeling they were in on some sort of private joke. Did everyone around me know a lot more about what went on in Killdeer than I did?

"How's your father?" Leif asked, giving me a warm smile. "He was soaked through when he stopped by that morning after the downburst. Well, both he and Virginia were. He catch a cold?"

"No, you know my dad," I said. "He's fine."

"It was good of Nathan to come and check on us. The rain was heavy, but we were spared the bad hail that Fable got. Size of quarters! That was lucky for us. We didn't have any damage."

That reminded me it was high time I put some pressure on my boss to get our crew out to my place and cut up that toppled cottonwood tree. It had cluttered my front yard for two weeks now. After I picked out a new shed and got that installed, my place would finally be back to normal.

"How did Virginia get so wet that night?" I asked. I didn't really care and was simply making conversation. Leif Gable was one of the nicest men I had ever met, and even though his wife was intolerable, I always made an effort to be friendly. That meant asking after Virginia.

"She thought we'd lost the dog. She went out to the back yard to look for him, when I had him in the bedroom with me the entire time. I swear sometimes she loves that dog more than she loves me."

Leif Gable was not what I considered "dog people." Virginia was. Her corgi, Saint Christopher, lived a better existence than half of the children in the valley.

Leif didn't talk very much about what he had done for a living before relocating to Killdeer five years ago. Something in international business. I always got the impression from him that he had been born poor and had come into money.

But only after years and years of hard work. He seemed more normal than he had a right to be.

"It's lucky she didn't catch a cold, then," I said, as nice as I could. Honestly, I didn't think it would hurt my feelings much if she had caught pneumonia.

"Oh, you know my Ginni. She's stout," he said. Then his eyes dropped down to his plate. He seemed to be remembering something. He frowned, his normal cheer replaced with a blank stare.

Then he looked up again, forced a smile. "Marley, do you remember what time it was you found Paul?"

That must have been what had made him look so glum. Well, it made me feel glum too.

"I think it was about a quarter to five," I said.

I kept glancing at the door, and when I saw the familiar splash of silver hair, and the shoulders that looked like they belonged to a bulldogger, I knew that Joe Martinez had just arrived.

At that moment Lewis Pritchett slapped an enthusiastic hand on Leif's shoulder, ending our conversation.

Lewis squeezed between Leif and me, and the two men started chatting about cattle futures. I said a polite farewell to Leif with a small wave and he gave me a nod. I inched my way towards the stacks of books that marked the biographies.

Joe had taken a spot in front of Julius Caesar and was busy with a tall glass of deep red wine. He was a difficult man to miss in a crowd. Joe was taller than almost everyone around him, wore nothing but tailored suits and had a pair of hands that could crack open coconuts. I scanned his orbit for Wendy. I spotted her, mousing her way to his side with a plate of grapes and a flute of champagne.

Joe looked like he could have taken a bite out of a live rattlesnake. His face was flushed, one fist was crammed into his jacket pocket and he was breathing like a bellows.

I eased closer to them, being careful to keep my back towards them so it didn't look like I was trying to eavesdrop.

Finn was suddenly standing directly behind me. He put a hand on the nape of my neck. "What are you doing?"

I stopped inching backwards and shivered involuntarily. His hand was very warm. "Nothing."

"Something," he said.

I meant to move away, but for some reason I couldn't. He had just asked a direct question and I considered my options. I decided the truth was always the best choice, even if it was strange. "That woman behind me? The one in burgundy, with the short blonde hair?"

Finn nodded without looking in their direction. "The one dripping diamonds."

"I need to talk to her. She may have seen something that will help me understand why Paul Nesbit died two weeks ago."

"The schmoozer," Finn said. "Not a heart attack, then?"

I shook my head. "I am starting to wonder about that."

"Why do you care?" he asked.

"Because I'm the one who found him."

It came out a little harsher than I had intended. But Finn simply watched me, waiting to see if I was finished with my explanation.

"So go talk to her," he said. He finally let his hand slide from my neck and took a small step back.

"Her husband doesn't look very happy," I said, hoping my blush didn't show.

Finn sighed. "Who cares what that bloke thinks? What's he going to do, embarrass himself in front of all these nice people?"

He had a point. If I started in with casual conversation what could Joe say? Push off, Snoopy? I decided it was worth the chance.

As I turned to zero in on Wendy a hand snagged my wrist and pulled me towards the dictionaries. A familiar wide face popped into view.

"Loy," I said, letting my irritation show. "I'm trying to go say hello to someone."

"We never talk anymore, Marley."

I looked him up and down, and was shocked to see Loy Shucraft wearing a suit. Granted, it was a bit rumpled and was mostly brown, but it was a suit.

"Look at you!" I said. "No baseball cap tonight?"

"I'm undercover." He gave me a grin and threw his arm over my shoulder.

Mayor David Jordan breezed by, pumping a man's hand wildly, thanking him for a recent donation. He looked half sober, his ruddy cheeks shining in the crowd-generated heat.

"Listen, Loy, I don't want to be rude, but I'm trying to go talk to—"

"I'm Finn."

Loy's gaze turned slowly towards Finn, like an iceberg that has just spotted a nice big ship to ram.

Finn took Loy's hand and shook it.

Hard.

Loy shook back.

Harder.

"Nice to meet you. You here with my girl Marley?"

Finn stared at the sheriff, his eyes as sharp as a sword blade, his expression blank. "I am. And I didn't know she was your girl."

"I'm not," I said, pulling out from under Loy's draped arm.

It was Finn's turn to grin. "Then I guess that means she's my girl tonight."

Loy looked like he had just swallowed a squirrel.

I didn't have time for this. I walked away, leaving the two of them to sort it out. I was heading straight for Wendy . . . where Wendy had just been—but wasn't any longer. She'd vanished.

"Oh come on," I said under my breath.

I scanned the crowd. She was here someplace. The romance section? No. I looked harder. There! She was hiding out in arts and crafts. I sprinted to the end of the stack, and then screeched to a halt before she saw me and pretended to saunter down the row towards her.

"Oh, hello Wendy."

She looked up from the knitting section, seemed puzzled that I'd said something, and turned her attention back to the books. "Hi Marley."

Wendy had always been very pretty. She was petite, in fantastic shape and had big brown eyes that made her look like a pixie. Her smile sparkled. Usually. But not anymore. Now she was defeated, utterly. I could see it plainly. Wendy was a husk of the normally chipper person I remembered chatting with in the grocery store from time to time.

Wendy and I had been close friends in high school. Back when we had been seventeen we both imagined such bright futures.

I was going to become a biology professor at a prestigious university. Wendy was going to graduate art school and become a famous designer.

She married Joe before she had a chance to finish her degree, and I had finished two years of junior college, run out of money and gone to work for the Fish and Game to make ends meet. Here we were, fifteen years later. Not much had changed for the better and plenty had changed for the worse.

"How are you?" I asked.

Her eyes reminded me of that deer I'd found in the ditch. She didn't answer me right away.

I nudged her with my hip. "How's inventory going at your shop?"

She looked at me. "I'm not taking inventory."

She was about to burst into tears.

I put a hand on her elbow and tugged her towards the big double doors behind us. "It's noisy in here. Let's go out in the courtyard so we can hear each other."

The courtyard wasn't deserted. A few smokers lingered by the stone benches taking the opportunity to escape the press of bodies inside. I found us a quiet spot and took a seat on the nearest bench. It was freezing cold and I sucked in my breath the moment I sat down. Wendy sat too, but didn't seem to notice the cold. Her shoulders were so hunched together they could have almost touched.

"I'm not taking inventory," she said again. "Joe doesn't want me to leave the house."

"Wendy," I said. "Whatever it is that's bothering you, it's okay to talk about."

She had managed to keep her lower lip from quivering.

Suddenly I had no desire to pry about what she had seen the day Paul had come to her shop for his publicity stunt. Wendy obviously had bigger problems.

"You have been hiding out at home all this time?" I asked. "Why?"

"Joe wants a divorce."

I blinked. I had not seen that coming. "What? But, he's crazy about you."

"He used to be crazy about me," she said. A tear escaped and trailed down her cheek.

"All marriages have troubles," I said knowingly, from personal experience. "It will pass."

She shook her head. "Not this time. Joe's pride's been hurt. And when his pride is hurt he doesn't ever forgive it."

"Wendy, husbands get mad sometimes. But they get over it."

"Not when their wife has an affair," she said, her face twisted up with shame.

She dropped her head and cried. Really, really cried.

I sat there, trying to think of something helpful to say.

I put a hand on her arm. "Does Joe just think you had an affair? Or does he know it?"

She looked in my eyes. "He isn't sure. He thinks I did. But he doesn't want to endure the embarrassment if it came out."

"Well, do you think the other man will ever make it public?"

Wendy made a sound halfway between a sob and a whimper. "Joe won't ever have to worry about that happening."

I suddenly felt a cold shiver run down my spine. "Wendy, look at me. Who was it?"

She fixed me with those hollow eyes. "It was Paul. It was only one time. It was the worst mistake of my life. I slept with Paul Nesbit."

CHAPTER 20

I think my mouth actually fell open. I stared at her. She looked back at me, horrified, and slapped a hand over her lips. I think she was shocked she'd said the words. "Marley, I'm so sorry. I forgot about Allen and that girl from Kalispell."

"Wendy, it's alright," I said. "Allen and I had a lot more wrong with us than a waitress who couldn't keep her knees together."

It was my turn to feel bad now. "Sorry. I didn't mean that you couldn't keep your . . . never mind. Let's just say I am not going to sit here and judge you."

Relief made her shoulders slump, and she ran a hand over her cheeks to wipe away her tears. "Joe accused me of staying late at the shop all the time so I could meet someone. He's furious and he will hardly speak to me."

I tried to pull myself together mentally. "Have you suggested going to a counselor?"

Wendy laughed bitterly. "I think he'd jump off a building before he would ever let anyone think he needed help."

We sat in silence for a moment. I was, for once in my life, speechless. I had no idea what to tell her.

The loudspeakers mounted on the walls inside the library crackled to life and the library director came out to announce that the auction was about to begin. Wendy used the hem of her silk shawl to dab away the moisture from her cheeks. She stood up. "I can't be gone for very long or he will get angry."

"Let's find the restroom and tidy up first," I suggested.

She smoothed the wrinkles on the front of her cocktail dress and nodded. "I don't want him to know I was crying. He might think I told someone what happened."

We walked back towards the door, and I was relieved that no smokers had been standing behind us eavesdropping.

As I pushed open the door and felt the hot air escaping, I led Wendy through the crush of the crowd, dodging anyone who even remotely resembled Joe and keeping my head down. We ducked inside the bathroom.

As I pulled Wendy along behind me towards the mirrors I almost ran straight into Virginia Gable. She took one look at me, sneered, saw Wendy's tear-soaked face and I could almost see her mind processing what she was looking at.

Perfect.

"Ladies," Virginia said.

"Wendy bit into one of those jalapeno poppers," I said quickly. "Boy have they got a kick."

Wendy immediately bent to the sink and started gulping water from the tap. She waved one hand as if she was in pain. "Who made those things? They should have a warning label."

Virginia was taking in our performance with a suspicious glare.

For some reason, Virginia reserved her most searing look for Wendy, and practically ignored me altogether.

"Joe is looking for you," Virginia said, conspicuously straightening her gold watch.

Wendy kept her head bent down and reached for a paper towel. I snatched one from the dispenser and handed it to her.

"Leif is looking for you," I said, trying to distract Virginia.

She was staring at Wendy the way a border collie watches a stray lamb.

"Not likely. Leif knows that when I attend these functions he shouldn't interfere with my networking."

"Is that what the kids are calling it these days?" I asked.

Virginia's gaze snapped on me instantly. "This is a couple's event."

"I have a date," I said, my tone smug.

"Oh? How nice for you," Virginia said, sounding anything but sincere.

"She came with that guy from the weather station," Wendy said, trying to shift the tone of the conversation.

This tidbit of information seemed to distract Virginia at last.

She tilted her head and looked at me down her nose. "Does he have a name?"

"Finn," I said.

"Does he have a first name?" Virginia asked, tossing her hair.

She wore a blood-red full-length formal dress with a plunging neckline. She looked like she was ready to receive her academy award.

I smiled, noticing that she had accidentally spilled a dollop of shrimp cocktail sauce down the front of her cleavage. There wasn't a chance in hell I was going to point it out to her.

"Just Finn."

"Like Yanni? Or Fabio?" Virginia said with a curve to her upper lip.

"More like Bono, or Shaq," I replied.

Wendy had covered her red nose with a dusting of makeup and was smoothing on a coat of lipstick. She looked almost back to normal.

The last thing Wendy needed was gossip floating around, courtesy of Virginia Gable. We needed to get out of there before the nosey woman found something else to pick at.

"I hope you and Leif win that seven-day fishing trip on the Wind River down on the Shoshoni Indian reservation," I said.

Virginia's eyes bulged. "Fishing trip?"

"I'm sure I saw him bidding on it," I said.

Virginia spared one last glare of contempt for Wendy and shot from the bathroom with a furious look on her face.

Wendy gave me a grateful smile. "Thanks. She is the last person who needs to think Joe and I are having problems."

I stopped Wendy as she reached for the door. I had a very bad feeling about the revelation that she had just shared. I tried to sound more concerned than alarmed. "Listen. There is something I need to tell you. Sometimes husbands can do amazingly stupid things when they are hurt. If you need anything, please call me. If Joe keeps isolating you, call Loy."

For a moment Wendy looked at me like I was slightly off balance.

I squeezed her hand. "I know it may seem like things are impossible right now, but it is more important for you to be safe than it is to protect Joe's pride."

Wendy looked confused. "Do you think Joe would hurt me?"

"I think Joe is in a lot of pain right now and may not be thinking straight. If you ever feel like he is trying to maintain too much control over what you do, where you go, that sort of thing, I think it would be a good idea to call Loy and have him over to your place for a talk."

She frowned. Her expression showed that she didn't want to believe me.

"Wendy, he hasn't let you go to your shop for an entire week. Don't you think that is a little bit strange?" I asked.

She twisted her huge wedding ring. "I'll tell Joe I'm going back to work Monday. If he gives me a hard time, I'll call Loy. Alright?"

"That's all I ask," I said. "Let's get back out there. I left Finn alone and there is no telling what's happened to him by now."

I found Finn in the romance section, pinned down by three of the women from the Rotary Club. When he saw me he stood up and leaned towards my ear. "Get me out of here."

I should have talked to Loy first, but I decided if Wendy called him in a panic he would know what to do.

Finn and I left early, not a few wistful stares trailing us as my date left the building. We climbed into his Jeep and he shut his door, but didn't start the engine.

"Is something wrong?" I asked.

"I watched you talking to that woman. I know what you are doing."

I sat next to him, but kept my gaze straight ahead. "It's not very smart, is it?" I said.

"You seem to not care about smart very much."

I bristled a bit at that. "Hey, I'm just trying to understand what happened."

"So you can feel better about yourself?" he said.

I shot him a look. "So I can learn the truth."

He waited a few moments before he spoke. I could tell he wasn't having an easy time of it, but he said the words anyway.

"You know why I ended up in Killdeer, Montana?" he asked. "I got shot. I got shot because I pushed something too hard, and for too long, and that's what it cost me."

"What happened?" I asked, not entirely sure he would tell me.

Finn stared at his hands. He grimaced and looked up at me suddenly.

"I used to be a private bodyguard in South Africa. I took a job doing security for a scientific firm contracted to evaluate some high-tech equipment the government of Namibia had purchased. After fraud charges were filed against a group of government employees, the firm I was hired to protect was brought in to determine if a shipment of high-resolution security scanners were legitimate or if they were worthless. The Namibian government paid millions of dollars for the scanners and they were basically robbed. The machines were supposed to detect explosives, but they couldn't detect a kilo of C-4 if it was lying on the scanner with the product label still attached. It was a mess."

He sighed softly. "I advocated leaving Namibia as soon as possible, but the local coppers were dirty and they wouldn't let us out of the city. They wanted the evaluation team to retract their findings. The scientists on the team were threatened almost every day and I started to think I could protect them better if I could find out who was after them. I couldn't look the other way. I couldn't let it go. It wasn't my job but I got obsessed. I investigated. I collected evidence."

He looked out the window and scanned the parking lot. "When it's going to storm, I still sometimes walk with a limp."

"But this isn't the same thing," I said.

Finn turned to look at me. "It's exactly the same thing. I made myself a target because I investigated something I should have left alone. I got shot because I let myself get distracted. It wasn't my job to find out who was corrupt. It was my job to protect the scientists."

"This isn't anything like what happened to you," I said. "I just want to know—"

"You want to know why your neighbor died. Seems harmless enough, right? But I want you to listen to me. You can't change what happened. It was rank bleak, and it wasn't fair that it happened, but it did."

I closed my mouth and listened.

"Marley," he said. "Killdeer already has a sheriff."

He was right. I knew it. And yet, I also knew sitting there that I wasn't going to listen to him. Not now. Not after what I had heard from Wendy.

Loy had told me to let it go, like Finn was doing now. But neither one of them knew what I had just discovered.

They didn't know at this moment there was a living and breathing solid reason why I should be very suspicious. There was a very real possibility that Paul had died unexpectedly from a bad case of revenge. It had always been my experience that revenge is not patient. And it was common knowledge that Joe Martinez wasn't either.

I couldn't tell Finn, and especially not Loy, about my suspicions. I knew what they would say. They would say that I was letting my imagination get away with me.

But it wasn't my imagination. Something about the way Paul had died was suspicious. But if I was going to snoop into what had really happened I would have to do it quietly. No sense making Loy or Finn worry.

I let my head drop a bit and pulled my seat belt on, clicking it in place. "Maybe you are right. Maybe I feel like this because I didn't have any control over the situation, and I wish that I had."

Finn nodded. "That's normal. It will pass."

"How long?" I asked.

He started the Jeep. "It took me three years."

"Three years?"

He pulled out of the parking lot and onto the quiet night street. "I wasn't the only one who got shot that day," he said.

"And what happened to them?" I asked.

Finn shifted gears. The Jeep bucked just a little, and then smoothed out. "She died," he said, never taking his eyes off the road.

CHAPTER 21

He drove me home, silent and focused on his own memories.

He didn't say a word until we pulled into my little driveway.

"You've got company," he said.

I lifted my eyes and saw Nick Wilcox sitting in his sheriff's truck waiting for me.

"Fantastic," I said.

Finn glanced over and gave me a grin. "No worries. This could be fun."

He parked the Jeep and climbed out, making a show of coming to my door and opening it for me. I stepped out and the moment my high heels touched the ground Nick was on me quicker than a chicken on a June bug.

"Where were you tonight, Dearcorn?" he asked.

He slammed the door on his truck as he waited for an answer, and seemed to have completely forgotten about his notebook.

"She was with me," Finn told him. He slipped a hand around my waist possessively.

"Where were you both?" Nick asked, leaning in towards Finn.

Nick was livid. I hadn't thought the deputy could muster the blood pressure to make a vein stick out on his forehead, but I was wrong.

"We were at the library auction," I said. "What's going on?"

Nick ran a hand through his hair. I decided he would be bald by the time he was thirty-five. "Can any witnesses attest to your whereabouts tonight?" he asked.

"About two hundred," I said.

"Did you ever leave the library?" he asked. He was huffing he was so angry.

"We arrived at the building at 6:29 p.m. and departed at 8:12, coming directly to this location," Finn told him. He was actually smiling.

"Did she ever leave the building?" Nick asked, thrusting a finger in my direction.

"She was out of my direct line of sight for eleven minutes while she was inside the women's washroom, from 7:39 until 7:50."

Nick blinked at Finn. "Are you sure?" He was incredulous.

"I am sure," Finn said. "She is my responsibility tonight."

His responsibility? I was clearly not a member of this conversation. I was the object of the conversation.

"Nick, what are you doing out here?" I asked.

The deputy looked at me, eyes glazed with frustration. "My job," he said.

He climbed into his truck and lifted the microphone on his radio, calling Loy.

I wanted to linger and try to catch as many words of the conversation as I could, but Finn steered me up the steps to my house, keeping his hand on my waist.

"What was that all about?" I asked.

Finn chuckled. "Something that has nothing to do with us."

"You look like you are really enjoying this," I said.

"Ah, he's a good bloke. Eager. Could stand to be taken down a peg or two. But smart."

I almost laughed. "Nick?"

Finn dropped his smile. "I didn't come up here to talk about the deputy with you."

He touched my chin, tilted my head back and kissed me without warning.

He tasted like chocolate and his hands found my neck as he leaned into the kiss, sending shock waves of electricity down to my toes.

I was too stunned to pull back. My eyes fluttered closed and when he stopped kissing me they still refused to open.

I blinked myself back to awareness as Finn sauntered down the stairs. He strolled past Nick, seemingly oblivious to the deputy, and hopped in his Jeep.

Nick glared in my general direction, then he said something into the radio, slammed the microphone down and started his truck. He tore out of my driveway, but instead of heading back towards town his truck bucked its way down the road leading farther into the valley.

Finn watched Nick until the deputy was out of sight. He started his Jeep and rolled out of my driveway slowly. I couldn't be sure, but I swore Finn turned to look back at me over his shoulder before vanishing into the night.

I went inside and pulled the door shut behind me, locking it. I leaned back and tried to keep my thoughts from crashing into each other.

Finn had kissed me.

Nick was furious about something.

Wendy and Paul had slept together?

But, the important thing here was that Finn had kissed me.

I slipped off my heels and let them drop to the floor, my pulse still pounding.

Irene was never going to believe this.

CHAPTER 22

"Joe Martinez killed Paul and made it look like a heart attack."

Irene stared at me. She drummed her trimmed fingernails on the counter. "Maybe we should put on a pot of coffee."

"Irene, listen." I sat in my usual seat at the counter of her café. She was closed down until eleven this morning, but I'd begged her to meet me before she opened for the day. I had to talk to someone who would understand. "Last night I talked to Wendy Martinez at the library auction."

"Who took you to the auction?" she asked.

"Finn."

"Finn? Not your dad's lawn boy?"

"No, Finn works up at the weather station," I said.

Irene nearly dropped the coffee carafe. "You did not go to the auction with the Area Forty-nine guy!"

"Did you hear what I just said? Joe Martinez—"

"Killed Paul . . . blah blah . . . yes I heard you. Tell me about the date! How did you find him? Was he a gentleman?"

"He was a gentleman," I said.

Irene shook her head. "Oh, Honey, that's too bad . . ."

"I think that Joe Martinez killed Paul because he was sleeping with his wife."

Irene's mouth closed slowly. "Whose wife?"

"Joe's," I said. "Paul had an affair with Wendy. Well, more like an encounter, I guess. And you have to swear to me you won't say a word about this."

I didn't need to make her swear. Irene liked to collect gossip. She didn't ever give it away to anyone other than me.

"How did you find out about this?" She pushed the start button on the coffee machine and it began burbling away.

"Wendy looked like someone had just shot her dog when she came to the auction last night. I got her alone and we talked. She told me about the affair and said that Joe suspects it."

Irene pulled a narrow bar stool from under the counter and propped herself up on one cheek. "Do you really think that Joe could do something like that? He's the bank president."

"And do you remember the time he coached the junior high girls' soccer team?"

Irene remembered. The entire town remembered. Joe had been quietly asked by the school board to never, ever involve himself in sports again. The coach of the visiting team had eventually been persuaded not to press charges. To say Joe had a temper was being kind.

Irene poured us each a cup of her signature blend coffee, and we stared at the countertop.

"Maybe," she said. "Maybe he could. But why isn't Loy asking around, investigating this?"

"He thinks it was a heart attack," I said.

"It probably was a heart attack."

"And what if it wasn't?" I asked.

Irene, oddly enough, was quiet a moment. "Okay, so if Joe killed Paul, how do we find out?"

I felt a surge of hope. "I haven't the foggiest idea."

"Think about it logically, I guess," Irene said.

"Logically," I repeated.

"How did you do it in your Fish and Wildlife office? Didn't you investigate stuff there?"

I felt my cheeks flush. "The investigators investigated. I typed."

"But you talked to them. You watched them. How did they go about doing it?"

I thought about Bruce Duvekot, the lead investigator who worked out of our office. I thought about the hours and hours we had spent going over case files, talking logistics and time lines and anything else that could be used to untangle a messy investigation. "Well, the first thing they would do is try to determine if the guy had the opportunity."

"So, we determine . . . what? If Joe was in town that day?" she asked.

"That would be the first step. Logically," I said.

She shrugged. "Well, that's simple. All we have to do is find out if Joe was in town that night, or if he was away on business. You know how much he travels. He's gone more than he's here."

"Right," I said. "How do we do that?"

"Marley, really. It's not that hard. We just go into his office and ask him."

"Why is he going to tell us anything?" I asked.

"If he's at work, he's going to be Mr. Reasonable, that's why. You have a better idea?"

I didn't have a better idea. Figuring out a case sitting in a nice quiet office was easier than actually finding out the facts in the real world.

Irene finished the last swig of coffee in her cup and set it on the counter hard. "So tomorrow you and I are going to the bank. And we are going to talk to Joe about possibly opening up a new line of credit for the café. And while we are there we will make small talk about the night Paul died. If he says he was in town, then I think you need to go talk to the sheriff."

I had to admit, Irene was fast in the planning department. "What time? I've got to work at seven."

"Tell Jack you need to get off early. Joe leaves by three-thirty every day, so we need to be there right before then. Meet me here at two-thirty and I can get the gals lined up for the four o'clock rush."

"I'll be here," I said. I stood up to leave and slid my coffee cup towards her.

Irene took it and we both stared at the countertop again. I didn't know what to say. I wanted to give an abbreviated version of a long speech telling her how grateful I was she didn't talk to me like I was crazy.

"Thanks, Irene. See you tomorrow." It was all I could think of to say.

I walked out into the chilly morning air and drove back home, relieved that Irene was willing to help me talk to Joe, even if my motivations for wanting to find out where he was the night Paul died were a bit melodramatic.

I drove home, excited about following up on my suspicions, and realized I'd completely forgotten to tell her that Finn had kissed me goodnight.

CHAPTER 23

I worked twice as hard Monday morning but not twice as smart. Everything I touched either broke, fell apart or crashed to the ground. Jack kept hissing at me to keep my head in the game. I was distracted and I knew it. I asked him to let me off early, and after the fourth time I snapped the string on the gas-powered weed whacker, he told me to just go home.

I drove too fast to Lil's. When I walked in, the place was empty save for a couple of brand inspectors sitting quietly in the back.

Irene cornered her two waitresses. "We will be at the bank, and if for some reason you need me, I want you to call over there right away."

The girls nodded. "Yes, Miss Baker."

"They will burn the place to the ground before we get back," she said as we climbed into her little red pickup truck.

She fired up the engine and we lurched wildly into traffic. Most people in Killdeer simply gave way when Irene was coming down the street.

"I saw his outfit so he's there," I said.

In Montana, an outfit wasn't necessarily what you wore, it was most likely what you drove to work every day.

We parked in the bank parking lot and I wiped sweat from my palms onto my jeans.

"Ready?" Irene asked.

I nodded. "Line of credit."

Irene set her jaw. It could have stopped a wrecking ball. "Let me do the talking."

We went inside and the bank tellers all crouched down, suddenly busy with their drawers when they saw us coming.

Irene had a reputation for being a difficult customer.

She ignored them and started walking up the stairs.

I followed her, not sure if we should be strolling past the receptionist like that.

"Miss Baker," the young receptionist said. She started to rise from her desk.

"I have an appointment with Mr. Martinez," Irene said.

"He's on the phone just now." She looked slightly terrified.

Irene walked past her and we went up the stairs. "I'll wait."

We went up, the receptionist trying to decide who she wanted angry with her, Joe or Irene. She settled for Joe and let us by without another word.

Joe had his back to the door, was swiveling in his chair and chatting, looking out the window towards the mountains.

Irene plopped down in one of the guest chairs and settled her black purse in her lap.

I sat down slowly, my pulse picking up the pace.

"No, no, no," Joe said. "It's not that I think it's a *bad* idea. Not one bit."

He laughed. "I think it's the *worst* idea I've ever heard in my life. Mark, don't quote me on this, but in five years I'm going to be out of this hellhole and so why in the blazes would I want to tie my money up in a project like that?"

Irene cleared her throat.

Joe spun around, blinking. "Mark, I've got someone here. I'll call you back."

He hung up the phone, looking at Irene like she'd just walked into his office holding a gun. "Miss Baker."

I tried to look casual.

My chair squeaked with every move I made. It was wildly expensive stuffed burgundy leather, and therefore ridiculously uncomfortable.

Irene plunged in. "Joe, I want another line of credit."

"Ah, yes." Joe's mouth tightened. His steel-colored eyes swiveled to me suspiciously.

Irene barely paused long enough to let him catch his breath. "My interest rate is too high and I want to close out that account and open one that's more in line with what the economy is doing now."

Joe pulled a file from his desk and opened it up. He didn't say anything, just read through the pages inside.

Then he looked up. "Says here that we have you set at 7.9 percent. That's pretty good, Irene."

"Well, I've banked here for—"

"As long as you've had Lil's," he said.

"And I'd like to keep it that way," she said.

My chair squeaked.

"Miss Dearcorn," Joe said, giving me a nod. He wasn't entirely clear on why I was in the room.

"Hi, Joe. How are you?"

His lip twitched. "Irene, I am not sure we can do better than this for a business line of credit. And I don't think you can get a better rate from over at the First Federal."

Irene drew breath to protest, and the two of them started in, arguing about the economy going all to hell, and the implications of that.

I noticed while they argued over rates that Joe's desk was covered with one of those huge calendars that has room to write on. Papers partially obscured it, but the month it displayed was October. I thought we might be able to get out of this without asking him where he had been two Mondays ago.

"Joe, I want 5 percent. It's not unreasonable."

He cleared his throat and loosened his mauve silk tie. It was to prevent him from saying what he really wanted to say. He paused a moment and forged on. "You know I can't do 5. Not for a business."

I sensed we were running out of time. I needed an excuse to look at that calendar. Before I lost my nerve I reached towards the Kleenex box on the desk and pulled out a tissue. I started to cough into it, not the delicate genteel cough of a lady. I coughed like a yak with tuberculosis.

Joe started to look alarmed. "Are you alright?"

I choked. "Water?"

Joe was on his feet and headed for the hall. Irene was looking at me like she'd never seen me before in her life. The moment he turned the corner I darted to his desk and pulled the files aside.

October eleventh was blank. The entire calendar was blank.

"Marley, what in the hell are you doing?" Irene asked. Her jaw was clenched.

Before I could answer Joe came running around the corner into his office holding a cup. I was standing at his desk holding an armload of files.

"She's looking for a cough drop," Irene said, glaring at me.

Joe's eyes shot sparks. I dropped the files and took the cup of water, mouthing a thank you while pretending to turn blue from coughing. I wanted to climb under the desk and die from embarrassment. Instead, I eased out of the room, mortified and trying to apologize.

I could hear Irene trying to cover for me, explaining that she'd brought me along so I could see how a line of credit for a business worked.

I slunk downstairs and drifted past the receptionist. Did Joe keep cups of water standing by in the hallway just for emergencies? Then I noticed the Culligan water dispenser sitting at the bottom of the stairs and felt like an idiot.

"Is Joe almost finished with Miss Baker?" the receptionist asked.

I nodded. "Oh, I'm sure he is."

"He's got a call on hold is all," she explained. Her dark hair was curled just-so.

I glanced at her name tag. Lindsey. "Joe must be a busy man."

She nodded. "Oh, it's a full-time job just keeping up with his schedule."

"I know he travels all the time," I said. "A couple weeks ago Irene was telling me she wanted to make an appointment to see him, but he was in Belize."

Lindsey looked confused. "I, I don't think so . . ." she said, pulling her appointment book from her drawer.

I was winging it, but, really, Belize?

Lindsey, the helpful sort, leafed through her appointment book and shook her head. "No, that would have been the eleventh? Mr. Martinez was down in Denver. He had a shareholders' meeting. He's impossible to reach when he's got a shareholders' meeting."

"Oh, that's right," I said. I tossed the empty cup into a wastebasket as Irene stomped down the stairs towards me.

"Are we leaving?" I asked.

She walked past and I fell into step beside her. Without a word she climbed into her little truck and I sat beside her quietly.

"Well," she said, letting her hand dig through her purse in search of the keys. "You are forbidden to ever speak to me again."

"I'm sorry," I said. "I blew it, I know. I thought that calendar on his desk would have his travel dates on it."

Irene looked at me, her forehead wrinkling. "Joe has no use for writing things down. He's got people to do that for him."

"He was in Colorado," I said.

"At a shareholders' meeting in Denver," Irene finished.

I looked at her. "How did you find that out?"

"I asked him," she said. She rammed the keys into the ignition. "So, it's impossible that Joe killed Paul. He wasn't even in the state. And you're crazy."

I pulled on my seat belt. Always prudent when riding in a vehicle with Irene.

"Look, I'm sorry," I said. "I was making it up as we went along. I thought we were running out of time."

"If you are going to figure out who killed Paul you are going to have to learn to be a lot more careful than that," Irene said.

She gunned the engine and we sped back to the café. She parked and shut off the engine. I watched her shove her keys back into her purse.

It took me a moment to realize what she had just said. Find out who killed Paul? So, I wasn't the only one who thought there was more to this than a heart attack.

"But Joe wasn't even in town," I said. I stared at the dashboard. "You still think there is something to figure out?"

She looked out her windshield. "I don't know. But something you said made me think about it last night."

I tried to remember everything I had told her. I couldn't remember saying anything too important. "What did I say?"

She watched her two waitresses suddenly pretending to be busy, now that they had spotted her truck in the parking lot.

"You said that Deputy Wilcox wanted to get a sample of your DNA."

I blinked. "And why is that important? He just wanted to make sure I'd really done CPR on Paul."

"He wanted your DNA because he and Loy found something that didn't add up," she said.

I looked at her, frowning. "And how do you know this?"

It was her turn to look a little embarrassed. "Because Loy asked me to tell him about it if you started poking into things."

My face flushed. I wasn't embarrassed anymore. I was angry.

"Why would Loy ask you to do that?"

Irene finally looked at me. "Because he said he was worried that you might get involved with something, like you did back in Helena."

I swallowed my anger, not surprised but frustrated anyway. The investigation that had gone so wrong in Helena had deteriorated quickly into an irretrievable mess, and I should have learned to keep my curiosity under control. I guess Loy knew me better than I knew myself.

Irene tapped her fingers on her steering wheel, thinking. "Joe had a really good reason for killing Paul. But he couldn't have because he was almost a thousand miles away."

I shook my head to clear it, rubbed my eyes and tried to think.

"But Loy found something that didn't quite seem right," I said. "So Nick wanted my DNA."

We sat together in silence for a few moments.

"He wanted your DNA so he could eliminate you as a suspect," Irene said.

Hindsight was telling me I should have been more cooperative.

"Well, what did they find in the house?" she asked.

"A bottle of wine. Open."

"Were there a couple glasses with it? Maybe Paul had a drink with someone and they poisoned him."

I shook my head. "No, it was only one bottle, and one glass. I know because I accidentally smashed the bottle on the floor."

"No wonder the deputy was interested in you. Marley, you tampered with a crime scene."

I nodded, my stomach feeling sour. "I know. The bottle was half full and it made a huge mess. I must have gotten it all over the place."

Irene was undaunted. "That seems odd. Paul wasn't a boozer. Not like David. I can see David drinking alone, but Paul always seemed the type who would drink only when there was an occasion. And he drank a half a bottle by himself?"

I considered that. "Maybe."

"Marley, isn't there anything else you can remember about that night?" Irene asked.

There were a number of things I could remember. All of them equally horrible.

"I thought it was odd that he seemed to be so warm. It's like his body was burning up from the inside out," I said.

Irene looked thoughtful. "Maybe he was poisoned? Could his system have reacted somehow to an overdose?"

"It's possible," I said.

Irene studied her hands. They were dry from so many hours spent up to her elbows in dishwater and detergent. "Let's say he was poisoned. What on earth could have that sort of effect on a person?"

I opened the door on Irene's truck and stepped out, pulling my car keys from my coat pocket. "I don't know. But I know who does."

CHAPTER 24

Deputy Nick Wilcox slammed the door on his patrol truck when he saw me walking towards him. He was in the parking lot of the sheriff's station, obviously getting ready to leave when I pulled up and got out of my car.

"I am twenty-four hours away from a warrant," he said, pointing at me with two fingers.

"You don't need a warrant, Nick . . . Deputy. I'll give my DNA."

"I spend a goddamned week working the phones to get a warrant and you stroll over here and just offer it up?" he said, his jaw clenched.

It wasn't attractive when a grown man whined.

"I'll give you my DNA if you tell me one thing."

He shoved his hands in his pockets. "I don't have to tell you anything."

I sighed. "I know you found something at Paul's house that doesn't quite fit."

He sneered, but didn't deny it.

"And I know you want my DNA so you can eliminate me as a suspect. Right?"

Nick hooked his thumbs in his gun belt. "Loy talked to you. Didn't he? I knew he was letting himself get compromised by this."

"He didn't say a word to me," I said. "I just know that something wasn't right with how I found Paul."

Nick watched me, trying to figure out my angle.

"Listen, Deputy. I know something else about that night that I didn't tell you when you interviewed me."

"Then you best cough up that data, Miss Dearcorn," he said.

"If I do, I want your word that you will tell me, honestly, what you think it means."

He folded his arms across his chest. "I'm not obligated to tell you a thing."

"No, you're not. But, I also know you are an expert in crime scene investigations. All I want is for you to tell me your opinion about what it could mean."

I hoped that flattering him would work where being evasive hadn't. He shuffled his boots once, but his curiosity won out.

"Alright. But understand me. I'll give you an opinion, but if anyone asks me on the stand if we had this conversation, I'll say I can't seem to recall it."

"It's only a hypothetical situation."

He shoved his hands in his pockets. "Go."

I supposed that meant it was my turn to talk. "Paul's body temperature was too high based on the time line I gave you, wasn't it?"

Nick gave a noncommittal shrug.

"It looked to the paramedics like he'd had a heart attack," I said. "But to you it looked like something else."

Nick gave me no reaction.

I tried to keep my temper in check. I was on his side and it would be a lot more productive if he were willing to work with me.

I tried again. "But because his temperature was so high you and Loy had doubts."

He nodded. "It seemed to contradict what you had reported. Loy told me a hundred times that if you said you'd been doing CPR for twenty minutes that it was true. I didn't believe him. We checked Paul's liver temp at what would have been about two hours after he had supposedly died. Body temps drop about 1.5 degrees per hour postmortem, and Paul was still at 98 degrees."

"If I had been there that long doing CPR, Paul should have been colder. Right?"

Nick spit on the asphalt. "So, what's this bit of info you forgot to tell me when I interviewed you?"

"It didn't seem that important at the time. But I've had a chance to think about it and maybe you can help me understand what it means. Paul's body was completely paralyzed," I said.

Nick turned his head to the side. "What do you mean by paralyzed?"

I forged on. "Exactly that. He couldn't move at all. His whole body was rigid. He couldn't even talk."

Nick squinted as he thought it over. "Like he was unconscious? Comatose?"

"No, his eyes were wide open. But he was totally immobile and he couldn't talk. It was almost as if even his throat was paralyzed."

He glanced away.

"Is there some kind of drug or poison that can affect a person like that?"

"Sux," he said.

"Well, yeah, it does," I said.

He looked at me like I was as stupid as a bag of wet hammers.

"S-U-X. Suxamethonium chloride. It's used in hospital emergency rooms."

I frowned and held out my hands. "Emergency rooms?"

He let out an exasperated snort. "When a patient comes in to an emergency room with severe trauma and the doctor has to intubate them. You know, shove a tube down their throat so they can pump oxygen to them? Sometimes the patient is thrashing around and the doctor can't get the tube down so they shoot them up with sux and it paralyzes the patient so the doc can get to work."

"It paralyzes them?"

Nick was frowning down at the concrete between his boots, thinking. "It completely shuts down the body's muscles, unless the anesthesiologist makes a mistake, shoots them up with too much of the stuff. Then they stop breathing. Literally, they die because their diaphragm stops moving. One of the signs of an overdose is hyperthermia."

"How would a paramedic know it was not a heart attack?" I asked.

He looked up, staring at me, his expression determined. "They wouldn't."

He reached inside his pocket, whipped out his notebook and began to furiously search through the pages, mechanical pencil poised.

"The stuff only takes about twenty minutes, maybe a half hour at the most to do the damage," he said.

"Does it matter how big you are?" I asked. "How much would someone need to give him to kill him?"

"A guy Paul's size? About two grams would do it. It's undetectable. No smell. No taste . . ." he wasn't talking to me any longer. He was staring off into the distance and seemed to be talking to himself.

I shivered. "This sux isn't easy to get, is it?"

He was already walking away, bounding up the steps of the sheriff's office, and seemed to have forgotten I was there.

"Deputy?" I asked.

"No," he called over his shoulder. "It's not easy to get. You have to be a doctor or an E.R. nurse to even handle the stuff."

He disappeared inside and left me standing in the parking lot.

I got into my car and drove straight home. I wasn't entirely sure that talking to Nick had been a good idea after all. At least before I had been blissfully unaware of how close I had come to being face-to-face with someone who was capable of murder.

As I climbed the steps of my little house another thought occurred to me. I hadn't seen anyone else at Paul's that night, but what if someone else had seen me?

The words that Finn had said to me at the library the night of the auction kept spinning in my mind.

Without even knowing it, I had made myself a target.

Purely by accident I had stumbled across a murder in progress. It was likely that the killer had caught a glimpse of me going inside the house. And if not, all they had to do was get the paper the following day and read the headline to see that I had been there.

And here I was, talking to the sheriff openly at Lil's, talking to the deputy in broad daylight in the parking lot of the sheriff's office, running around asking questions and generally making my curiosity about Paul's death obvious. Anyone who knew anything about the goings-on around Killdeer would have figured out by now that I was very interested in finding out what had happened that night.

Before shutting off the lights and turning in for bed, I made sure that every door and every window were locked up tight.

I was convinced that my little hometown was harboring a killer. I didn't know who it was, but there was a good chance that the killer thought I did.

CHAPTER 25

I woke up to the sound of someone pounding on my door. I rolled over and tried to focus on the clock. Four-thirty-something. This wasn't a social call. I went to the door fast, worried that I was going to be getting some bad news.

Loy stood in the doorway, glaring at me, furious. "Marley, what, exactly, did you say to my deputy?"

I gaped at him. "It's four in the morning."

Loy's eyes were bloodshot and he looked like he hadn't showered in a week. "Nick's contacted the Major Case Section of DCI, and they have opened an investigation into Nesbit's death. What did you say to him?"

I shook myself awake. "I told him that I knew you and he found something that didn't fit."

Loy's face fell. "I asked you to let all this go. I told you to let all this go."

"Because you knew that I would stir things up?" I said.

"Because there is a killer in my town and I haven't the goddamndest idea who it is," he said, completely exasperated.

I had the good sense to look contrite.

He finally took a breath to calm down and came inside when I asked.

He sat down on the little sofa. "I had a feeling from the start it wasn't natural causes that I was looking at."

"Is that why you asked me all of those questions about what I had seen when I first got there? To see if someone else had been in the house before me?"

He sat back with a groan. "It is. I knew because you had been the one to find Paul there could be a chance whoever killed him would think you were some sort of threat. I've been watching your house for two weeks."

This surprised me. "I had no idea you were doing that."

"I'm good at my job." He did not display his usual grin when he said it.

I sat down next to him, leaned against his shoulder with my own, and folded my hands in my lap. "Do you have any idea at all who it could be? Any hunch?"

He looked crestfallen. "Nothing. It could be your dad for all I know."

"It's not my dad," I said.

"I need you to understand that I am in the dark, Marley. Paul was not a popular man."

"Well, it wasn't Joe Martinez."

Loy shot me a look. "And you know this how?"

"He was in Denver. Shareholders' meeting."

"Why would you think Joe had anything to do with Paul's death?"

"Because Paul and Wendy had an-"

"Jesus, Marley. How many people know you've been poking into this?"

190

"I may have mentioned to Irene I had my doubts about it being a heart attack."

He looked pale. "Please tell me nobody else knows you think that."

"Your deputy knows."

"How did you find out about Wendy and Paul?"

I swallowed. "She told me at the library auction."

"Where everyone in the entire building could see you talking to her. So, you have not been careful."

I started to feel shaky all over again.

"It's four-thirty in the morning, and I am awake. What's wrong with this picture?" I said. It was time I got an explanation from him.

He put a big hand over my knee. "I saw someone driving down your road and I came to make sure you were alright."

"It might have been my dad. He sometimes gets up and can't go back to sleep."

"It wasn't your dad. I don't know who it was."

"Did Nick tell you what I said?" I asked.

"He told me you put a bug in his ear."

"I told him something else that I didn't mention that night. I didn't realize at the time it was important. But it turns out I was wrong about that."

Loy hadn't removed his hand. I tactfully slid my knee away and turned to look at him. "Nick thinks that Paul might have been poisoned with something called Sux. It's used in emergency rooms."

The sheriff processed this. "He mentioned the paralysis. I think maybe it was a move, the kid calling the state."

"You do?" I asked.

"Might not be a bad idea if you go stay up at your dad's place for a few weeks. Just until the autopsy results come back and we determine if that's really what happened."

"So you think it was someone from Killdeer?"

He squeezed my knee. "I don't know. Until I do know I don't want you to spend time alone."

"Loy, I can't go hide up at my father's place for the next month."

He waved a hand, frustrated. "I've been sleeping in my truck for two weeks and living out of the Information Center's rest-stop bathroom so I can keep surveillance on your property. I'm tired, and I want to sleep in my own bed tonight. Will you just do this one thing for me? Please?"

"Why is this so important all of a sudden?" I asked.

"Someone broke into the evidence locker at the station," he told me. He stared at his hands. "We have no idea who it was. They did it the night of the auction after I left the station and went to the library. They were watching me, Marley. They knew when I was gone."

I felt that familiar pressure squeeze my chest. "What did they take?"

He shifted uncomfortably. "Nothing. Whatever it was they were looking for, they didn't find it. So, will you please go stay with your dad for a while?"

He looked worn-out. I didn't have the heart to turn him down. "Sure, Loy. I can do that. Just until this is sorted out. I'll go tomorrow, alright?"

He relaxed and adjusted his cap.

"Thank you. And while you're at it, don't talk to anyone else. I wish I could stay here and tell you everything that's going on, but I don't have the time."

I felt terrible now. I had no idea I'd been putting him through so much trouble. "What should I tell my dad? He's going to wonder why I want to stay up at the house."

"Tell him that I said there's been a few break-ins at farmhouses the last couple weeks."

"He might buy that, but then again he might not. I think I'll stick to the truth," I said.

"Maybe it would be better if he knew what was going on. But you only need to give him the facts, and you don't need to worry him with my suspicions."

"I'm already worried enough for the two of us," I said.

I walked Loy to the door and gave him a hug. He held on a heartbeat longer than I did, and for a moment there was that awkward sensation that he was getting a lot more out of the embrace than I was.

He finally stepped back and automatically checked his gun. I could see how haggard he appeared. I almost worried that he wouldn't make it home before he fell asleep.

"I'll be alright," I said.

"Yes, you will." He turned and clomped down the stairs to his truck. He looked back over his shoulder three times before he was out of sight.

I couldn't go back to sleep, not after what Loy had told me. It was still pitch black outside and I jumped at every sound I heard, even if it was just the house settling or the wind hooting through the old stovepipe in the kitchen.

I turned on every light in the house and made coffee to keep myself busy.

False dawn warmed the sky just as I climbed out of the shower. I stood dripping on the linoleum with my head cocked to the side, trying to identify the strange sound coming from the driveway. Was that a chainsaw?

I toweled off and threw on the first clothes I could lay hands on. When I pushed open my front door the Reliant Landscaping truck was sitting beside the downed cottonwood tree in the driveway. Jack was busy sawing the branches off, cheerfully oblivious to the fact that a chainsaw might actually wake a person up. I shook my head, smiling.

"Doesn't anybody ever sleep in this town?"

Jack grinned and waved when I went down the stairs. I handed him a cup of coffee. He killed the chainsaw and set it at his feet.

"I thought it was time we got this out of your front yard," he said. He took the coffee and gulped it.

I sipped mine. Steam moistened my nose. "So that means you got caught up on those jobs in town?"

He beamed. "I made a mint off that storm."

I shook my head and smiled back. "Gonna charge me a mint for doing this job?"

Jack laughed. "Chicken Little, I wouldn't worry about it if I were you. I'll take it out of your check a bit at a time. You won't even notice."

My boss was good people, as far as I was concerned. I wasn't sure I would ever know why my father didn't like Jack.

I zipped up my old canvas coat, shivering in the chill morning air.

After I managed to get a couple bucks ahead, I vowed I would buy a new coat that actually kept me warm and didn't have stains all over it.

"Let me go get my gloves and I'll come down and start getting these branches into the trailer," I said, gulping the last of my coffee.

Jack handed me his empty cup and picked up the chainsaw. "This shouldn't take more than a few hours. We'll be done by lunch."

Just as he was about to pull the cord and fire up the chainsaw, Jack looked over at my deck and froze.

"Holy hell, Marley."

I turned. "What?"

I saw it at once, and I almost dropped both cups.

It was impossible to see from above the stairs. But down by the toppled cottonwood tree I had a clear view of the space beneath my deck. The sun squinted between the pines, casting a faint light, and a shape swung back and forth in the breeze.

We walked closer to the deck and both of us bent our heads to peer under the stairs. With a noose made of twisted yarn, a strawberry blonde doll had been hanged as though in effigy from the beams crisscrossing the redwood bottom of the platform. It was wearing a cream-colored dress. Blood, or something very much like it, dripped from a painted gash across the neck. A toe tag dangled from one foot, words scrawled across it grotesquely.

The tag bore one word. I looked at Jack and he reached for the doll with his left hand, pulling the tag closer so that he could read it.

I felt the hairs on the back of my neck rise up. "What does it say?"

He scanned the scrap of paper and then looked up at me, his face angry. "Snitch."

He let the tag go and it twirled in the light breeze.

"What does that mean?" I asked.

"It means I will be shorthanded today," he said, glaring out at the shadows between the thick trees. "You are taking the day off."

CHAPTER 26

Jack walked up the stairs to my house and went inside without a word. I knew he was making a phone call, and I sat down hard on the remnants of the cottonwood tree.

It was a very good thing I was sitting down when my father roared into the driveway. I had started to feel sick.

My father threw his truck in park and reached for something on the seat. He had a shotgun in one hand as he slid out. For once he was cordial to Jack.

Jack didn't say a word, just pointed to show my father what we had seen.

My father examined the doll. "Son of a . . . Marley, go in the house please."

I looked up and nodded, my feet none too steady. But I couldn't sit there and look at that thing under my deck for another minute.

I went inside and had a sudden urge to pull all the blinds closed.

Jack and my father spoke quietly at the bottom of the stairs, but I picked up a few words of the conversation.

"Something to do with Helena?" Jack asked.

My father said something angry, and that was the end of the conversation.

Jack stayed by the stairs while my father walked around the outside of the house, staring at the ground. I supposed he was looking for any sign of who could have been there.

Nick Wilcox's sheriff truck pulled into the driveway, lights flashing but no siren. He jumped from his vehicle and trotted to the deck. He had a camera with a lens sprouting from the front powerful enough to photograph the moons of Jupiter. He asked Jack to move and started unrolling the crime scene tape.

I groaned. When my father came inside I had moved on from worried to downright scared.

"Think I'll come stay with you for a few days, Dad. If that's okay."

My father nodded. "Get your things. As soon as Nick says it's alright, we're leaving."

My mouth was so dry I couldn't respond. I packed quickly, taking only what I needed and nothing I didn't. Everything fit nicely in a shoulder backpack. When I walked down the steps Nick glanced up from his work.

"Who found this?" he asked.

Jack stood next to his truck, looking grim. He lifted a hand. "I saw it."

The deputy seemed to be in full-on cop mode. For once it wasn't irritating. It was reassuring.

"Nathan, I need your permission to search the property and the interior of the house in case there is anything we may have missed," Nick said.

My father nodded. "You have it."

Nick set aside his camera and stood beside me, flipping open that notebook. "What time did you come home last night?"

I had to think to remember. "It was just after I spoke to you at the station."

Nick flipped back two pages. "Five-thirty. Did you see anything when you got here?"

"It was dark."

The deputy gave me an irritated look. The last time I'd said that to him I was being uncooperative. Today I was simply stating the truth.

"What time did you notice it this morning?" he asked Jack.

"Twenty minutes ago. About seven?" Jack said.

My father had finally put his shotgun back in his truck. "Where's Loy?" he asked, standing beside me with arms folded.

Nick didn't answer immediately. "He's in a meeting."

I told Nick the significance of the cream-colored dress, that I had been wearing one the night of the auction.

My father and Jack exchanged looks, but didn't interrupt. They were obviously wondering what the auction had to do with this.

"I'm sure Loy told you about my conversation with Wendy," I said.

Nick met my eyes. "He mentioned it. I don't think it has much to do with this situation."

Meaning that Nick and Loy had come to the same conclusion that Irene and I had reached. That Joe Martinez was not responsible for anything other than having a bad temper and poor relationship skills.

The last thing I should be doing at this point was thinking that this was no big deal.

I decided the best possible course of action was to treat this threat seriously.

Jack and my father had a short, heated negotiation about what would happen next.

They argued about whether or not I would be going to work for the rest of the week. Usually I would argue when other people were making decisions for me, but not this time.

I was rattled. It was sinking in how much trouble I had gotten myself into this time. It was Helena all over again, only worse.

"You can come stay with me if you like, Marley," my boss said. His quiet voice betrayed his concern. He was looking as nervous as I felt.

"No. She'll stay with me," my father said. He stared Jack down, sparks shooting from his eyes.

Jack relented and shrugged. "Sure, Nathan. That's probably for the best anyhow."

"Marley, maybe you should consider leaving town for a while," Nick said.

"That's overreacting a bit, don't you think?" Jack said.

My father was at the end of his tolerance. "She's staying with me."

He made a show of taking my backpack and walking towards my car. He set the backpack on the passenger's seat and after closing the door he climbed into his truck with purpose.

"I guess we're going," I said.

Jack gave me a worried smile, while Nick started the process of searching the property. Since my father had already walked around the outside of the house twice, I doubted that Nick would find anything.

The old pickup truck fired to life, and I climbed inside my car, taking my father's cue.

We drove in tandem to the ranch. I settled into my old room and tucked my few items inside the empty dresser.

The ranch house had changed over the last few years, but not much. It hurt my dad too much to see old photos of my mother. So instead he'd spent a fortune on landscape paintings, and had hung them on every empty square inch of wall space. If you didn't look at the old brown hardwood floors and paneling on the walls, it could have been an art museum. My room was now affectionately known as the hay bale bedroom. Three paintings of golden round bales graced the walls. My grandmother's old quilt covered the bed. I sat on the corner of the bed and ran a hand over the worn stitches of the pale blue quilt.

I heard my father come into the room and watched as he wordlessly propped a shotgun in the corner. He bent down enough to give me a quick kiss on the forehead and went back to the kitchen.

I stared at the shotgun and a horrible feeling iced my chest. Paul had guns at his house too, for all the good they did him.

A few hours later Nick called to say that the doll had been bagged and removed from my place. He would call if he discovered anything important.

Jack phoned the ranch too. He had called Donny and Shepherd down to my house, after Nick had given the all clear, and the three of them finished with the tree. When I was able to go to my little house again, at least it would be back to normal when I got there.

My father puttered around the house for the rest of the day, hovering over me while trying to look like he wasn't hovering.

I spent the afternoon feeling my emotions traveling from scared, to irritated, to downright angry. I fell into bed that night, worn-out and surly.

When morning came my father was gone. A note told me to stay in the house, that Jack would understand if I didn't show up. How long could I go on not living my life? I had bills to pay and obligations to think of.

In spite of the note, I showered, dressed, loaded the shotgun into my Honda and left. I had a good reason for leaving, and in the bright morning sunlight I felt unrealistically safe. But I had a purpose for my drive. And I thought the risk was worth taking.

CHAPTER 27

I parked not far from the ditch where I had first met Finn. I sat there for almost a half hour, but eventually the black Jeep came around the corner and flipped a U-turn, and parked behind me.

I had no idea why, but I trusted Finn, and I needed his advice.

Finn walked to my car, opened the door and jerked his head towards his Jeep. He said without smiling, "Get in."

He went back to his Jeep and opened the passenger door for me. I left the shotgun in the backseat of my Honda, but at least had the sense to lock the doors.

When I was in the Jeep sitting next to him I finally relaxed. It had been a tense half-hour wait for Finn to arrive. Had the circumstances been different, I think I would have started asking myself some hard questions concerning this man. But as it was, I had other things to worry about.

"You shouldn't have been out here alone," Finn said.

He was different today. Not that he wasn't always alert, but today he was charged like a Taser.

"Don't tell me you already heard about the doll?" I asked.

"Small town," he said.

"Is this where you get to tell me that curiosity killed the cat?" I asked.

He didn't smile. He hadn't taken off his sunglasses and I couldn't see any expression on his face. If Finn ever decided to play poker professionally, he'd be lethal.

"I need some advice," I said.

"Will you take it?" he asked.

I felt my cheeks go pink. "I might. You said you were a bodyguard in Africa."

He nodded. "Other places too."

"So, what can I do to stay safe?"

He looked at me. "Really?"

I smiled, as much as I could smile.

He tossed his sunglasses on the dashboard and propped a hand on the steering wheel. "I could tune ya all day about threat assessment levels, safe movement procedures and the like, but it wouldn't mean much."

I noticed his accent seemed to get thicker when he looked unhappy.

"Can you give me some basics?" I asked. "Nothing too complicated, just some good advice I can follow?"

"Yes, leave town."

I blinked. "Where would I go? I can't go to Sweden for six months and live at a ski resort. I live in reality-land and I don't have a money tree planted in my back yard."

He gave a short laugh. "Right."

"If you were me," I began.

"What would I do?" he asked.

"Can you give me the short version? I don't think I have time for Navy SEAL training. Mrs.

Gunderson's yard needs to be aerated before it snows."

He almost cracked a smile. Almost.

"Marley, use your head. For the average person, common sense is a lot more valuable than special training."

"Special training. Like being able to kill somebody with your thumb?"

He shrugged. "There's three ways to do it."

I tried to see if he was joking.

He looked out the window, past my shoulder into the trees. He always seemed to be scanning his surroundings.

"Don't stay outside for prolonged periods of time," he said.

"I'm a landscaper."

He dropped his head. "Do you want my advice? Then listen. You can't eliminate all risk. It's impossible. But you can maneuver to avoid risk. If you use your head."

His expression made it plain he doubted that I would be able to do that.

"I'm listening," I said.

"Patterns are your enemy. If you follow a daily pattern, you are easy to track and easy to target. Vary your route each and every day. Do not repeat your movements. Check your house top to bottom at night before you go to sleep. Lock everything. Lock your windows and doors, your car. Don't sleep in the same place at night. Sleep on the floor in the closet. Sleep behind the couch, with a pistol right beside you. Sleep in places that no one would expect to find you, and have an early warning system."

I must have looked confused.

He studied my face. "An early warning system is nothing more than something that makes noise to alert you of an intruder."

"Like what?"

"Like, stack up a bunch of empty soda cans by a point of entry to your house. Have a string strung across a doorway that is attached to something light that will fall and make noise if it's tripped. Always, always have an escape route. Do you know how to use a weapon?"

"Yes," I said.

"Then carry one. If you don't feel comfortable with it, practice. Keep multiple weapons close at hand. Always have a primary and a secondary weapon within reach. You don't want to rely on one weapon. You always need a backup."

I let out the breath I had been holding. "You actually live like this, don't you?"

"Assume nothing," he said. "You don't know if the threat is someone you know or someone who is a stranger. Being around other people can sometimes make you feel safer but unless you have your threat identified you could be standing right next to a killer and never even know it."

"I think in this case, the threat is probably someone I know," I told him.

He smirked. "There you go, making assumptions. What if it isn't?"

"Does it make sense to try to find out who is after you? Wouldn't that help?"

"It could. But it could also box you in. What if you are certain of the identity of the threat, but then it turns out to be someone else you hadn't expected? You've spent all of your time and energy focused on trying to tailor your defense to one person, then it turns out to be the wrong guy and you have left yourself vulnerable in key areas."

"But if you know who it is—"

"Bollocks," he said. "Your goal isn't to go get the bad guy. You're not the coppers, Marley. That's their job. Your job is to keep breathing."

I thought about that. Maybe he was right.

"What if the threat uses poison?" I said.

Finn rubbed his chin. "Like, what kind of poison?"

"Hospital grade medicine."

He slumped back in the seat, thinking. "Administered how?"

"Maybe in a glass of wine," I said.

He thought some more. Then he looked at me. His eyes were searching my face.

"How do you know all this?" he asked.

"Paul Nesbit. He probably died from an overdose of a hospital drug used in emergency rooms."

"And you found him," Finn said.

We were both quiet for several minutes, each absorbing what the other had said.

Finally Finn shifted in his seat and faced me. "It doesn't change anything."

"But don't women use poison more often?" I asked.

"Do you want to fall back on pop culture to tell you what will save your life?" he asked.

"No."

Finn watched me. "Stop trying to identify the threat and concentrate your energy on staying safe."

He did have a point. But the thought still lingered in my mind that if I could only find out why

Paul had been killed it would point me to who had done it.

"I should get home," I said. "My father will be calling the FBI anytime now."

"He knows where you are," Finn said.

For the first time, I noticed there was a black radio attached to the underside of the dashboard that looked similar to my father's CB radio, but this one had a lot more buttons. No wonder Finn was certain my father knew where I was.

"I'll think about everything you've said," I told him. I opened the door and got out.

"You should leave town," he said.

I nodded. "I know."

He looked frustrated, and angry. I tried to think of something else I could say. Something reassuring.

"If the sheriff doesn't figure out who put that doll under my porch, I could always rent a room to you for a while," I said, a corner of my mouth turning up.

Finn put his sunglasses back on. "I could never provide effective security for you. I'd be too distracted."

He started his Jeep and I swore he winked at me under his sunglasses. He waited until I was back in my car and pulling away before he headed toward the road that would take him back to the weather station.

In a funny way, I liked this man. Well, I felt safe around him. But he was so odd.

I drove back to the ranch, and when I walked into the house my father was cooking eggs.

"Lunch, Kiddo? Irene finally let me have her Chicago omelet recipe."

"I didn't know Irene ever gave out her recipes to anyone."

My father chuckled. "She doesn't."

Well, well. My father had some secrets after all.

We lunched on the back deck, until I remembered what Finn had said about not being outdoors for prolonged periods of time, and we ended up heading back inside. My father left to patrol the pastures and see to any fences that were in need of repair before the snow started to come down. Winter would be here any day. We all felt the chill in the air.

Before he left he lectured me about not opening the door for anyone and staying in the house.

I felt like I was five years old.

When the house was quiet and the thick trees around the back yard whispered in the breeze, I made a cup of hot cocoa with heavy cream and four tablespoons of chocolate syrup. I figured I could use the comfort food.

The fireplace was loaded with wood, crackling and popping with life, and I curled myself on the old couch to think. The flames danced, casting a comforting warm glow over the room. It gave me a place to rest my eyes while I turned everything over in my head.

The way I saw it, I had two choices. Either I could do what Finn had suggested and lay low, keeping myself locked up until Loy and Nick figured out who was behind the doll incident, or I could do the opposite and go on living my life.

Why was that doll left under my stairs? It was meant to frighten me. Why? Because I knew something, or the person responsible thought I knew something, and wanted me to be worried about the doll instead of Paul. It didn't do me any good to think the threat was not related to my involvement with what had turned out to be a murder.

Finn had given me good advice. I'd follow it as far as possible. But unless I wanted to live in hiding for the rest of my days I couldn't wait around for things to magically work themselves out. I had to do something.

But what?

I thought about the facts I'd been able to establish.

Who would want to see Paul Nesbit dead?

Irene and I had already been able to prove that Joe Martinez couldn't have killed Paul, but he certainly had a solid motive for it.

What if Wendy wasn't the only woman in Killdeer Paul had seduced? It could be that a jealous husband had put an end to an affair by putting an end to the man.

Irene had said there were a lot of people who were not fond of Paul.

Mayor David Jordan was one. He had been on the verge of losing the race and now he was certain of victory. Was it just a coincidence that David had gone from certain defeat to running unopposed?

I weighed those two possibilities and it seemed more likely that the latter was the better guess. But Finn had said not to make assumptions. I needed solid proof.

If I wanted to find out if David had been desperate enough to eliminate a political rival it meant taking a huge personal risk.

I finished the last of my hot chocolate and picked up the phone.

Copies of my paperwork from Reliant Landscaping sat on the counter, and I dug through the stack until I found the twelve-page detail of David's pine tree removal job.

I scanned the page until I found his phone number and dialed his home.

He didn't answer. I let it ring twenty times, but no machine ever picked up.

I hung up, and then I called the courthouse and spoke to the receptionist.

She sounded harried. "Yes, David is in. But you will have to hold. He's talking to Boyd about the cemetery fertilizer storage unit and they are not having a good conversation."

I had to smile. The beauty of small towns was the fact that folks would tell you anything. "Can you say how long it will be until he is available?"

"From the way it sounds, could be close to an hour."

I thanked her and hung up. Having the mayor stuck at his office for the next hour was giving me a window of opportunity I hadn't expected to get. If Mayor Jordan was going to be at the courthouse, I knew one place that he wouldn't be. He wouldn't be at home.

I was feeling the overwhelming desire to do something incredibly reckless.

It went against everything that both Finn and Loy had told me to do, but I was a firm believer that if I was going to get my life back together, the only way I could do it was to find out who had been responsible for Paul's death. Since the mayor seemed to be the most logical person with a motive, I would begin with him.

It wasn't much to go on, but it was better than sitting around waiting for trouble to find me.

The last thing anyone would think at this point was that I would keep digging into this. So, that's exactly what I would do.

I didn't believe if you kept your head down and hoped for the best a problem would resolve all on its own. It was far better to face a bad situation head-on.

I picked up the phone and called Irene.

"Honey, are you alright?" she asked. "I heard about what happened at your place Tuesday morning and I was worried. Are you at the ranch? I tried to call you."

"I'm fine. Really. It sounded worse than it was. I called to ask you a favor. Can you meet me at David Jordan's house in about a half hour? It's important."

The phone was silent for a moment. "Marley, does this involve something stupid and risky?"

"It might," I said.

She sighed. But it was the sound of resignation. "I'll be there."

I grabbed my stained canvas coat and pulled it on with the knowledge that my next move was incredibly dangerous. But I had made up my mind.

The shotgun was exactly where I had left it in the backseat.

As I drove into Killdeer I remembered my conversation with Finn and his sage advice that I leave well enough alone. In the world according to Finn, hunting for monsters was a good way to ensure that you would find one.

But in the world according to Marley Dearcorn, not hunting for monsters didn't necessarily mean that the monsters wouldn't hunt for you.

CHAPTER 28

When I pulled up in front of the mayor's house I tossed my canvas coat in the backseat of my car to hide the shotgun. The bite of winter was in the air, but my sweatshirt would have to do. My breath came out in white puffs. I pretended to be checking a clipboard and I scratched nonsense on the empty forms. Irene pulled up and got out, coming towards me with what looked like a bag of carry-out food.

"Good idea," I said, taking the sack. "Make it look like you are bringing me lunch."

She rolled her eyes. "I am bringing you lunch. What in God's name are we doing here?"

"You see that window on the second floor?" I asked.

Irene nodded. "What about it?"

"It sticks. David never has been able to shut it all the way because he got a bunch of water damage years ago and so now he leaves it open a crack so it won't swell shut permanently."

She held out her hand. "You owe me six bucks."

It was my turn to sigh. I juggled clipboard, sack and pencil to pull out my wallet. I dug out a ten-dollar bill and handed it to her.

"I'm going to climb up there and go inside, and I want you to wait out here and call me if anyone comes this way."

She stared at me. "What? You don't even have a cell phone. And what do you want to go burglarizing David's house for?"

"Can we talk about this later?" I said.

"How am I supposed to call you?" she asked.

"Call David's house on your cell phone. Can you get a signal here?"

Irene pulled out her tiny flip phone and studied the face. "I've got a signal. Barely, but I've got one."

"Call the mayor's house and let it ring once if you see anyone coming. If the phone rings once and stops then I'll know it's you warning me and I'll head for the back door."

Irene was hopping from foot to foot. "It's freezing out here. And I don't know his phone number."

I tore a square of paper off of my landscape form and scratched the number down. I handed it to her.

"Will you do that for me please?" I asked.

"As long as I can wait in my car. And don't you think it will look strange when you get out a ladder and climb up on the mayor's roof?"

"The roof is sloped down to almost ground level on the back side and I can step right up onto it from there. I'll climb up the back and you'll only see me for a second when I come down the other side. I'll be through the window so fast nobody will even know I'm up there."

Irene looked around the deserted street.

All of the people who lived in this section of town were at work this time of day.

She shook her head and grimaced. "Fine. But make it quick. I left Judy Isley in charge at the café and if I don't get back soon she will have shorted the drawer. The girl couldn't count four quarters to make a dollar if Stephen Hawking was helping her."

I took the sack lunch around the back as if I was heading for a place to sit down for a break. I saw Irene head for her vehicle, and when I got to the back yard I heard the engine on her little truck fire up. She revved the engine once and let it idle, but I could tell she was sitting in the same place and not moving. She was warming up.

I stashed the sack of food under the eave next to the back door and left my clipboard beside it. The back yard was taking on the usual pallor of winter, and all the trees were bare and gray. I pulled on a pair of heavy work gloves to protect my hands and scrambled onto the roof. I crab-walked up the slippery shingles to the top. When I poked my head over the edge of the rooftop, all I could see was Irene sitting in her truck, pretending to fiddle with her radio. The rest of the street was empty in both directions.

I threw a leg over the rafter, inched my way over the roof, slid down the other side . . . and kept right on sliding.

The roof was steeper on the front and my momentum propelled me towards the window so fast I started digging my gloved hands into the shingles to slow down. Shingle pebbles tumbled down the roof, and I nearly shot past the window.

I managed to slip a hand underneath a loose shingle, grabbed it tight and used it to stop my fall.

I'd torn it in the process, but I wasn't sliding anymore.

I scrabbled towards the window and snagged one hand on the window frame. Using it to pull myself up, I tried to get my footing to boost myself the rest of the way. The torn piece of shingle peeled off under my foot and tumbled down the roof. It caught in the gutter, teetered there for a moment then fell into the yard.

Not exactly textbook breaking and entering.

I didn't have time to worry about it now. I muscled myself the rest of the way up, put my hand on the windowpane and pushed hard. For one brief and horrible moment I thought the window was stuck shut, but on my second shove it popped open and I eased one arm inside the frame. The window was just large enough for me to squeeze through, and I fell inside the upstairs bedroom headfirst.

I had the sense to close the window behind me before I got to my feet. I stood there, trying to get my bearings, and the phone rang. I froze.

It rang a second time.

I let out a huge breath. It rang again. And again. I counted fourteen rings by the time I had reached the downstairs. Seriously, who didn't have an answering machine? I was so rattled I picked up the receiver and held it to my ear.

Silence.

"Marley?"

"Irene, you are not supposed to call me when I am busy breaking into someone's house."

"I thought you were going to kill yourself out there. Are you all right? It looked like you almost fell off the roof!"

"I did almost fall off the roof."

"Well do you see anything?"

"No I don't see anything because I am talking on the phone," I said.

"Well get off the phone and hurry up," she said. "I saw Harvey Wilson drive by and I am almost sure he saw you."

She hung up.

I set the receiver back in the cradle. I had no idea what I should even be looking for but the first place to start would be locating an appointment book or a calendar. David kept an office at the end of the hall on the first floor. He had a wall safe behind the desk and I'd seen him pay Jack out of it before. If there were anything useful or important that David had written down, it would be in the office.

I headed down the hall being careful not to touch a thing. David's house was old, but it was well kept and had a classy feel instead of a dated appearance. Our mayor wasn't rich, but this home that he had inherited from his parents sure gave the impression that he had money. The rugs were all tasteful, Persian, and looked very old. The walls were olive with dark trim. It was a much nicer house than I had ever lived in.

I hurried down the stairs and rounded the corner into the office. A huge oak desk dominated the space. I scanned it and started to sift through the few items lying on the blotter. An appointment book lay beneath a folder. I snatched the date book and read through it quickly. It was meticulously marked. Each tiny white square that represented a day of the month was filled with appointments, times and names.

I flipped to October eleventh and found it was full with lunch meetings and times for fund-raising events.

Of course I didn't find anything scheduled for the evening hours. As if David would have penciled in a time to drive out to Paul's house to murder him.

This was ridiculous. What did I expect to find?

I set the date book aside and sifted through the remaining papers. A couple of bills for cable and Internet. Two tickets to the high school play for Thursday night. The Man of La Mancha.

This was getting me nowhere. I had to find something that might tell me if David was a murderer, not determine if he paid his cable bill on time.

I turned around slowly and my eyes fell on the wall safe. It wasn't hidden behind an oil painting the way you would expect a safe to be. It was simply mounted in the wall behind the desk. My boss had a safe. Not Jack, but my old boss from the Fish and Wildlife office. He had a small safe, about the size of this one, behind his desk back in his office in Helena. He kept documents in it, and the occasional file folder loaded with photographs.

When my old boss was in the office, he kept the safe closed, but it wasn't technically locked. He kept it on what he called "standby." Which basically meant it was unlocked; but that he had to turn the dial one-quarter turn and then he could open the handle.

I hoped that David also used that little trick.

But which way to turn the dial to open the safe? Right or left?

I closed my eyes and tried to picture my old boss, chatting and working the dial.

He was left-handed. I remembered that. And he'd used his left hand.

He'd turned the dial to the right so many times, accidentally relocking the safe, that he actually had a little ritual of saying "left is right" every time he opened it from standby.

It was probably a waste of time, but I didn't have anything to lose. I took off my gloves, shoved them in my back pocket and touched the dial. It turned easily in my hand. I spun it slowly one-quarter of a turn to the left and I almost jumped back when I heard the safe click.

I think I was more surprised than happy. I took hold of the handle and pulled. It rotated down ninety degrees and the safe opened.

"Ha!"

I put my hand over my mouth. I had to be the world's worst burglar.

Now that the safe was open the best thing to do would be to take everything out in one stack and go through it on the desk methodically.

The pile of papers wasn't that big, so I grabbed them all and set them on the desktop being careful not to shuffle them around.

The usual forms and folders were in the stack. I started going through copies of tax returns, David's last will and testament, some lawsuit that had been filed against him years ago by a woman demanding palimony. That was old news in Killdeer.

This was getting me nowhere.

I went through the entire contents of the safe and I didn't see one thing that could be associated with Paul, the mayoral race, nothing. There sure as hell wasn't a bill of sale from a Mexican pharmaceutical company or a handbook for the amateur poisoner.

Frustrated, I started to stack the papers back in order. Just as I was about to get them organized again, the phone rang.

Once.

"Oh no."

I snatched the stack of folders and shoved it back in the safe. One errant yellow sticky note drifted down from my hands and fell under the desk. I crammed the rest of the papers back inside the safe and dropped to my knees, searching for the sticky note. Just as I hit the floor the back door of David's house opened and I heard the sound of booted feet coming down the hall.

I crouched under the desk with my knees tucked to my chest.

Someone walked slowly down the hallway past the office, making the floorboards creak. I held my breath. Heavy footsteps started to move up the stairs. I grimaced, waiting for my chance to peek around the desk to see if I could make a run for the back door, and when I leaned forward to get in position I saw a white envelope taped to the bottom drawer underneath the desk. The only thing a person would tape to the bottom of a desk was something he didn't want other people to see.

I didn't pause to think. Snatching the envelope, tape and all, I crammed it into my sweatshirt pocket, held my breath, and fished for the sticky note. I found it with my hands while nosing up just high enough over the top of the desk to see the stairs. I peeked sideways through the partly open office door until I could just glimpse the upstairs hallway. I saw a man easing towards the top step. At the angle he stood, it would be almost impossible for him to see me.

He was too tall to be David Jordan. Someone else was in the mayor's house with me, and I wasn't about to wait around to see who it was. I stood up and stuffed the sticky note back in the safe, closing the door as softly as I could, my heart hammering and my hands slippery on the dial. It clicked. I'd just accidentally locked it.

Hoping when David came home he wouldn't be able to remember if he had locked his safe or not, I inched towards the hall and listened hard. I heard a faint creaking from the far bedroom. The room I'd broken into.

Whoever was upstairs, he was searching the back bedroom. Looking for me.

It was time to get the hell out of there.

I toe-heel walked around the corner as softly as possible, down the hall, and sprinted straight for the back yard. Pausing long enough to scoop up my clipboard and my lunch, I straightened up and took a hard right turn for the driveway. The driveway was invisible from the upstairs and I headed for it at a run.

When I rounded the side of the house and reached the front yard I scanned the street for Irene. She was gone. She'd zipped away, most likely right after ringing David's phone.

It wasn't difficult to figure out who was inside the house searching it room to room, and if he managed to catch me in the act, he would be furious.

I headed for my car at a dead run.

CHAPTER 29

I dove for my Honda, tossed my clipboard on the seat and jammed the key three times before finally getting it into the ignition. The engine hiccupped to life and I peeled out and sped away, headed towards Main Street. I turned onto Main and deliberately slowed my pace, checking my rearview mirror frantically. I expected to see a sheriff's truck roaring down the road after me any moment.

I drove as casually as I could to Lil's café, parked in the parking lot and went inside. My knees were shaking like hot rubber. I didn't exactly sit down on the stool. It was more of a collapse.

Irene stood at the counter like someone had shoved a steel ramrod down her spine. Her expression was all business but her cheeks looked flushed. I was still panting with effort and adrenaline from the sprint to my car.

Irene poured me a cup of coffee and set it in front of me with one smooth motion. Her eyes darted towards the door and she shot me a piercing look.

I'd taken two sips from my coffee when Loy Shucraft pushed through the door of the café.

He stood in the doorway and I could almost feel his eyes on my back.

Loy clomped over, leaned on the counter beside me, reached down and took a drink out of my coffee cup.

His sheriff badge was level with my nose. "Marley. A word?"

I was almost panting from the race, but I managed to nod and give a casual smile.

"What's up?" It took everything I had not to gasp for air.

"Got a call someone broke into David's house through the upstairs window. You just happened to be there going over the job site from that downed pine tree—at least that's what I imagine you were doing—which makes me think had there been anything to see you would have been in prime position to see anything funny going on over there."

He took another drink of my coffee, pale blue eyes boring through me like a drill press.

"Uh . . ."

"Did you see anybody come out of the mayor's house?"

"Nope."

It was the truth, after all.

He pressed his lips together. "Because it would be a damn shame if someone got themselves shot while doing something stupid, in the pursuit of a goal or objective of equal stupidity."

I felt inside my sweatshirt pocket.

The envelope was still there, undisturbed.

"You want some more coffee, sheriff?" Irene asked.

She smiled innocently.

"No thanks, I should go lock up David's house for him. Funny, but the back door was open. You'd think if someone was going to break into a house they would check for something like that."

He gave me the hairy-horse-eye, glaring like a man who had just found out he was missing several head of cattle.

Loy headed for the parking lot. The usual late lunch crowd was in the café and they collectively watched the sheriff climb back in his truck.

Judy Isley, the waitress Irene sometimes referred to as a dim bulb, stood next to the counter popping her gum. "What's the sheriff all in a twist about?"

"He's upset that it's not meatloaf day," Irene said.

Judy shrugged and lugged a gray tub of dirty dishes towards the kitchen.

As soon as the girl was through the swinging doors, Irene leaned down and glared at me, one hand on either side of my coffee cup.

Irene's lip curled up. "I hope you had a really good reason why you felt like going on your little field trip today."

I took the envelope out of my pocket and placed it on the counter between us.

She looked at it.

I lifted my eyebrows. She lifted her eyebrows in response, snatched the envelope up and used her index finger to open the seal. She held out her hand and tipped the envelope upside down. A photograph fell into her palm.

I leaned in. She turned it right side up and we both stared at it.

"Holy Schlitz."

I saw what she meant. In her hand, Irene held a photograph taken from outside of Wee Wooly's Yarn Shop. It had been shot through the big picture window from the street. The photograph showed Wendy Martinez and Paul Nesbit, in what could only be loosely called an embrace. It was night, but the lights inside the shop were burning brightly and the image was unmistakable.

"They're . . ."

"Not knitting," I said.

She stuffed the photo back inside the envelope. She laid it on the counter and I left it there, not wanting to pick it up.

"This isn't good," I said.

"Well, you think?" she said.

I heaved a sigh. "It means that David didn't kill Paul after all."

Irene blinked. "How do you figure that?"

She poured herself a cup of coffee to give herself something to do with her hands.

We were both keeping our voices down, but she still kept glancing around to make sure we weren't overheard.

I rubbed my forehead, thinking. "Well, if David was so worried about losing the election, then this would have clinched a victory for him. All he would have had to do was show this dandy to Paul a couple weeks before the election and threaten to make it public. Paul would have had to drop out of the race."

She scowled. "That sounds like something David would do. He always did like to handle things privately. If anything, it would have given Paul a reason to kill David."

I snatched the envelope and shoved it back inside my sweatshirt.

I sipped my coffee, feeling nothing but disappointment. "He knew the whole time he was going to win. David only made a show of playing the role of the underdog, but he didn't have anything to worry about. There was no way Paul would have won with this photo floating around Killdeer."

I slumped on my stool. Another dead end. Every time I felt like I was making progress I ended up right back where I had started.

"What are you going to do with the photo?" Irene asked.

"I don't know. I think the best thing to do will be to give it to Loy. He needs to know in case he ever considered David as a suspect."

"Poor Wendy," Irene said. "I think she showed extremely bad judgment, but I'll bet she never thought it would come to this."

I could sympathize. "Maybe I should go talk to her?"

Our eyes met and Irene shrugged while I tried to weigh the options.

"Do you think David will wave it around town that he has a picture like this?" Irene asked. "I doubt it. If you hand it over to Loy, I doubt anyone will ever see it again. But if you want to go talk to Wendy and let her in on the fact that other people besides you know about her and Paul that is your call."

I set a couple of dollars on the counter, but Irene shoved them right back. I didn't argue and wordlessly folded them inside my thin wallet.

"I might drop by the yarn store just to say hello," I said.

Irene gave me a sad look. "That might be for the best."

We both knew that if David Jordan was aware of an affair between Wendy and Paul, it was probably only a matter of time before other people knew about it too. David had a horrible habit of getting stone drunk at rodeo weekend and telling stories. The photograph might never surface, but the rumors would fly. I thought Wendy at least deserved to know what might be coming.

"I'll see you later, Irene. Thanks for ringing the house to warn me."

"I don't know what you are talking about," she said. She turned her attention back to the café, giving me a smirk as I walked out.

I drove past Wee Wooly's and to my surprise it was open. The lights were all glowing brightly, and it looked cheerful inside. I parked and went in. Two women were busy trying to read a sweater pattern and determine how many yards of baby brown alpaca they would need for the project.

"Hi Wendy," I said.

Wendy was behind the counter, stacking up skeins of new yarn she was taking out of a shipping container. She gave me a smile. "Hey, Marley. How are you doing?"

She looked better. Not so pale, at least.

"I wanted to see how inventory went," I said, giving her a smile and letting my eyes rotate towards the two women. I didn't want to talk about her problems with Joe in front of other customers so I worded my conversation in a way that would let us chat without drawing attention.

It was edging towards four in the afternoon, and the two women were close to wrapping up their purchase anyway. Wendy totaled up the yarn, and after the doorbell rang behind them as they left, she hefted another box onto the counter.

"It's over," she said, her face sad.

I looked for a place to sit, found a worn chair and eased into it. "That doesn't sound very good."

She looked resigned. "Joe is filing for divorce. He said it is too much of a liability to have a wife he can't trust."

"Too much of a liability? Did he say it like that?" I asked.

"Joe has never been very sentimental," she said.

"Has he ever been supportive or affectionate?" I asked.

She laughed. "In his mind a woman who needed him to be supportive was weak. I think he hasn't loved me for a long time."

"But he seemed so protective, or at least, other folks have mentioned that."

Wendy fiddled with the skeins of yarn. They were a deep indigo with shades of plum. "Joe was very concerned about how we looked to others. He had definite ideas of what his image should be. I had the look he wanted."

I hoped it hadn't been as bad as all that. I hoped for Joe's sake that he at least had enough of a heart to have been protective of his wife because he loved her, and not because he wanted to look masculine.

"What are you going to do?" I asked.

"Run my shop," she said. She smiled a little. "Try and find a cheap apartment here in town."

"Does your shop make enough money?"

Her face flushed and she scrunched her eyebrows together. "No. But I won't need much. I can cut back expenses and try to make a go of it."

I thought about going from a huge, pristine mansion to a tiny, drab apartment and I wondered how long it would be until Wendy broke down and moved to a bigger city. I gave her six months.

"You could always go back to school," I said.

She laughed, but a tear escaped her and fell on the pile of yarn. "That's what Paul said. He told me it wasn't smart for me to depend on Joe for everything. He told me that I should build up my skills so I could get a good job, if I ever needed to. He even said he could look into university programs that offered distance education and send me some websites to check out."

That was not like the Paul Nesbit that I knew. "Really? He said that?"

She wiped off her face with the back of her hand. "He was right. I do need to get my job skills up."

I decided the last thing Wendy needed was to hear about the photograph. It was bad news that could wait for another day.

I gave her a sympathetic look. "What else did Paul tell you?"

She fingered the yarn, remembering. "He told me that I was special. Things all men say to a woman to get her to like him. He told me I was smart, and pretty."

"Didn't Joe tell you those things?"

"Joe said I was hot. Paul said I was pretty, like a summer day."

He had quoted Shakespeare to her? No wonder he had been so successful at seducing women. He had appealed to them, not made them into a conquest.

I wondered if there were any other women he had appealed to.

"Wendy, did Paul ever say anything to you about other women he knew here in Killdeer? Maybe a woman who he had been involved with?"

She tugged her lip with two fingers. "He did once. But he said it was too intense and he had to break it off."

I winced a bit when I asked, but I had to know. "Did he ever say who it was?"

She shook her head. "He didn't talk about it because he said she was married too. He came to my knitting class, you know, a couple of weeks ago? He was really shaken up about something. He tried to talk to me, but there were too many people around. I got the impression, because of some of the things he kept saying, that he wanted me to stay away from him. The woman he'd once been with wasn't too happy about him calling it off with her."

How many married women lived in Killdeer who would have been attractive enough to get Paul's attention? Not very damn many. And if this woman had not been happy about Paul breaking it off with her, maybe I had jumped to the wrong conclusions about it being a jealous husband.

Maybe a jilted lover had murdered him.

Shepherd had told me that the day Paul had been in the yarn store he'd taken ill suddenly. Maybe the spurned woman had walked in while Paul was trying to warn Wendy to stay away from him.

That would make any man turn six shades of white.

"Do you remember who came to your knitting class that day?" I asked.

She shook her head. "Jill was there, but she is always around when there is a free class. Marissa, Judy from the café. But mostly it's a blur. There were a lot of people there to see Paul try to knit. It was a circus. I don't think I could remember everyone who came that day."

Wendy fumbled with the shipping container and she looked like I had the day I had filed for divorce. My heart went out to her and I wished there was something I could do to help.

I stood up and rummaged for my car keys, being careful not to let the photograph slip out of my sweatshirt pocket. "My father has a place out towards the foothills. Really, it's way too big for him to handle alone. I was thinking about moving back in with him and that would leave my little caretaker's house empty. I know it's not much, but it would be better than you living in an apartment here in town."

She looked confused. "You want to rent it to me?"

"We can talk about rent later. If you need a place, it's empty now. I'd just have to move out my clothes and you could move in whenever you liked."

She looked down, her lip quivering. "I'd appreciate that, Marley. I really, really would. Thank you."

"Just promise me one thing," I said.

"Sure."

"Promise me that once you leave Joe for good, you won't ever go back to him."

She thought about it for a moment before she answered. Her eyes looked sad but she held her head up. "That's a promise."

CHAPTER 30

I left Wendy to her work and drove over to the sheriff's station. Loy's truck was there, Nick's deputy vehicle wasn't. That suited me. Although I could understand what motivated the deputy, it still didn't mean I had to like him.

It was just before five, but Valerie, Loy's dispatcher and office manager, didn't seem to be at the front desk when I went up the steps.

I walked into the station and the sheriff was behind the dispatcher's desk at the computer, clicking the mouse furiously.

"Irene called," he said, not looking up. "Told me you would be by."

I took the envelope out of my pocket and gave it to him. He slipped it into his lap. "If it had been anyone else, I'd have pressed charges."

He was beyond being angry. He was over that now and had settled on weary. We both knew I had been the one who had snuck inside the mayor's house, but I was the only one who could appreciate the fact that I would manage to avoid going to jail because the sheriff nursed a soft spot for me. I could tell by Loy's expression that if I didn't bring up the incident at David's house, he wouldn't either.

"Did Irene tell you what was in that envelope?" I asked.

"She did."

"So you know what it means," I said.

"It means David Jordan is a blackmailing pervert who stalked a political rival, for starters," he said.

"It also means he probably didn't kill Paul. With that picture he could have ruined Paul's reputation and that would be the race all sewn up for him."

Loy clicked a few more times. "I know the file is not found," he said to the computer. "That's why I keep asking you to look for it."

He leaned back in the office chair and yawned. "I can't understand why Valerie had to go to a concert in Billings now. She can talk to these damn things."

After a few more angry clicks he gave up and pushed away from the desk.

"Are you staying out at your dad's?" he asked. He watched me, worried eyes searching.

"I'm probably going to move back in with him. At least for a while."

That news seemed to calm him a bit.

"I think Wendy may come and stay out at the caretaker's house until she can get her feet under her. Joe and she are splitting up," I said.

Loy didn't look too surprised. "I never did like Joe," he said.

I fiddled with the zipper on my coat. "Listen, I'm sorry to have put you through so much trouble the last few days."

He smiled at me.

It was the sort of smile you'd give a five-year-old who had dropped her ice cream cone.

"Marley, don't apologize to me," he said.

"If I was doing my job better I would've caught the son of a bitch by now and you wouldn't have to worry about being harassed."

I studied the old tile floor. "So you think the same person who left that doll under my deck was the same one who killed Paul?"

He laced his hands together behind his neck. His biceps were straining the fabric of his brown shirt. "I do. Tuesday I couldn't come to your place to see the doll and I had to send Nick. I was over in Billings getting the results of the autopsy report. It was pretty clear Paul had been overdosed. We still don't know how. There wasn't much left of the wine, but besides cutting it with a bit of juice there didn't seem to be anything wrong with it. The pathologist didn't find anything out of the ordinary in his stomach, either."

I let my eyes drift out of focus as I thought about conversations I'd had. "Nick seems to think that the person would have to be a doctor in order to get ahold of that kind of drug."

"It's impossible to have a confidential investigation in this town," he said. "I need to talk to that boy. He's smart, but he has a lot to learn about being in law enforcement."

"But he was right, wasn't he?" I asked. "Only a doctor could get it?"

Loy thought about that, and reluctantly nodded. "It might be possible for someone who wasn't in the medical field to get their hands on it, but it would be damn difficult."

"What do you think the person who broke into the evidence locker was looking for?"

"Maybe they thought we had found something incriminating?" he said.

"And wanted it back?" I said, speculating.

"I'm not altogether sure about that. They didn't take anything, which worries me more."

"Why?" I asked.

Loy studied my face. "Because that means they didn't find what they were looking for and it's out floating around somewhere."

I pondered that. "What do you think they were looking for?"

"If I knew that, I'd have figured this mess out," he said, irritated.

"What about a—"

"You done asking me questions now?" he said with a stern expression.

I was done. I could see from his face that Loy was not going to share notes with me any longer. Anyway, I needed to talk to Jack. Something he'd said was tickling my memory.

I hooked my thumbs in my belt loops. "I'm having Irene deliver you an early supper. You like lasagna?"

He laughed. "I will eat anything Irene puts in front of me."

"You will eat anything, period," I told him.

His eyes still looked sad, but he seemed to have relaxed. Maybe it was self-centered of me to think it was because I would be living at the ranch house now, maybe not.

I left him to his computer work, drove by the café and ordered up a supper to be sent over to the sheriff's office. It was the least I could do for being such a cocklebur under his saddle over the last couple of weeks.

I drove by Jack's shop and was surprised to see that the Reliant Landscaping truck wasn't parked there. It was late in the day for Jack to still be working.

Jack's shop was nothing more than a tall steel building he'd built himself to house all of the tools of the landscaper's trade. It was plain, white, and usually disorganized, but it served its purpose.

I parked, got out of my car and went inside the back door of the shop. It was dark and quiet, so I flipped on the light switch and went over to the big steel desk where Jack kept all of his appointments. He didn't use a blotter or an appointment book like most people. He wrote all of his jobs down on scraps of paper and tossed them on the desk, relying more on his memory than anything else to keep all the clients straight. The clients who paid quickly, or who paid a lot, were automatically a priority.

I sifted through the piles of paper, looking for the current date to see if I could determine who he was working for today. I didn't see any notes for this afternoon and was possible he was doing a last-minute job for someone who had called that morning.

I kept my eyes on the door as I sifted through the scraps of paper. I knew walking around like nothing was wrong was not the smartest thing I could do, but I was determined not to give up my life because of some unseen threat.

I flipped over a glossy pamphlet hidden in the stacks of paper that looked like a Forest Service publication. It was an informational brochure about the pine beetle infestation that had swept the western states over the last several years. Killdeer hadn't been spared. We'd suffered damage to huge swaths of pine trees in the forested area surrounding the town. The beetles had progressively gotten worse, and eventually something would have to be done about all of the dead trees.

I scanned the desk for anything helpful, and thought about calling Mrs. Gunderson in case Jack had stopped by there to check up on her ponds. Then I heard someone rummaging around outside in the storage shed behind the shop.

I turned out the lights and left the shop, and saw Donny wheeling the big air compressor over to the shed. He went inside and I went after him.

"Where's Jack?" I asked, poking my head inside.

Donny looked irritated. "Oh, you still work here?"

I didn't have time to listen to a whiny teenager. "Where is he, Donny? I need to talk to him."

"He's over at Lewis Pritchett's. Again." Donny parked the heavy air compressor beside the workbench. He struggled to find a clean space on the surface to set a small box of rubber gaskets, gave up, and just tossed them on the piles of scattered tools. The kid looked like he was having a bad day.

The shed was normally a mess, but today it was in particular disarray.

Donny was pecking through the hand tools, searching for something, when a shiny box slipped off the bench and clattered to the floor.

He leaned down and snatched it up. "I don't even know why we have this thing!"

He tossed the box back up on the bench. I could see it was an air compressor, but it was tiny, too small for commercial use. I vowed that when the snow started to fall, I would come back and help Jack clean out this shed. It was a disaster.

"He say how long he would be at Lewis' house?" I asked.

"Till after dark. You going over there now?" Donny asked me, his hair flopping into his eyes.

"Yes, I'm going to try to catch him before he quits for the day."

Donny squinted and gave me a nod. "You see him, tell him the bank called."

I nodded. "You alright, Donny?" I asked.

The kid kept his back to me, but he let his shoulders slump down when he answered. "Jack gave Shepherd a raise."

"Wow," I said.

Donny hadn't had a raise in two years. I sensed that there was trouble in our little family.

"Don't worry about it, Donny. I don't think Shepherd wants to live in Killdeer forever. He'll be moving along anytime now."

"Yeah? I wish he'd move now," Donny said.

He found the part he'd been searching for, a hose clamp we used for underground sprinkler systems, and stomped past me to finish with his day. He called over his shoulder to remind me about the bank calling, and to tell Jack.

I went back to my car, feeling guilty. I know both Shepherd and Donny were not very happy I hadn't been around pulling my weight. I wasn't too happy about it either. It was time I stopped living like a hermit and got back to work. I decided that it didn't make any sense to hide out. Everyone knew where the Dearcorns lived.

CHAPTER 31

The sky was dimming now, leaving a pink splash of color on the few remaining clouds. Jack would be wrapping up soon. He never worked after dark. I drove through town and headed south until I saw the big sign with the stylized mustang carved into the heavy wood. I turned into the entrance of the Mustang Ranch.

I drove to Lewis' house and got out of the car, vowing I'd tell Jack that I would be at work, on time, tomorrow morning. It would be Thursday by then and I would have lost out on three days' pay.

As soon as I shut my car door, a beige and white blur shot from the yard and charged for me with a vengeance.

Someone called from the porch. "Saint Christopher. No!"

I jumped back, not sure what to expect, as the Welsh corgi Virginia Gable owned went for my ankles. I braced for impact, but instead of biting me, the corgi yipped and danced around my feet with excitement. I looked down and saw the remains of a very tattered ball resting on the brown grass.

Saint Christopher jumped back and forth, ready for the game to begin. Smiling, I scooped up the ball and tossed it.

The corgi tore after the ball, snatched it and growled as he chewed it mercilessly. He brought it back to me, dropped it at my feet and panted while he accepted a petting.

I looked up and Virginia was standing on the porch with Lewis. She watched me pet her corgi and looked murderous.

"Saint Christopher, bad dog. You don't bother the help."

The help. I had to bite my tongue.

Lewis was holding a bulging Falcon Realty folder, thumbing through it with both hands and looking confused.

"Virginia, I don't quite understand this. All I want is an appraisal so I can refinance my house."

Virginia tipped her head to the side. "I think we need to keep all of our options open here, Lewis."

He shut the folder. "I'm not selling my house. This write-up on my property is nice and all, but it don't do me a bit of good."

She had her cell phone out, something I considered to be unbearably rude, and was busy dialing while Lewis tried to hand the folder back.

"Lewis, keep it. It's for informational purposes only. The appraiser can't come until next Wednesday so I thought I'd draw this up just in case. . . . Hello? Miranda? It's Virginia calling from Falcon. I've got an appointment for us to take a look at that duplex in half an hour. Miranda? Can you hear me?"

Virginia held up her finger to Lewis, indicating that he should wait. He was starting to lose patience.

"Fine," she said. "I will meet you there. I said, I will meet you there . . . damn thing."

She hung up her cell phone, tossing it in her handbag with a look of utter disgust.

"If I lived in a real city I would be able to actually have a conversation with someone," she muttered. "When is this place going to allow itself to be dragged kicking and screaming into the twenty-first century and wake up to the fact that it needs to keep up with the times? Killdeer needs to install a cell tower."

I shared a pained look with Lewis as he waited for her to address him again. She seemed to have a different purse every time I saw her. One for each pair of shoes, I guessed.

Lewis looked like he was trying not to be rude. He shoved the folder into her hands.

"Thanks all the same, but I am not interested in selling."

She stammered. "But the home owner association fees here must be killing you. If you wanted to trade up, I could get you into a property with acreage on the face of the mountain. You can't beat the prices right now."

Lewis was old school, and therefore too polite to simply walk away from her. Instead, he held out his hand and waited until she took it. He shook it once. "Thanks for coming by."

He did not take the folder, and left her on the porch. He walked towards me and ignored the corgi.

Unless a dog was actually herding cattle at that very instant, it was just furniture to Lewis. Not that he was a cruel man, he simply didn't have time for things that were not useful.

Lewis looked relieved to see me.

He used my arrival as an excuse to get away from Virginia.

"Marley, I expect you'd be looking for Jack. He's out back laying out lines for the gazebo and moving that pile of trash from the old glass table that broke. I'll go let him know you're here."

Gazebo? There was only one reason I could think of that he would be even considering building something that was purely decoration. In all things Lewis was a practical man, until it came to Dr. Rebecca Winthrop. Love made us do crazy, crazy things.

Virginia snapped her fingers and ordered her corgi inside her black BMW. He reluctantly jumped into the backseat, mouthing his ball.

She slammed the door of her SUV, looking peevish.

Lewis walked around the back of the house and Virginia marched towards me, heels sinking into the yard. She hobbled to a stop, blonde hair looking a bit frazzled.

She stood in front of me, holding the folder. I noticed her manicured nails matched her dress. They were painted crimson.

"Here," she said. She thrust the folder at me. "Take this and leave it someplace he will find it."

I wasn't in the mood to cater to Virginia. I needed to talk to Jack about something that had occurred to me.

Virginia held the folder out to me, insistent. I made no move, and let my eyebrows rise up on my forehead. I must have looked like someone who was trying desperately to give the impression that she cared, unsuccessfully.

When I didn't take the folder she turned and tossed it like a Frisbee towards the porch.

Papers scattered on the steps. She looked at me as if I was the one who had forced her to do it.

"If I can get a man to do what I want just one time, one time, it will be a miracle."

"Leif always does what you want," I said.

Her eyes flashed. "Yes, but if only I could get him to do something that mattered."

She hobbled back to her BMW, high heels still sinking in the grass, threw her purse on the floor in the backseat and pulled herself in. If Virginia weren't such a snake, she would have been a very beautiful woman.

For the sake of the property, I went to gather up the scattered papers littering the front porch. When I had them neatly bundled I glanced back and saw Virginia sitting in her BMW stabbing her finger at the screen of her GPS unit. The back window was lowered halfway down for Saint Christopher. I thought I would do Lewis a favor and slip the sale folder in the backseat of Virginia's vehicle, and save everyone some heartache.

Virginia was so engrossed programming in the next location on her GPS she looked right through me as I walked past her BMW. Saint Christopher, an ever present satellite orbiting his neurotic mistress, actually licked my hand when I dropped the folder onto the backseat. I gave him a scratch behind the ears.

"He just had his flea treatment," Virginia said, hanging up the phone.

I shook my head. "I'll be sure to wash my hands."

Saint Christopher, though not a big dog, was having trouble navigating the backseat of the big vehicle.

He was sharing the space with two large boxes that left him little room to sit. I read the labels. Chateau de Roques.

"It's French," Virginia said, taking in my puzzled expression. She buckled her seat belt and started the engine.

"You and Leif having a party?" I asked. There had to be at least twenty bottles of French wine in those boxes.

She gave me an annoyed glance. Are you still talking? She threw the SUV into gear. "They are for my clients," she said. "I don't drink."

She pulled into the street without looking, her tires chirping as she hit the gas too hard, and I stared after her.

She didn't drink.

Twenty bottles of wine were packed into her backseat, but she didn't drink. Virginia was married . . . and she was attractive.

Paul liked beautiful women. He liked married, beautiful women.

When I had run upstairs to get Paul's inhaler, there had been an open bottle of wine beside the bed, but only one glass. Irene had said she didn't think Paul was the type to drink alone. But what if he hadn't been alone? What if a spurned lover had come to have one final drink with him? Someone who toted around two boxes of wine in the backseat of her SUV . . .

It was like getting slapped in the face with a wet horse tail.

Finn had told me not to jump to conclusions about who might be responsible for the doll, for the murder, but I couldn't believe that what I had just seen didn't point me straight to who had killed Paul Nesbit.

I finally shook myself back to reality and went around to the back of the house in search of my boss.

I was thinking so hard I jumped when Lewis came around the corner and popped into view.

He gave me a sheepish smile. "I simply cannot tolerate that woman," he said. "Sorry I left you there to face the dragon."

I had forgotten all about asking Jack what I'd come here to find out in the first place.

Thoughts were crashing into each other in my head. I knew the answer was staring me in the face. I just had to ask the right questions.

"She is the single most aggravating person I know," Lewis said. "All I asked for was an appraisal and she writes up a for-sale brochure for my house. Like I ever want to move. But she has to have it her way."

"Virginia can be a mite tiresome," I said. I was struggling to work things out in my head. There was something critical here. I knew it. How did I make sense out of the questions that had log-jammed up in my brain?

Luckily, my mouth was way ahead of me.

"Lewis," I said, struggling to piece the mess together. "Didn't you say that a few years back a big fire burned over where Leif and Virginia live?"

Lewis scratched his head. His ever present Stetson cowboy hat had left a ring on his forehead. "It was about forty years gone by now," he said.

"And didn't you tell me that a few firefighters got killed?"

"I know the story is that a dozen men burned up in that fire, but I think it was only four or five of them that died. Not that five men dead isn't bad enough," he said.

"But one of them survived. You said that he ended up on top of the cliff behind where Paul built his house. Did anyone ever figure out how he got up there so fast?" I asked.

It was starting to come together.

"No, nobody ever did. I was about ten years old, but I remember most folks just being thankful it hadn't been six men who died that day."

I could see it all clearly in my mind now.

The downburst had hit my house at the same time that Paul was being poisoned. I had driven up to his place to check on him, but I hadn't passed a single car on the way. If anyone had driven up to Paul's I would have seen the car. It was impossible for me not to. The road was narrow, lined with trees, and there was no place to conceal a car. That meant whoever had poisoned Paul had walked there. And I had just figured out how they had done it without being seen.

I needed to get to the library. I needed one more piece of information and I knew I could find it there.

I looked over Lewis' shoulder and saw Jack standing behind him. I hadn't heard him walk over, but I was glad to finally catch up to him.

"Hey, boss. I wanted to let you know I will be in to work tomorrow. That sound alright to you?"

Jack's face brightened. "Sure does. I've got a lot of winter prep to do over at the polo field. The owner promised me a check tomorrow."

"Oh, that reminds me," I said. "Donny told me to let you know the bank called for you."

Jack flinched. He managed to compose his expression and pasted a smile back on his face. "Probably want to change the layout of that branch landscaping design. Again."

"I have to go, Jack. I need to go look something up. So, I'll see you tomorrow?"

"Bright and early," he said. His cheerful tone was forced. I knew Jack was concerned about the bank calling, and I should have slowed down long enough to give him some reassurance or at least some moral support, but I couldn't wait. I had to go find the last piece of the puzzle that would tell me without a doubt that Virginia Gable was responsible for killing Paul.

It was all coming together and there was only one thing left for me to find out. I had to discover how she had gotten up the cliff so quickly that night.

I left and drove straight to the library.

CHAPTER 32

We were blessed in Killdeer. Our library boasted an archive of local historical records that rivaled collections in much larger cities. It was called the Montana Room. Though not a very imaginative name, it was accurate. All things Killdeer were carefully filed and stored in the archive.

I told the reference librarian what I was looking for, and in ten minutes I had been handed the two weeks' worth of newspaper clippings pertaining to the fire that had cost the lives of those firefighters so many years ago.

The newspaper articles had been transferred to microfilm records to save space. A large magnifier projector sat against the wall, and it was quick work to load the microfilm and scroll through the stories after the librarian had shown me how to use the machine.

I looked at each carefully labeled box. They were labeled with dates and abbreviated titles from the newspaper headlines. I was looking for one thing in particular.

Names.

I found them in the third box.

Two days after the tragedy, the names of the men who had been killed had been released.

After a quick investigation it had been determined the fire was caused by a lightning storm. It started as a slow burn and then a light breeze kicked up which fueled the growing flames. A crew had been sent in promptly, after a day of smoke choked the valley.

A few hours after the firefighters had reached the Gables' property, called more accurately the Wilson Ranch back then, the wind had picked up fiercely. The valley had been considered safe to enter, since the prevailing winds had consistently blown from the east, allowing the men to enter the area without facing the smoke and keeping the flames moving away from them. But the day the firefighters entered the valley, without warning the winds had shifted to westward and started eating up the dry grasses lining the pathway to the drought-stricken trees. In less than an hour all of the men were trapped when the fire blew into an inferno. Five firefighters had been killed, and their names were printed in a column that had run in the local paper. At the bottom of the article I found what I was searching for. The name of the man who had survived.

I had to read it twice before I realized who it was. Michael Shepherd. Shepherd? That was an old family name. The Shepherds had been in the valley for several generations, like my family. It took me a moment to realize I knew a Shepherd. He worked with me. And he hated my guts.

We all called him Shepherd, but really his name was Tom. Thomas Shepherd. He was, what? Twenty? I knew that because he had gotten an MPI over the summer. He was on the verge of twenty-one, but on the verge didn't count when the officer in charge was Loy Shucraft.

Retired firefighter Michael Shepherd had passed away in 1992, according to the archives I requested of obituaries for Killdeer. He would have been eighty-eight years old today. That would make him too old to be Tom Shepherd's father. At eighty-eight, he was most likely Tom's great-grandfather. The last person I wanted to talk to about this was Tom. That meant there was only one other person left to question. That person was Tom's mother, Lila. She couldn't be more than forty, maybe forty-two at the most. I didn't know who Shepherd's father was, because Lila had always used her maiden name and had passed it on to her son. We all assumed it was because she was ashamed of who Tom's father was. But I knew Tom's mother. And, more to the point, I knew where to find her.

I had just figured out how Paul had been killed, and how the killer had gotten away with nobody seeing her. And I was convinced now that it was a *her,* but I had to be able to prove it.

I sat back in the chair, feeling a mixture of triumph and trepidation.

"Did you need anything else?" the librarian asked. She didn't wear her hair in a bun or have a pair of reading glasses on a chain around her neck. She wore slacks and a ruby-colored blazer. Librarians were chic these days. "We close up here in ten minutes."

She was cordial, but not warm. I decided I had learned everything I could.

"Thank you, but I'm finished."

I got up to leave and stopped. "Do you have any topographical maps of Killdeer?" I asked.

The librarian gave me a practiced smile. They probably got that question a lot.

"You can get them up at the Forest Service office. They are $9.99."

I left, driving faster than I should have, but by the time I got to the Forest Service office up on the hill they were already closed, and had been for more than an hour. I would have to wait until tomorrow to pick up a map. That was fine. There was more than one way to get the information I needed. Bless these small towns.

I drove back to Main Street and turned on Turtledove Lane, which was a pleasant name for a very unpleasant street. Turtledove housed the two most popular bars in town. Well, two of the only three bars in town. I parked in front of the Broken Spoke Bar, where most nights Shepherd's mother could be found slinging shots to locals and testing the capacity of the human lungs for tolerance for smoke inhalation.

When I walked in I saw Lila behind the bar, leaning down to fill two mugs for a pair of coal bed methane workers slumped at a table. She glanced up and registered my face, then frowned, and went about her task. Lila wouldn't be making any money off of me today.

Everyone who lived in Killdeer knew I didn't drink. Since alcohol was the reason my mother had died when I was seven, I never touched the stuff.

Lila Shepherd had been a beautiful woman, once. She looked weary now. She also didn't look like she was in the mood to chat.

I took a seat at the bar, noticing I stuck to the old wooden stool a bit. Probably from years and years of spilled drinks and oil-stained clothes pressing into the grain. I pulled out a five-dollar bill and when she came back I ordered a Coke.

She quickly pulled me a Coke from the bar, her ash-blonde hair molded in a beehive of teased strands and shellac, mascara painted on so thick it looked like two spiders clinging to her face. She wordlessly plunked the Coke down and I slid the five across the bar.

She squinted at me. "You work with my son."

"He's a hard worker," I said. It was the only nice thing I could find to say about Shepherd.

She took the five. "Jack's gonna train him up to be an arborist," she told me.

I was surprised. "That's a good job."

She lifted her chin. She had damn little to be proud of, and I could tell she would cling to any amount of recognition offered. She made change for the five. I left the change untouched.

"He wants to move to Martha's Vineyard and go to work for those tree trimmers up there," she said. Her hands were busy searching for her purse under the bar.

"He'd be a good climber." I made a point not to stare at her, and focused on the bar instead. It was worn from years of holding up the sad elbows of the drunk and dispossessed.

She found her bag and fished through the contents, sifting hairbrushes, tampons and wads of crumpled lottery tickets.

"Lila, wasn't your granddad a mountain firefighter awhile back?" I asked.

She pulled a cigarette out of her purse and lit it. "Yeah."

She took a long draw. "Guess working around trees runs in the family."

It was dim inside the Broken Spoke. I thought the place could use a few more lights, but then again . . .

"Didn't he work a fire in Killdeer years back?" I asked.

Lila let the cigarette wander around her lips while she thought. "He told me about that once."

"Pretty amazing he survived," I said. I waited. People liked to talk about near misses.

Her brows bunched up. "He always said it was so stupid."

"Oh?" I said, sipping my Coke.

"Those other guys wanted to try to make a run for it, back up the canyon, and hope to reach a river or something," she said. Her face brightened a little with the spotlight of telling a tale.

"What happened?" I asked, trying to look casually interested.

"Granddaddy said the guys were yelling and arguing, and he knew they were all done for. They could see the fire coming up the trees and it was rolling like a tidal wave. That's what he called it, a tidal wave. He said they should try to find a place along the cliff that didn't have as many trees, maybe find a place where the rocks had fallen and made a shelf. Then they could stand up on that shelf and they might have a chance."

I couldn't pretend to be casual anymore. "What did he do?"

She drew on the cigarette, shaking her head. "He went one way and the rest of them all went the other."

"Did he find a shelf?" I asked. I was almost certain he'd done better than that.

"He found a cave."

I blinked. A cave?

At that moment one of the methane workers called for another round, and Lila lost her rhythm.

"Same?" she called to them.

She left me sitting there while she refilled their drinks. When she came back she filled herself a Coke and took a long sip, her eyes unfocused and taking on that thousand-mile stare.

"Is that how he got to the top of the cliff?" I asked. "He went up through a cave?"

She stubbed out her cigarette butt in a stained ashtray and blew out the last puff of smoke, finishing it off with a rattling cough.

Lila didn't know it, but she had just helped me piece everything together.

She glanced back at me, her stained fingers tapping on the bar. "Sure he went up the cliff through a cave. What else could he have done? He said one minute he was sure he was gonna die and the next he was walking back to Killdeer."

CHAPTER 33

The phone rang and Lila started a lively conversation with a screechy female voice on the other end. From the sound of it, she would be chatting for a while.

I left the change and the rest of the Coke, went to my car and fumbled with the keys in the darkness.

All the caves around Killdeer were limestone. They were deep, meandered along with no goal in sight, and often ended abruptly. If Lila's grandfather had found a cave then it was a safe bet it went from the forest floor somewhere close to Virginian's house and up to the top of the cliff behind Paul's house. No wonder Virginia had managed an affair with Paul, for who knows how long, without anyone guessing. She had literally used a secret passage to go back and forth between her place and his. I felt a sudden pang of sympathy for Leif. I thought he topped the list of all the people in Killdeer who actually deserved a loving and devoted wife.

I drove around the corner, headed south and went to Lil's café. It was a busy Wednesday night. Cars filled the parking lot, and when I walked in I found Irene up to her knees in alligators.

"Marley! Get an apron and start cleaning off these tables!"

I gapped at the chaos. "Where's Judy?"

"She quit, and Toby has the mono," Irene said. She was busy at the register, a pot of coffee in one hand and a twenty-dollar bill in the other. She was making change while a couple waited. Toby was the busser, and Judy was her only waitress for Wednesday nights. Irene was in a tight spot.

I took a breath, went to the kitchen and did exactly what she asked. An apron hung on the back of the staff door and I pulled it over my head. Then I grabbed one of the deep gray dish tubs and set about clearing off tables.

The tables were piled with dishes. I cleared them fast and set the tub back in the kitchen. Back out on the floor, folks waited for coffee refills, so I grabbed a pot and set about with that. Then I took the water pitcher around, topped everyone's glass and finished clearing tables. I had never waited tables in my life, but since everyone in the café knew everyone else, the event of Judy quitting with no notice turned into a community project. Even Harvey Wilson deigned to rise and fill his own coffee cup when I was in the middle of fetching a couple plates of pot roast for two dudes from the Lazy Ox-Yoke Ranch.

Loy Shucraft came in, having gone by and seen the parking lot overflowing, and took a seat at the counter. He gave me a pinch on the cheek as he went by. It should have felt like a condescending gesture, but somehow, tonight it felt affectionate.

The Chan twins, a couple of sharp teenagers from the high school, were more than helpful and had gotten up to fetch their own dinners from the cook's window. It felt like New Year's Eve.

The first round ended and I was about to sit down and ask Irene for her help, again, when the second shift lurched into full swing.

Loy finished his dinner and left, vacating the seat to allow others to sit. Three rowdies from the Broken Spoke, mostly drunk, had come in to try and sober up before making the long drive back out to a dilapidated and almost forgotten trailer park we in Killdeer affectionately called "The Burbs."

The residents of The Burbs were as skinny as a man can be and still hold up a pair of pants, and just went day to day and tried hard to keep their heads above water.

Sometimes they came into town to drink around other people, for the novelty of the act. Nobody in Killdeer mocked a man for being poor. It was a condition shared by a two-thirds majority of the population. They waited patiently, calling me ma'am, while I tried to take down their order. After intense negotiation, they all finally decided on a round of BLT sandwiches.

While I served them they tossed spit wads at each other, speculated on the validity of the last episode of The Simpsons, and generally clowned their way through dinner. But they didn't bother anyone else and Irene looked relieved they didn't seem to want trouble tonight.

I had just finished setting the BLTs on the table when I saw Finn walk through the door. He gave me a nod, unzipped his black jacket and sat at the counter.

Irene positively beamed when she asked him if he would like to see a menu. She was finally getting her chance to size the man up, and she wasn't going to miss it.

I was so busy with the crowd I didn't have a chance to find out what she was saying to him, but her face was a dead giveaway. She was laughing, teasing, and every minute or so she would stare directly at me shamelessly. I felt my cheeks go red more than once.

Finn had the soup. Crab bisque. Irene doted on him until he finally stood and left money on the counter. As he passed me on his way to the door, he leaned towards me.

"I'll be outside when you are finished here."

"It might be another hour," I said.

He just smiled and walked out.

Irene waggled her eyebrows at me. I rolled my eyes at her and started to gather up the remnants of dishes and cups.

It looked to me as if the worst had passed. I returned the last of the dishes to the kitchen, gave the cook a sympathetic smile and went back out to sit at the counter.

Irene patted my hand. "Thanks, honey. You really helped me out. Judy decided she couldn't wait any longer for her big break and has run off to cosmetology school in Parkman. Toby's mother called an hour before the rush to tell me he was laid up. It was a mess."

I poured myself half a cup of coffee and shrugged. "I was glad to help out."

"But you shouldn't linger." She gave me a sly grin.

"I know, I know," I said. "But I wanted to ask you something first."

Irene wiped her hands on a dishrag and started rounding up the coffee mugs that had collected on the counter. She stopped and gave me a look.

"What," she said. "You have another suspect in mind?"

I couldn't tell her everything, as much as I wanted to. Even though she had been far too patient with me already. This time I would only ask a favor, and not get her tangled up in the rest of my speculations.

"I was hoping that this Friday night you could do something for me," I said.

She pulled her stool out from under the counter and propped herself on it, eying me suspiciously.

"Does it involve breaking and entering?" she asked.

I felt a twinge of guilt. "No. I was hoping you could go look at a piece of property for me."

She looked even more suspicious now. "Where, at the Mustang Ranch?"

I laughed. "No. I was hoping you could give Virginia a call and ask her to show you one of those new ranchettes she keeps trying to sell up on the slope of the mountain."

"Marley," Irene said. "I can't possibly afford one of those. Do you know how much those parcels are going for?"

"I just want her to be occupied for a couple of hours," I said. But I didn't say anything else.

Irene watched me. I could tell she wanted to ask me a dozen different questions, but considering our escapades over the last week I could see she was not too sure she really wanted the answers.

"I would consider it payment for today's work," I said.

She grimaced. Irene knew I was up to something, but she also knew a good deal when she saw it.

"What time am I meeting her?"

"I know the café is busy on Friday, but could you meet her at five sharp?" I was pretty sure I could get Jack to let me off a bit early, maybe around four-thirty. For the task at hand, I figured I would need no more than an hour, maybe an hour and a half at the most.

"Five, that's going to be tricky," she said.

"It's important," I said.

She set the coffee cups in a gray tub and wiped her hands again. "Alright, I'll do it. But Marley, you have got to get another hobby pretty soon or it will start costing me business."

I breathed out a sigh. "I'm thinking of taking up knitting."

She laughed and we shared a smile.

"And Irene," I said, as I rose to fetch my coat. "It has to be Virginia. If you can get Leif to go with her, that would be even better. But Virginia has to be the one to show you that house."

"Why would Leif want to go with her on a viewing?" she asked.

"I don't know, you could always tell her that you want a man's opinion about the place and see if she will let him tag along. Let's just say it would be a good thing for the Gables not to be home for a couple of hours Friday night."

"Well, Leif is back in D.C. so it won't be an issue," Irene said, giving me a stern look.

I paused. "Why is he in Washington?"

"Visiting the son," she said. "I know that boy isn't even Leif's child, but he treats the young man better than Virginia does."

Even better. All I had to worry about now was Virginia.

"Thanks, Irene. I think all this mess will be sorted out pretty soon."

"You be careful," she said. "I mean it. I don't want to be reading in the Billings Gazette about you."

I put my hand over my heart. "I promise."

I walked out and headed for my car. Finn was leaning against his Jeep beside it.

I stood in front of him. "Hi, Finn."

"You don't take advice much, do you?"

I couldn't help myself and smiled. "Worried about me?"

"Worry doesn't do a bit of good," he said.

"More of an action man than a planner," I said.

"I plan. But, yes. I tend to enjoy the execution more than the strategizing."

"Me too."

He grinned back at me. "Bollocks. You make it up as you go along."

"It doesn't hurt that I have been pretty lucky," I said.

His grin faded. "In my experience, there is no such thing as luck. Why don't you try being sensible for a change?"

A flippant retort sprang to mind, but from the look on his face I could see that Finn wouldn't think it was funny. I softened my expression. "I'm sure Loy will be wrapping up this investigation in no time."

"Until he does, you should not be messing about so much."

I had the sense to drop my gaze and nod. "That's good advice. Maybe I will take you up on that suggestion."

He bent down and kissed the top of my forehead. "Good. Now get home and stop spending so much damn time alone."

I felt my face flush. I tried to say something, but he turned and climbed into his Jeep before I could speak. He drove off without looking back.

I stood in the parking lot like an idiot for a few seconds, trying to figure out why I was trembling slightly. Finn was the most mysteriously aggravating man I had ever met.

One flickering streetlight hung over the parking lot, forming pools of darkness behind the parked cars. The air was sharp with cold. My sweatshirt wasn't nearly enough to keep me warm, and I fiddled with my keys and opened the back door of my car.

My stained canvas jacket was gone.

In its place a thick black coat rested on top of the shotgun, exactly where I'd left my old canvas coat. I pulled it out and ran my hands over the fabric. It was heavy. The fabric was matte black and smooth to the touch, and it was a much warmer coat than my old jacket. I slipped it on and marveled that the zipper actually went all the way up to the top.

"Finn," I said, knowing that he had somehow gotten inside my locked car and replaced my old jacket with this sleek new coat.

It was too late to argue with him. He was long gone.

I felt inside the pockets for a pair of gloves, but they were empty. I shrugged that off and told myself to be grateful for the gift, and not greedy that he hadn't included a new pair of gloves as well.

I drove back to the ranch as nervous as a plump hen before a barbeque.

Knowing who had killed Paul wasn't making me feel any better. I wouldn't be able to sleep soundly again until Virginia Gable was enjoying the comforts of a Yellowstone County jail cell.

Virginia wouldn't be arrested until I could prove to Loy beyond a shadow of a doubt that she had access to Paul's house, and that she had a solid motive for wanting him dead.

But in order to find the proof I needed, there was one more risk I had to be willing to take. When it was all over I would finally be able to put the ordeal behind me and get on with my life.

CHAPTER 34

Thursday turned out to be a typical work day filled with frustrations and numb fingers. Donny and I worked at Rebecca Winthrop's house, servicing her koi pond and prepping it for winter. I shook my head over the impracticality of having a koi pond in Montana. This one was a constant problem for Jack. It was always springing a leak from the deer making themselves at home when they came to drink and punched holes in the bed liner with their sharp hooves. In the summertime the blue herons would come by and snack on the expensive Japanese fish that had been lovingly placed there. At least it was a moneymaker for Jack. The pond was such a hassle for Rebecca that she paid Jack a fortune to maintain it for her. She liked the peacefulness of the garden behind her house, when she wasn't fretting about the expensive fish or cursing the deer, that is.

When work wrapped up for the day I met Jack back at the shop, intending to ask him if I could leave a bit early on Friday. As it turned out I didn't need to ask. He informed the crew, during an impromptu staff meeting, that we would be working a short day on Friday so that he could get the snowplow attached to the front of the truck.

We all groaned, knowing that winter was coming and there wasn't a thing we could do about it.

The weather report for the next day was calling for snow at midnight.

This was not particularly good news for me. If I was going to find the evidence that Virginia had access to a cave leading to Paul's house, I'd have to do it quickly. I'd never find the spot after the forest was buried under several feet of the white stuff.

I had managed to snag a topographical map from the Forest Service office on my lunch break, and I took it home that night to study.

It wasn't as much help as I had hoped it would be. I knew that the caves all around Killdeer were limestone, and the cliff behind Paul's house was also limestone. How could I find a find a cave amidst that mass of rock?

I searched the map for clues to the location of a cave entrance, and finally gave up and folded it away in my desk drawer. I should have gotten a geological map instead. But if my hunch was right, I would be able to find a well-trodden path behind Virginia's house without too much difficulty. After all, she had probably been using it for weeks.

When the Friday workday began I found myself sweating before the first hour had passed.

A pile of paving stones left over from a patio job had to be loaded up and hauled back to the shop, and I spent the better part of the day moving the load an armload at a time.

The stones were heavy and awkward, so by the time lunch rolled around I was nearly worn-out.

It was not the best situation.

I needed to be fresh.

I told Shepherd and Donny that I would spend the rest of the afternoon typing invoices into the computer. They hated the job, and for once did not argue with me about the task I'd chosen.

I was sitting at the computer when the phone on Jack's desk rang. I answered it.

"Reliant Landscaping."

Irene's voice greeted me. "Jack said you'd be in the office. Well, Virginia was not happy, but she said she'd do it."

I leaned back in the old swivel chair. "Why was she not happy?"

"They won't let her take Saint Christopher out to the ranchettes," Irene said.

I chuckled. Well, no. The properties had a strict no dogs allowed policy. The subdivision flanked a sheep ranch, and there had been a few incidents.

"But she said she would meet you?" I asked.

"The lure of profit outweighed her loyalty to her dog. I'm still not clear about why the blazes I am going up the slope of the mountain," she said.

"Because your truck can make the trip, and my Honda probably can't," I said.

Irene believed that story like she believed politicians have their constituents' best interests at heart.

I tucked the phone under my chin, finished typing in the last invoice and set it aside. One of Jack's business cards was lying on the desk underneath the last invoice, and when I saw it I fiddled with it while I tried to explain. "Listen, I don't want to get you mixed up in any other stupid schemes of mine, so it's better that you don't know."

She was quiet. Not a very good sign.

"Irene . . ."

"Fine. How long do you want me to keep her there?"

"An hour should do it. If it takes me longer than that, I'm probably guessing wrong."

"Girl, what are you into this time?" she asked.

I flipped over the business card and saw my name written on the back. I frowned. This was the card I'd left in Paul's mailbox. I guess Jack didn't want Reliant Landscaping doing any work for the Nesbit estate after all. "Nothing serious. I just need to check something out. I'll call you when I get back from the Gables. Alright?"

"Alright. Be sensible, Marley. Please?"

"Thanks, Irene. I will. Talk to you in a couple hours."

She hung up and I tossed the business card back on the desk. I glanced at the clock. It was time to go.

I heard a crash behind me and I spun around in the chair. Jack was standing with his back to me, digging through a stack of music CDs that were piled on top of an old bookcase. He was mumbling.

"Marley, have you seen that Bruce Springsteen disc I left here?"

I caught my breath. I'd been so focused on my thoughts I hadn't heard him come in. "I think it's in the truck," I said, getting to my feet. I pulled my new coat from the back of the desk chair and slipped into it.

Jack bent to round up the CDs that had fallen to the floor, and I knelt beside him to help.

He stacked them back on top of the worn bookcase, his movements weary.

"Long day?" I noticed his tired expression.

Jack left one hand resting on the stack of plastic cases, and tilted his head as he appraised me.

"Listen, you and I are friends, right?" he asked.

I was surprised by his question, but I nodded. "Sure, Jack. You know that."

He watched me, his soft voice matching his expression. "So, you wouldn't mind if I gave you some advice, would you? Just between friends."

"Advice is free," I told him.

"Sure. But it's also priceless." He smiled a little.

"What's on your mind?" I stuck my restless hands in my back pocket.

Chatting with Jack was eating up the time I'd allotted for my drive out to the Gables' house.

He lifted the corner of his mouth when he answered. "I've been talking to Loy."

He waited a moment for that to sink in.

"Okay," I prompted.

"And he seems to think that for some reason, somebody here in Killdeer may have it in for you over this deal with Paul."

Did Loy hand out informational fliers about my personal life?

I let my head drop a bit. "Could be."

"Look, I don't have time to worry about whether or not my employees are going to make it to work because of some sort of trouble they might be in."

My face grew taut.

Was he about to fire me?

"Now, I have only missed three days of work, Jack," I began.

He held up a hand to cut me off.

"I'm not worried about that. I just think the best way to sort this out is if you make sure that nobody has any reason to come after you."

I let out an exasperated laugh.

"Well if I could figure out how to do that you can bet I would."

He kept his eyes on me. "I'm not accusing you of anything. But it seems to me that there must be some reason why you've got yourself in trouble in the first place."

"Some reason I got myself in trouble?" I asked.

He gave me a sympathetic, sideways smile. "Maybe, while you were in the house that night you found Paul, just maybe you touched something? Or took something? I mean, why else would someone be after you?"

"Took something," I said, thinking hard.

Jack turned his head in a half shrug. "Loy seems to think that when you were there that night you might have accidentally picked something up that you shouldn't have. That's the only reason he can think of that you would be having trouble now. You know Loy, he's too darn soft to tell the whole truth when it comes to you. Since I know he's worried sick about you, I thought I would pass it along. Did you handle anything that night in Paul's house you didn't tell him about?"

I felt my eyes grow wide. There was something that I had picked up that night, but I had forgotten all about it.

I'd picked up Paul's inhaler when I had gone up to his bedroom.

Reflexively my hand darted to my coat pocket and I patted it, suddenly remembering that I'd stashed it there.

But this was the wrong jacket. I'd left it in the coat Finn had taken from me at the café.

As soon as I was finished at Virginia's house I needed to find Finn. He didn't know it, but he could be carrying around a very important piece of evidence.

"Jack, I've got to go," I said. I headed for the door.

He took a step towards me. "Hey, don't take everything Loy says as gospel. If he's wrong, he's wrong and you shouldn't lose any sleep over it. Alright?"

I stopped in the doorway and spared a glance back. "Jack, thanks. But I've got to run. See you on Monday."

I hurried to my car, checking my watch as I drove. Damn. I was running out of time.

I'd asked Irene to keep Virginia busy for an hour and I would have to drive fast if I was going to make it to the Gables in time to find that cave. The inhaler could wait.

As I drove, my fingers ached from holding on to the cold steering wheel. The wind was picking up and the temperature had dropped ten degrees in the last two hours. It hurt to touch the steering wheel and I desperately needed a pair of gloves. My house was on the way to the Gables' place and it would only take a moment to run in and grab a pair.

By four-thirty I was headed down the road towards home. I pulled into my driveway and killed the engine. I bounded up the stairs and turned the key in the door. When I pushed open the door and went inside, I was shocked. The house was freezing inside, and for one horrible moment I thought that the power had gone out again and the furnace had stopped.

But when I listened I heard the furnace working hard. The blower was busy trying to warm things up. I went through the kitchen and saw that the back door had been carelessly left open.

"Damn, Nick Wilcox. Were you born in a barn?" I said as I pulled the door shut. It had been four days since I'd been to the house. No doubt Nick had left the back door wide open after he had searched the property. The heating bill was going to be a killer this month.

I kicked off my soggy work boots on the kitchen floor and scrounged in my bedroom closet for my heavy hiking boots. They were warm, and dry, and I'd need them where I was going. As I rummaged through the closet searching for a pair of warm gloves I noticed that a few of my dresser drawers had been pulled open. Frowning, I glanced through the top drawer of my dresser and it was obvious someone had been pawing through my clothing.

That deputy was going to get a piece of my mind the next time I saw him.

Nick could have been more careful searching the place. Why he needed to go through my things was a complete mystery to me.

But I didn't have time to worry about it now, and shut the front door tight before jogging back to my car. The wind grabbed my door as I opened it and I had to hold on with both hands to keep it from whipping shut on my leg. As I drove towards Virginia's, it never once occurred to me that it might not have been the deputy who had searched my house.

CHAPTER 35

The sun was quickly vanishing behind the cliffs when I pulled up to the Gables' place. I'd tossed a heavy flashlight in the glove box earlier and pulled it out now, comforted by the weight. Two extra D-cell batteries rattled around the inside of the glove box beside the flashlight, and I shoved them in my coat pocket. If I was going inside a cave I wanted backup batteries just in case I needed them.

The big log house was quiet, and when I got out of my car and shut the door a gust of wind shoved me back on my heels. I zipped up my heavy new coat as high as the zipper would go and shoved the flashlight inside the deep pocket.

I trotted past the back of the house and headed down a footpath leading through the trees. The path meandered, like a pleasure trail does, taking advantage of the prettiest places instead of the quickest. I jogged until I reached the cliff and started searching. If there was a cave entrance here, I had to find it fast.

I systematically walked the bottom of the cliff, checking every crevice and nook that could possibly be an entrance. I told myself it couldn't be obvious, or everyone would have known about it.

Still, I didn't expect it to be invisible, which it apparently was.

I kept searching. The light was fading quickly, and I started to lose hope that I'd be able to find an entrance before darkness fell. I resorted to turning on the flashlight to see in the low light of dusk, and realized I was not going to be successful unless I had a serious stroke of luck.

I had to be able to prove that Virginia could have gotten from her place to Paul's, and that she had been able to do it easily. That would have given her enough time to make it back to her house by the time my father had driven down to check on her and Leif after the storm, and enough time to have poisoned Paul and gotten home before Paul had succumbed. I shuddered at the thought of someone being so coldhearted.

Inside the shadow of the high cliff the light was nearly gone. I started to trip and stumble with logs and branches hindering me. I kept searching, and soon I had to admit that this idea was not going to work. If there was a cave here, I would never be able to find it. As much as I hated to, it was time to start back. Irene would only be able to keep Virginia busy for so long before the woman got impatient and returned home.

But to come all this way and give up now seemed like such a waste. There had to be something here that could point me in the right direction.

Maybe there was something inside the house that would give me a clue? It was the longest of long shots, but maybe if I took a quick peek inside the Gables' place I would find something that would give me a hint one way or the other if Virginia had been having an affair with Paul.

I'd been lucky at David's house and had stumbled on the photo of Paul and Wendy. Maybe my luck would hold out a little bit longer.

I stumbled my way to the house, buffeted by the strong winds, and went up the back steps. If Loy could see me now he would have handcuffed me without hesitation, but I promised to take care and not snoop for very long. I was desperate to find the truth, and I had a higher purpose, after all.

The door was unlocked and when I stepped through the back door I was shocked to see an expensive alarm control panel right next to the light switch. No buzzers or klaxons went off, and when I peered at the panel I could see that it hadn't been turned on. It seemed Virginia didn't feel the need to bother with a little thing like setting the security system on her house before she left. I let out a huge breath from relief. That had been too close.

The back utility area was neat and tidy, a row of hiking boots was lined up along the wall on a floor mat and a high-efficiency washer and dryer were tucked against the back wall. A coat closet stood open, displaying jackets arranged carefully. The floor was slate, beautiful and expensive. Even in my haste I could see that this house really was a work of art.

I was about to pass through the utility door and go into the kitchen when I heard a low growl. I froze.

Standing in the doorway that led to the dining room, his head lowered and his teeth bared, was Saint Christopher. He growled again.

"Hey, boy," I said.

He stopped growling and watched me.

"Saint Christopher, come here boy," I said.

At the sound of his name, and maybe the familiarity of my voice, he wiggled happily and put his teeth away. I knelt down and he came to me, ears down, apologizing for the growl.

I scratched his ears. "What are you doing home?"

Then I remembered that Virginia couldn't take him to the ranchettes. That must have chapped her.

I stopped scratching him and stood up. She took him everywhere.

I looked down at Saint Christopher. He barked once, game for action or hopeful for a treat.

I walked to the back door and he followed me. I opened it and he raced into the back yard, yipping with excitement.

Then I said the magic words all dogs long to hear. "Go for a walk?"

That had the desired effect. He exploded in barks.

He dashed down the footpath like a rabbit, disappearing in the gloom, and I had to sprint to keep up.

We had just reached the base of the cliff when I called out to him, hoping that my flash of inspiration would work.

I knelt down and patted the corgi. "Let's go see Paul, Saint Christopher. Let's go see Paul!"

He cocked his head at me and glanced back at the cliff, a bit uncertain.

"Go see Paul?" I said again.

He barked once and trotted down the path. I flicked on the flashlight and followed.

I didn't know where I was going, but apparently he did.

The little corgi trotted down the path without hesitation. I stumbled once and went down hard on my left knee, swearing, but managed to get back up and follow.

I almost lost track of him but saw the flash of his happy white tail dart between two tall trees. He led me down a narrow cut in the landscape that dropped sharply towards the cliff, and then turned a corner and simply vanished.

I stood there, swinging the flashlight from side to side uselessly.

"Saint Christopher?"

His head poked up from beneath a low pine branch and he yipped.

I focused the beam on him, then bent down low and saw that he was standing in a depression behind the tree. I ducked under the branch and followed, watching as he went around a tight bend in the cliff to the left and disappeared beneath a narrow cut in the stone. I didn't hesitate and dove after him.

If ever there was a cave likely to house a sleeping bear, a nervous nest of rattlesnakes or hordes of bats, it was this one.

I lifted the flashlight and it seemed to strain with the effort of lighting the dank space. The stone walls, rising up to a tall ceiling stretching into the darkness overhead, swallowed the beam.

The roof of the cave arched high above like a cathedral, only to bulge out as it descended towards the floor, widening out into a space that could have easily hidden a string of stolen ponies. Though the entrance to the cave was nearly impossible to see, the cave itself was wide enough to produce an echo.

I stopped gawking and remembered I was not there to be a spelunker. This cave should lead to the top of the cliff behind Paul's house, and if I could climb up to the top in under a half hour, it would be obvious Virginia had been able to murder Paul and make it back home with time to spare.

I started moving.

Now that I was inside the cave, I could see a well-worn trail leading up into the darkness. It was almost as easy as climbing a flight of steps. I was careful as I went up, but I moved as quickly as I could. Saint Christopher had scampered on ahead but I could hear him scrabbling along the stone trail excitedly.

It was steep going, but the ground was dry and I had good traction. I guessed with the angle of the trail that I would pop out someplace well behind Paul's house, probably in the trees not very far from the cliff edge. But as I climbed I counted three switchbacks, and I changed my mind. It was more likely I would come up right on the edge of the cliff.

The cave narrowed abruptly. The ceiling was now so low it was within reach. I shivered in the chill air and saw beneath the beam of my flashlight multiple paw prints heading towards a low crawl space, and after a quick search with my light I could see it was a shallow mousetrap tunnel. With the ceiling so close, I hoped there weren't any bats lingering inside.

I had to crouch but the roof of the cave never sunk so low I needed to crawl. I expected it to be damp but the stone floor was perfectly dry. After inching along in a crouch for perhaps fifteen feet, I felt a blast of cold wind and realized I'd made it. I'd found the top of the cliff.

Another gust hit me as I stood up straight and walked out of the cave. I spun the flashlight around to get my bearings and could see plainly that the cave exit was only a dozen yards away from the edge of the cliff.

I angled my flashlight, illuminating the numbers on my watch to see if the climb up through the cave could be made in less than a half hour. I had made it with several minutes to spare.

As I lowered my flashlight the beam danced off of something that shouldn't have been there. Saint Christopher was barking at something. I raised the light and pointed it straight ahead. As the beam illuminated the corgi, I could see that he was dancing back and forth playfully. He wasn't barking at something.

He was barking at someone.

CHAPTER 36

My boss, Jack Parks, stood not ten yards away, watching me.

He didn't seem surprised to see me. I started to ask him what he was doing there. Then I saw the gun.

It was the little pistol I'd seen in the glove box of the work truck. I knew it was loaded.

He pointed it towards me, looking sad.

"Hey, boss," I said.

He said nothing, simply stared. He cocked the pistol.

"Whoa, Jack. Take it easy."

I felt my heart start to race. What the hell was he doing?

"I was really hoping I wouldn't see you up here, Marley. I really was," he said. "Move away from that cave. Now."

I stood still, my mind in a panic. Saint Christopher yipped and played at Jack's feet, wanting in on the game.

Jack swung a hard kick at the corgi and I heard Saint Christopher yelp in pain. "Get out of here! Damn mutt."

I heard the scrabble of paws as the corgi dashed by me and ducked inside the cave.

It hit me all at once.

I'd been wrong about everything. Everything. Virginia hadn't killed Paul. She had nothing to do with it.

I had just made the worst mistake of my life.

I took a breath, hoping to reason with him. "People know where I am. If you shoot me they will know it was you."

"No, they don't know where you are. They think you are down at the Gables' house."

I swallowed. My mouth was so dry I could hardly speak. I felt my heart hammering in my chest. I had to do something.

I stood my ground, still gripping the flashlight. "Jack, listen to me for a second."

He aimed the pistol and shot the ground at my feet. I heard the bullet ping off of the rock surface and I cringed, my eyes squeezing shut.

He cocked the pistol again.

"Move," he repeated.

I moved. My legs would barely support me, but I moved. I was so scared I thought I would be sick.

I wanted to keep him talking. I knew at the most I could probably only stall for about three minutes. But damn it, I wanted to live for those three minutes.

"How did you do it?" I asked. "How did you get him to take the sux?"

He looked a little bit surprised. Then he looked angry. "Why don't you hand me that inhaler you took from Paul's?"

I fingered the pocket of the jacket.

Then I remembered doing the exact same thing back at the shop.

I'd given myself away.

All this time I had been carrying the murder weapon around in my coat pocket and hadn't even known it.

"I don't have it," I said.

He closed his eyes and swore under his breath. "Yes, you do."

My chest ached from fear. "Is that how you did it? You put it in his inhaler?"

"Paul never leaves the house without one," he said matter-of-factly.

"And that's what the little air compressor in the shop was for," I said. I was trying anything I could think of to keep him talking. "You filled it with sux and let him poison himself."

"Marley, I want you to turn your pockets inside out."

"I don't have it."

He lifted the pistol again and I held up one hand. "Okay, okay."

Slowly I reached inside my coat and pulled out each pocket. The spare batteries tumbled out and I held them up so that he could see them clearly. "That's it. Nothing else."

He was losing patience. "Where is it?"

I swallowed, trying to keep my hands from shaking. "I don't know. That's the god's honest truth."

I kept the flashlight pointed at his face. Why hadn't he told me to drop it?

Because it gave him a clear target to aim for.

"That night I found Paul, you were there, weren't you?" I said, saying anything I could think of to keep him talking. "You were in the house. I heard the front door slam shut, but I thought it was the wind."

"Why did you have to come up here and check on him?" he demanded. "Why?"

"Paul never did anything to hurt you. Why did you kill him?"

Jack's face twisted in a snarl. "Because the bastard had the election all sewn up."

I was squeezing the flashlight so tight my fingers hurt. "You killed Paul for David?"

He looked suddenly ashamed. "David didn't know. He and I had an understanding. But if he wasn't going to be mayor anymore . . ."

"What understanding?" I asked.

Jack looked stricken. "The city contracts. We had an agreement. I did free work for David, and he made sure I got all of the jobs that came up for bid."

"But that's only a few thousand dollars," I said. "Why would you do something like that for a few thousand bucks?"

"Four hundred thousand dollars," he said. "That's how much the pine beetle mitigation contract was going to be worth inside the city limits. Killdeer got a federal grant."

"And Paul wasn't going to give it to you," I said.

"I couldn't take that chance," Jack said, shrugging with regret.

"Jack, it's just money. It's not worth killing someone."

"It is if you owe that much," he said. He looked wretched as he confessed. "I owe at least that much, maybe more. My business has been failing for years. I had to borrow money just to hand out paychecks. I even borrowed money from Nathan."

"My father? Why didn't you sell the business and quit?"

"Mom dying an inch at a time in the damn nursing home. Her social security wouldn't cover a third of what it takes to keep her in there. Equipment falling apart, hanging on by the skin of my teeth, waiting for clients who have more money than they know what to do with to pay their bills. How could I quit?"

"Loy suspects you," I told him.

"Loy will be too busy searching for you after you go missing," he said.

I thought my knees would buckle but I managed to stay upright.

"If you hadn't shown up that night I could have walked right out the door holding that bottle of wine and the inhaler, gone back down the cave and past the Gables' house and Loy never would have even investigated it. But you came barreling in there and I had to get out of the house before I could grab anything. Dammit, Marley."

"You stole the sux from the nursing home," I said.

"I stole a lot of drugs from the nursing home," he told me. "Virginia and I had a good deal going on with the OxyContin. Leif always thought I was just coming over to do yard work. Virginia backed me every time. I guess she figured since I was selling her pain pills she could confide in me about her thing with Paul. She's the one who told me he was sure to win the election."

"But Jack, he wasn't going to win."

He stopped his rant and stared at me. "What the hell are you talking about?"

"David was going to blackmail him. He had a photograph of Paul and Wendy together. He was going to force Paul to drop out of the race. Jack, you killed him for nothing."

He looked around wildly, his eyes not focusing.

I took a step backwards, bracing myself. I was going to have to run for it and hope he would miss me in the darkness.

There was no other way I would make it out of this.

I gave him a pleading look. "If you kill me, it will be exactly the same thing. It will be for nothing."

His mouth fell slack as he grasped what I had said. He wanted to deny it, but I could see he was starting to believe me.

Jack seemed to come to a decision. He raised the pistol.

"I'm sorry, Marley. I really am. But I just can't. I've still got a chance to salvage this, and you could ruin everything."

I shifted the flashlight to my right hand, tested the weight, and gripped it tight.

"I'm sorry too."

I threw the flashlight at him as hard as I could. It spun end over end but I didn't wait to see if it hit him and dove for the cave headfirst.

I was engulfed in total blackness instantly. I couldn't see a thing but fear drove me forward. I had just come through the cave and the memory of the path I'd taken was still fresh.

I hoped that Jack's memory wasn't.

I scrambled through the low entrance, my breath ragged. I used my hands like cat's whiskers, feeling my way along as fast as I could move.

I heard Jack yelling behind me and I knew it would only be seconds until he was on my heels.

He had a flashlight.

I didn't.

When I felt the low ceiling open up, I straightened cautiously, feeling along the wall until I got my bearings.

My feet scraped along until I found the first steps leading down. Frantic, I slid down to my butt and inched along the path using my feet to probe the darkness. But I was moving too slow. At this pace Jack would catch me before I even reached the bottom.

But if I stood up and moved too quickly, he wouldn't need to shoot me because I would break my neck when I fell.

I didn't have any choice. I stood up and took a long step forward. My breath caught with surprise as I fell forward, but mercifully my foot found a flat surface and I realized I'd landed on a perfectly level rock right in the center of the path.

I rummaged in my pocket and pulled out the two spare batteries. I laid one battery on its side exactly where I had stepped. Then I laid the second one right in front of it.

I didn't pause to make sure the batteries stayed put, I kept moving.

I could hear him behind me, gaining ground.

"Dammit Marley don't make me chase you!"

My heart sank when I saw the movement of a flashlight beam behind me bouncing off the walls of the cave in the darkness. I had hoped the light had been damaged when I'd hit him. I hadn't been that lucky.

He would be able to move about three times faster than I could.

I refused to stop and try to hide. I had to keep going.

A bullet ricocheted off the walls of the cave. I cringed at the sound. It was so loud I reflexively slapped my hands over my ears and stopped.

If I stayed where I was I would be an easy target. I forced my feet to keep sliding down the steps.

I saw a flicker of light behind me and realized he was gaining much faster than I was able to move. I nearly fell when I felt the floor of the cave drop sideways and I knew I'd found the first switchback. I angled my way around it to the left and kept inching my feet across the uneven rock.

I didn't bother to try and keep quiet and kept going.

Jack was pounding down the path behind me, gaining ground fast, and then I heard him yelp with surprise. A sickening thud followed by the clatter of a flashlight against stone echoed through the cave. He'd just found my battery trap.

It was a small victory, but I would take it, and gladly.

I felt the path snake to the right and I crawled along the second switchback as fast as I could manage.

I heard him moaning behind me, shuffling and trying to get to his feet. That told me the fall had slowed him down but that he was still able to move.

I suppressed a sob of anger and fear and shuffled on.

The darkness was hiding me, but it was also hindering me. I forced myself to breathe in steady breaths. I felt the panic rising in my throat and I had to keep myself in control.

It was almost impossible.

I was desperately moving my way towards the third switchback, knowing I had to be getting close to it, when something brushed my leg and I almost screamed. I froze and listened.

I heard panting.

I knelt down and my hands found the wet nose of the corgi. He'd been there waiting for me the entire time.

I leaned down as far as I could and whispered in his ear. "Let's go home, boy."

He lunged away but I had a tight grip on his collar. When he moved, I moved. I had to bend down so far to keep my hands in contact with him that I was almost crawling. But I kept my feet under me.

The corgi had traveled this route more times than Jack and I put together. He knew where he was, even if I didn't.

I stumbled hard, twice, and nearly crushed him, but Saint Christopher kept us heading down. It was all I could do to keep up with his pace.

My heart sank when I saw a flashlight waving through the cave behind us. Jack was up and running.

And gaining.

I sensed the cave opening up and I knew we were close to the end at last. When the corgi led me across the great empty room that marked the bottom of the cave I urged him forward frantically.

I was gripping him so tight he whined once, but kept scrabbling on over the rocks, leading me to the way out.

I ducked my head as Saint Christopher pulled me towards the opening, up and out of the cave.

Then I felt the rush of air and the blackness turned into an inky twilight. I let the corgi go and stood up, my muscles screaming from being bent down for so long.

I pushed my way out from under the pine bough, turned away from the cliff and ran.

I ran for my life.

I heard tree branches snapping behind me, then a wild gunshot rip through the night, but I didn't look back.

If I could make it to the house I could lock myself inside. I might have a chance then.

The way ahead was scarcely visible but I didn't slow down. I couldn't.

Then my boots snarled in a tree root.

Branches and leaves cracked as my arms and chest hit the ground hard. I sucked in a breath and shook my feet free of the root, lifted myself up and staggered on.

The dark outline of the house came into sight.

A crash erupted from the trees behind me.

"You can't make it, Marley!"

I could see the flashlight bobbing through the gloom.

He was right on top of me.

Somehow my legs carried me onward even though they trembled with fatigue and fear.

I broke through the tree line and saw the back of the house.

Almost there.

I heard Jack burst into the clearing right behind me.

I looked over my shoulder and saw his shadowy outline planted in a shooter's stance.

The gunshot knocked me to the ground and pain like I'd never felt ripped down my left arm and across my neck.

For a moment I couldn't move, but fear forced me to shake off the shock and I rolled up onto my right side just enough to look back.

Jack came further into the clearing, limping.

He stopped several yards away and propped himself on his knees to catch his breath.

Then he stood up straight, lifted the flashlight again, and pinned me in the beam.

All I could think at that moment was I would be damned if I was going to die lying down. I clutched my limp left arm and struggled to my feet. Then I turned to face him.

My entire body burned, from pain, the run, but mostly from pure anger.

I lifted my chin and shouted. "I want you to remember this moment when they strap you into that electric chair you son of a bitch!"

Jack steadied the flashlight and lifted the pistol.

A man's voice broke through the darkness behind me.

"Jack, stop!"

His flashlight darted frantically away from me as he searched for the source of the sound.

I turned my head and saw the hunched form of a man nearly thirty feet away. I couldn't see his face, but I knew his voice at once.

Loy Shucraft held his ground, even as the flashlight beam zeroed in.

"Lay it down," Loy called. "Lay it on the ground."

Neither man moved. It was as if they were both frozen in place.

Then I realized why.

I stood directly between them.

If I tried to run it would distract Loy, and Jack would just kill us both.

If Jack shot me first, he would be dead a half-second later.

It didn't matter who was quicker. This would come down to one thing.

Who had the better aim.

"You're not going to shoot me," Jack said. "Not with her there. You won't take that chance."

Loy's ice-cold voice didn't waver when he spoke. "I'm not aiming for her."

For the space of a dozen heartbeats, no one moved.

Jack stared ahead in total silence. He wasn't looking at me anymore. His flashlight stayed on Loy, motionless. Almost like he was calculating his chances.

And then his arms drooped and the flashlight rolled to the ground at his feet. He seemed to wilt as his body caught up with his mind, and he tossed his pistol a few feet away and lifted his arms up in surrender.

He was willing to kill today, but he wasn't willing to die.

Loy walked forward and around me, careful to keep his weapon and his eyes trained on Jack.

"Marley, you all right?" he asked.

I gritted my teeth. "Awful glad to see you."

Loy pulled out his handcuffs and cautiously moved to where Jack had slumped to the ground on his knees. He retrieved the dropped pistol, handcuffed Jack and searched him up and down for any other weapons.

Satisfied, he put his boot in the middle of Jack's back and shoved him to the ground facedown.

"You get the urge to make a run for it and force me to club you Jack, and I won't hold it against you," Loy said.

But Jack stayed still, his bruised body limp and defeated.

I suddenly felt queasy with pain but managed to ease myself to the ground before I fell over.

The sheriff was beside me in an instant. "Marley?"

"I think I got hit."

Loy stared back at Jack as though he were seriously contemplating committing some police brutality. But he holstered his weapon instead and knelt by my side.

"Where did he get you?"

"My left arm, I think." I eased my head to the ground, stars swimming in my eyes. There had to be blood somewhere. But I couldn't feel any dampness.

"I'm just going to take a look-see, so lie still."

I wasn't in any position to argue.

He unzipped my coat with slow, careful movements.

"You think you're a doctor or something, Loy?" I asked, flinching as he placed his hands on my neck.

"No, but I've seen a few gunshot wounds." His face looked rigid with concentration.

A sharp jolt of agony ripped through my neck as he ran his hands over my left shoulder, and I couldn't suppress a groan.

The burly sheriff sat back on his heels and breathed out a thankful sigh.

"Hun, you are going to be fine."

I sputtered. "I don't know that I *feel* particularly fine."

His hands slid over the material of my coat and he thoughtfully rubbed it between two fingers. "I think whoever gave you this jacket deserves a fruit basket or something. If you hadn't been wearing it, this might have gone differently."

Loy sat down hard beside me. He rubbed his eyes once, and breathed out another sigh. "Irene called me. She said you might be in trouble. I got here as quick as I could."

"Who says there's never a cop around when you need one?" I asked, trying to laugh but only managing a sob.

My face felt wet. I'd been crying and just now noticed it.

"Nick is on his way. He was right behind me. We can take you to the hospital as soon as he gets here."

"Why can't I feel my left arm, Loy?"

"Because you've got a broken collarbone. But the last time I checked, those aren't fatal."

I tried to thank him but darkness seemed to be closing in from all sides. He edged closer to me and gripped my right hand tighter. He covered my limp fingers with both his big paws, and I could feel him shaking.

"Is now a bad time to ask you to marry me?" he asked.

Mercifully, I picked that moment to black out.

CHAPTER 37

Irene sat in a plastic chair reading me the get-well cards stacked on the table. Four vases of flowers lined the tiny windowsill of my hospital room, and she was having great fun reading the notes and interjecting her own interpretations as she went.

"'Get well soon, Love, Loy.' He forgot to put on here that the only reason he hasn't arrested you is because he is trying to figure out a way to get you in the sack."

I didn't mention his spontaneous wedding proposal.

"Daisies from your dad. He's the sweetest man. He wants you to come home soon."

I smiled. I was in the Parkman hospital, and my father had raced over as soon as he'd gotten the call from Loy. He had spent the night sleeping in the chair so I wouldn't be alone if I woke up. I wanted to go home, but apparently people who get shot have to be kept for observation for twenty-four hours.

Even if they had been wearing a bulletproof jacket.

"These calla lilies are from Leif Gable," Irene said. "He just wrote the words 'I'm sorry,' nothing else."

Irene looked up at me, her face sad. "He wired these from D.C. He's filed for divorce from Virginia, you know. I guess word got out about her and Paul."

I shook my head. "I suppose he's sorry I got shot on his back porch?"

She let that go and went on to the next card. It came off a vase filled with white moth orchids. "I told you so," she said.

"Well, yeah . . ." I started to say.

"No," she said, shaking her head. "That's what the card says. That's all it says too. There isn't a name."

Finn. It was his style.

I couldn't argue with him. It also dawned on me that he had saved my life, even though he hadn't actually been there. I was going to thank him personally for the coat. And I could certainly do better than a fruit basket.

"Loy stopped in, but the doctor told him you couldn't have more than one person visiting at a time," Irene said. She looked smug. She was currently the one person.

"Is he alright?" I asked.

"Oh, he's blaming himself, convinced he should have gotten to the Gables' house sooner. You know. He's Loy. He also said that the inhaler was dropped off at the station. I didn't know what he was talking about, but I said I would tell you."

"Did he say anything else?" I asked. I tried to adjust myself and felt a jolt of pain. It was going to be many weeks until I was back to normal again.

"He said that the wine had strawberries in it. I guess he was talking about the wine they found in Paul's bedroom?"

I eased myself into a more comfortable position, wincing. "Strawberries."

Irene leaned over me and manhandled the pillows until they cooperated. "Paul was allergic. Very allergic. I knew that from the café. Whenever he came in he always reminded me that he couldn't eat anything that had strawberries in it. I think that Jack had left a bottle of wine in the bedroom, and Paul had assumed it was from Virginia. You know, a parting gift since they had ended the affair."

"And it had strawberry juice in it. That would have made him have an asthma attack for sure," I said.

Irene shuddered. "Unbelievable. That someone could do such a thing."

I could believe it. I had seen it firsthand.

"The asthma inhaler Loy was talking about had the sux in it," I said. "That's how Jack did it. He needed to make sure that Paul was the one who got poisoned. That was the only way he could be certain. He laced Paul's asthma medicine."

Irene pressed her lips together with disgust. "And Paul dosed himself without even knowing it."

"That's why Jack put that doll under the deck of my house," I told her. "He needed to get rid of me so he could search for that inhaler. It was the only thing that could prove how the sux had gotten into Paul's lungs."

"I think they have all the evidence they need at this point," Irene said.

I shut my eyes, thankful that the nightmare was over at last. Now I could get back to normal life again. But that had its downside too.

"What am I going to do?" I asked. "I can't work for six weeks until this collarbone heals."

Irene patted my feet. "You don't even have a job anymore. Remember? Anyway, you have bigger things to worry about right now."

"Like getting out of here," I said.

She stood up. "I should let you sleep. I've got an interview today. A young man wants to come work for me at the café." She waggled her eyebrows.

"You're a dirty old woman," I said.

"No I'm not. There is only one man I've got eyes for and I think you know that. I want to hire this young man because I think it will improve my professional woman's lunch crowd. There are a lot of gals who work in Killdeer who can appreciate an attractive waiter."

Irene. Always thinking about the bottom line.

I eased myself into a partial sitting position. "Thanks for coming by with my things. I needed to brush the scrunge off my teeth and all the toothpaste here tastes like soap."

She gently tucked the covers around my feet. "Your dad told me he will be by to pick you up tonight when they discharge you. I'll drop by the house to see you tomorrow after you get settled."

"See you later, Irene."

She gave me a long look before she left. I'd scared her pretty good, and I vowed to stay off of rooftops for a while.

She left me alone with my thoughts. I felt drowsy, and still exhausted.

I knew that while I was stuck in the hospital my father was busy helping Wendy Martinez move into the caretaker's cottage. He was doing that on two hours of sleep. I marveled at the fortitude of my family tree and wished I had some of that strength at the moment.

Now that the shock had worn off I had time to reflect on how close I had come to dying, and that thought was enough to shock me all over again. Normally noise was a bother when I was trying to sleep, but hearing the busy sounds from the hospital hallway was a comfort. It reminded me of normal.

I looked out the row of windows in my room and watched as a few snowflakes drifted down. Six or seven mule deer grazed on the remnants of grass in the hospital's vast yard. They looked up periodically and peeped inside the brightly lit window, watching me.

I had no idea what I would do once I was discharged now that I didn't have a job.

I vowed that as soon as I was home I would start sifting through the help wanted ads until I found something I could do. I felt lost without work waiting for me. At least a cast didn't hamper me. I couldn't wear a cast for a collarbone break. The only thing that would offer my bone time to heal was a sling, and so I was allowed some pretty powerful pills. I know the painkillers I was taking started working at some point, and I drifted off to sleep for a couple of hours.

When I woke up, I blinked and let my eyes drift around the room and I relaxed as I took in my surroundings. It would take some time for me to feel safe again.

When I focused on the chair Irene had sat in, I saw that someone else had been there while I had been sleeping. I smiled. Finn's black coat was draped over the shoulders of the chair, waiting for me to put it on when I finally went home.

FOR *"THE WRECKING CREW"*

A fourth generation Wyoming native,
Jessica McClelland is a librarian, avid archer
and spent a decade hunting dinosaurs in the
Jurassic formation in the foothills of the
Bighorn Mountains, a stone's throw away from
where the Johnson County Cattle Wars
occurred. She is the author of the
Marley Dearcorn novels, a series of murder
mysteries set in South Central Montana.

www.ingramcontent.com/pod-product-compliance
Lightning Source LLC
Chambersburg PA
CBHW020235180626
46810CB00006B/2201